Colonel Belchamp's
Battlefield Tour

Colonel Belchamp's Battlefield Tour

Adrian Crisp

Matador
9 Priory Business Park,
Wistow Road, Kibworth Beauchamp,
Leicestershire. LE8 0RX
Tel: 0116 279 2299
Email: books@troubador.co.uk
Web: www.troubador.co.uk/matador
Twitter: @matadorbooks

ISBN 978 1788036 818

British Library Cataloguing in Publication Data.
A catalogue record for this book is available from the British Library.

Printed and bound by CPI Group (UK) Ltd, Croydon, CR0 4YY
Typeset in 11pt Aldine401 BT by Troubador Publishing Ltd, Leicester, UK

Matador is an imprint of Troubador Publishing Ltd

To Ronia

and in memory of Alec Jay and Denis Saaler of the Queen Victoria's Rifles who fought at Calais in May 1940

About the Author

Adrian Crisp studied Medicine at Cambridge University and University College Hospital, London. His postgraduate education at Guy's Hospital, London and Harvard University was followed by thirty years as a consultant physician at Addenbrooke's Hospital, Cambridge. He is a Fellow of Churchill College. This is his first novel.

"Though he was greatly drawn to art and history, he scarcely hesitated over the choice of his career.
He considered that art was no more a vocation than innate cheerfulness or melancholy were professions… a man should do something useful in his practical life. He settled on medicine."

Doctor Zhivago by Boris Pasternak

"Calais was the crux. Many other causes might have prevented the deliverance of Dunkirk, but it is certain that the three days gained by the defence of Calais enabled the Gravelines waterline to be held, and that without this, even in spite of Hitler's fascinations and Rundstedt's orders, all would have been cut off and lost."

The Second World War, Volume 2: Their Finest Hour
by Winston Churchill

"He had often reflected that if experiences and conversations were not set down they were irretrievably lost. They might exist for fleeting hours, or even years, if memorable, but after the death of the players they vanished as if they had never lived."

Irises by Adrian Crisp

Acknowledgements

Two military campaigns are pivotal in James Butland's war: the defence of Calais in May 1940 against overwhelming German odds and the defeat of the Axis forces in Tunisia in May 1943. Correlli Barnett, the military and political historian, encouraged me to read the papers of Admiral Sir Bertram Ramsay in the Churchill Archives Centre at Churchill College, Cambridge. I learnt that Ramsay was as keen to evacuate the beleaguered Calais garrison as he was the 338,000 men from the more celebrated beaches of Dunkirk. Winston Churchill, in order to demonstrate to the French that Britain was not deserting them entirely, ordered Ramsay not to save the men of Calais and condemned them to death or imprisonment.

I have known two veterans of the Queen Victoria's Rifles who fought and were captured at Calais. I played cricket with Alec Jay in the 1960s but it was only after his death in 1993 that I learnt that he had served at Calais. The account of Alec's life by his son, John Jay, in *Facing Fearful Odds* (Pen and Sword, 2014) is an excellent resource for those interested in the defence of Calais. Airey Neave's *The Flames of Calais* (Hodder and Stoughton, 1972) is also essential background. Denis Saaler most generously allowed my wife and me to interview him about the campaign shortly before he died. I emphasise that James Butland is a product of fiction and not a depiction of any known member of the Queen Victoria's Rifles, although a handful of men evaded capture by escaping to England in a small boat.

My interest in the Tunisian campaign of 1942–1943 was

sharpened by a "battlefield tour" in 2008. A B Austin's *Birth of an Army* (Victor Gollancz, 1943), Rick Atkinson's *An Army at Dawn* (Abacus, 2004) and James Holland's *Together We Stand* (Harper Collins, 2005) are superb references.

Although James Butland did not fight in Italy, his expedition in 1938, when he was at school, and his return in 1947 as part of his post-war recovery, are critical episodes in his history. The massacre of civilians in Moggiona by the Germans in 1944 is fact, described in Danilo Tassini's *Moggiona,* (Pro Loco Moggiona, 2012). The Countess of Ranfurly's *To War with Whitaker* (Arrow Books, 1998) describes the role of the monastery and Eremo of Camaldoli in assisting British officers evading recapture. James Holland's *Italy's Sorrow: A Year of War (1944–1945)* (Harper Press, 2008) is invaluable on this period of Italian history.

With deep gratitude I acknowledge the account by Peter Milner of *Quainton Hall School: The First Hundred Years* (Peter Milner, 1997). The school is thinly disguised with great affection as Dayton Hall School in this novel. The names and circumstances of past pupils who were killed during the Second World War are reproduced accurately in the spirit of remembrance which we owe to those who gave their lives. The quotation from *Doctor Zhivago*, by Boris Pasternak, is reproduced with the permission of Penguin Random House. While this is an independent work of fiction, I am most grateful to Curtis Brown and the Estate of Winston Spencer Churchill for permission to record Churchill's statement on the importance of the defence of Calais in May 1940 from *Their Finest Hour*, the second volume of his account of the Second World War.

I express my thanks to Allen Packwood, Director of the Churchill Archives Centre at Churchill College, Cambridge, for helping me to breathe the bittersweet air of 1940 and to Christopher Catherwood for helpful discussions and encouragement. I owe an enormous debt of gratitude to Piers Brendon of Churchill College, Cambridge, for his critical and constructive comments which have strengthened my work. I reserve my special thanks to my wife, Ronia, who has turned my fountain-penned manuscript into a legible text and for her patience with the adventures of James Butland.

Weston Colville, 2016

May 1964

One year of despair and one healing spring had passed since the death of his son. It was a Saturday morning, no work, and James Butland was awake with no impulse to jump out of bed and face the day. On weekend days Alasdair would often sneak into his parents' bed and knead his knees into his father's back to test his level of consciousness. On that May morning James jerked with the same sensation in the small of his back and was flooded with the soaring relief that his son was alive, defying recent history. He smelt him. He threw back his hand to cap the offending knee but when he corkscrewed around to see his son he had already gone. It had been no dream sequence.

It had been a dream one night back in the long winter, stretched and blackened to pitch by desolation. He had taken photographs of his family on holiday with two other families in a farmhouse in Charente-Maritime. Alasdair was there, tall for his age, crinkling his eyes in the glare of the sun. He was jostling with his friends so that the children were spoiling the upright symmetry of the adults, all trying to smile with the restrained intelligence of their breed. The dream then fast-forwarded to the scene two weeks later when the Kodak oven-gloved envelope arrived with the developed pictures. Everyone was in the picture but not Alasdair. There was an empty space where he had been standing, and the other, shorter children were almost toppling over without their buttressing friend.

Shroud-like curtains hung lifelessly, admitting prisms of light, obeying gravity. Alasdair was dead – dead in spite of his cruel resuscitation and reincarnation by dreams. James twisted back towards his alarm clock: 5.15 am. He wondered why he bothered to set the alarm. He never allowed it to fulfil its strident cockerel destiny. Always well awake before zero hour, James pressed down the alarm button so that Alice, his wife, and Sarah, his daughter, would not be disturbed. Alice always seemed to sleep so efficiently. When sleep was truly empty of dreams with no distorted theatre of recent history he could awake in high spirits looking forward to the new day, especially in spring. But within seconds, heavy reality coshed him and forced him to remember.

On this day James felt marginally more positive, though awaking each morning was always a profound disappointment. Sleep is only a diurnal rehearsal of death after all. On almost every night after struggling with a few pages of his book, he prayed that he would not wake up and that he could mercifully die in his sleep and be liberated from life. I suppose we all hope for that kind of death. His dreams would travel back to a time when they were happy, an intact family with tremendous potential for busy and fulfilled lives in Cambridge, refugees from the suffocation of London. Awaking brought hostile reality and hard-nosed truth.

Instead of the usual work at Addenbrooke's Hospital where he had been a consultant physician for the past two years, James had arranged a week's leave. A month or two before, he had been scanning his thick Sunday newspaper, full of the usual trivia. All seemed trivial against the background of what his family had been through. The Second World War was still so vivid to so many of all generations. Everyone over forty played some part in the war and even those in their thirties had been infected with war virus in childhood so that all later events had to stand in comparison with those intense six years. "During the war…" prefaced so many conversations, providing shallow or deeper perspectives on every subject:

"Everyone spoke to each other, helped complete strangers

and seemed cheerful in spite of worries about husbands and sons in danger overseas."

"Now it's everyone for himself. The pursuit of pleasure and money dominates everything. So many spend their time despising others. The dockers and the car makers hate the bosses. The middle classes at worst have contempt for the workers, or at least patronise them. They have never forgiven the coal miners for striking during the war."

Boys' comics like the *Eagle* and the *Lion* seemed to exploit the principle of thirds: one third focused on science fiction with red-eyed green-bodied humanoids who everyone assumed must be living somewhere out there. One third exploited the ageless obsession with football, with heroes such as Roy of the Rovers who always played fairly and firmly by the rules and who was always rewarded for his high principles. The dominant third was war and fed the stereotypes of the moral British and the devilish Germans. There was one exception to this Punch and Judy show of gridded squares and balloon conversations. Foxy Schultz was a wily, hard German in North Africa who fought fairly but was outwitted each week by the more cerebral British, dressed in scout-like khaki shorts. His exasperated cry of frustration after each military setback: "*Donner und Blitzen!*" – "Thunder and lightning!" – became a favourite school playground curse and even competed with the obscenities of older school boys.

The advertisement in the Sunday newspaper that pinioned James's attention was for Colonel Belchamp's Battlefield Tours. After the First World War, which some fathers and grandfathers still called the Great War, some sad expeditions had been made in the 1920s to France and Belgium, mainly for those who had been bereaved so that they could visit graves. The simple wooden or iron crosses recording the brief details of the fallen were gradually replaced by the white headstones that now flecked the sites of battles. Those with no known graves were recorded on massive memorials at Menin Gate or Thiepval. It did not take much imagination by the bereaved to conclude that their relatives had been vaporised by artillery shells with the obvious consolation that there would have been no haunting "suffering" while awaiting death. Immediately after Alasdair's death one year ago, James had chosen that he would be vaporised by flames as he was haunted by the claustrophobic image of a cold corpse in a very tight wooden box, awaiting the bacterial decay of stinking flesh. Alasdair's favourite soft toy, named Baby Sarah after his sister, had been his inseparable companion on journeys and holidays. James extracted a promise from the undertaker that it would be tucked under his arm "all the way". Out of sight but never out of mind.

Colonel Belchamp was planning coolly academic rather than emotional tours of World War II battlefields, which were a respectable two decades away and which were now history rather than reminiscence. One tour in May 1964 was to the May and June 1940 battlefields in France and Belgium. Nice touch to arrange the tour at the corresponding time of year so that relevant weather conditions and vegetation would play their part in the theatre. James shuddered as he swallowed the advertisement. Twenty-four years had fled since that year of growing up and growing old in weeks. He had been there. An eighteen-year-old youth ready to go where so many from previous generations had passed already.

On that day in late May 1964, James stumbled to the bathroom and ran his bath. The Niagara roar of water surging from the taps in the early morning always startled him in contrast to the day without sound. He shaved with long continuous strokes, taking care on this day to draw no blood. James usually avoided more than a fleeting glance at the image of his face in mirrors but, on this day, he studied his features which would soon confront new acquaintances. The doctors had made an excellent job of his right eye. The glass was an exact copy of his left one, the blue uncannily accurate. His round, full face and sandy hair, reflecting

4

his inheritance of East Anglian Anglo-Saxon genes, stared back. He then made a careful descent of the stairs, daring them to creak although rebelliously they always did. Before eating his cereal standing up he slipped into his study to check that his passport, travel insurance and generous supply of French and Belgian francs were arranged neatly on his desk. His eyes walked down the long grass path towards the gate into the field. He had created this corridor between the dense shrubbery but only rarely now did he venture into that field. It was too harrowing. The children used to play in the field claiming it as their territory. Alice had no such qualms, striding out down the path twice daily with the two Labradors, Pepper and Flora. The dogs played their parts very successfully as surrogate children. On some days standing or sitting in his study he could almost convince himself that nothing had really changed. One day, children from the village across the field had ventured as far as the gate and, for a flash, he thought that they were Alasdair and Sarah still defying the awful events of one year before.

James picked his way upstairs again with slow deliberate steps and dressed in another bedroom where he had arranged his clothes the night before. Blue shirt, blue blazer, grey trousers and heavy black brogues. He would not wear his regimental tie and he had not packed it. He would keep a low profile and stay quiet on this trip. Healing osmosis was his prescription for himself. His suitcase was already packed in the hall so that Alice and Sarah would not be woken. James slipped into his bedroom and touched his dry lips on his wife's forehead. That was the limit of their physical contact now. They slept in separate beds and would have preferred separate bedrooms. James coped with his sleep-touched nights by reading hungrily until the book dropped from his hands for a few intervals of unconsciousness, but this was not Alice's technique. If they moved into separate bedrooms now that would have been a clear acknowledgment that they were finished. It was too early and too raw for that cremation.

He controlled his door key to keep the lock open until he had closed the door. He then released the bolt and withdrew the key. Bird chatter seemed more intrusive that day. The gravel was an octave higher than usual, like treading on exploding large black beetles with a satisfying plop. The key bit into the lock of the Jaguar. The teeth of key and lock always grated a little until resistance was at an end and the key could be turned. James almost dreaded the single heavy thump as the boot closed over his suitcase. Even the birds' chatter abated for a few timeless seconds. As he dwelt on this paradox another oxymoronic thought delayed him: the loud silence of the graveyard. In stressful and not so stressful times James often spoke out loudly to himself and on that particular morning he heard himself say, as if a companion were speaking to him:

"It all comes down to heightened awareness; an extra discharge of neurotransmitters in the brain. Probably the cortex or perhaps a more fundamental burst from the brainstem."

Nonsense of course. His loud speech rather shocked him when his whole will this morning had been dedicated to silence. They were his first words of the day.

This was his first escape on his own since Alasdair had been killed the year before in a road "accident". Nine years old. The word accident roused his ire as if it was an act of God like lightning or an earthquake. No, it was in ascending order of guilt: road incompetence, road crime or even road murder. James withdrew the last thought and, very generously he reasoned, substituted road manslaughter. A rational explanation for the collision had not emerged at the inquest and responsibility was buried by the verdict of "accidental death". If any religious faith had survived from his early life he could have accepted that an act of God was as good an explanation as any. He recalled when one of the children had knocked over a glass of water at the dining table, or had dropped something, that they would say that it was an accident. Without fail he would reply, "There's no such thing as an accident."

It was twenty-four years to the month since Calais fell in 1940. James had never returned there, purposefully choosing Boulogne, Dieppe or Ostend for occasional forays across the Channel. Colonel Belchamp's tour would cross from Dover to Calais, and would first trace the retreat of the British Expeditionary Force from its defensive position in Belgium around Louvain back to Dunkirk. The group would then return to Calais and review the resistance of a small British force in Calais which played its part in shielding the main defensive perimeter at Dunkirk. The Calais Brigade prevented 10th Panzer Division from hurling itself against the main evacuation port. Calais in May 1940. That was the start of James's war.

The drive from Cambridge to Dover was long and tedious but passed quickly. As he approached London James almost turned back, convinced that he was making a huge error in confronting the distant, painful past when his spirits were so fragile with more recent events. This might break him for good and cause what the newspapers and his patients called a "nervous breakdown", whatever that is. As he struggled with his indecisiveness, he reasoned that if he could survive 1940 reasonably intact he could survive 1964 and anticipate some sort of quality of life which seemed impossible at present. He drove on to Dover. Colonel Belchamp had offered two possible rendezvous. Most had chosen to board the coach at Victoria Coach Station in London. James could imagine the scene of nervous, clumsy and self-conscious introductions. All recording the temperature of the expedition like new boys in a new school. Clearly the motives of those joining such a tour were likely to be diverse. Some might have fought in the campaign. Others may have had relatives who had fought. Would-be military historians, who had only struggled with the too firmly screwed cap on the ink bottle on their desks, might be there too. The bereaved. It was all possible.

James, in spite of a lifetime in male society and medical practice, was fundamentally shy and he had chosen to avoid Victoria Coach

Station and to join the expedition at Dover. In making his cool decision he had already excluded himself from the centre of attention and from being "one of the lads", an uncomfortable theme in all male-dominated societies. He parked the Jaguar in the coach car park as instructed by Colonel Belchamp and carried his suitcase to the coach proudly emblazoned with COLONEL BELCHAMP'S BATTLEFIELD TOURS and a rather disconcerting crossed-swords emblem. At least it had avoided crossed Bren guns or even crossed bayonets, the unspoken nightmare of every new infantryman whose imagination flickered between the sensation of forcing the blade between hostile ribs and the icy squelch of steel dividing his own intestines.

He deposited his suitcase in the coach's luggage hold and climbed aboard. As he stepped between the rows of seats he roared "good morning" to everyone with all the warm military bonhomie which he did not feel. James hoped to find a double seat all to himself as far away as possible so that he would not have to trade small talk with his fellows. He smiled to left and right in an almost royal progress down the aisle and near the rear of the coach found the seat which he had specified for himself.

Colonel Belchamp stood up at the front of the coach, microphone in hand.

"Now the company is complete we can get down to business. A warm welcome to you all once again and especially to those who have joined us at Dover." That was James and one other recluse who had boarded just before him.

"I am Nicholas Belchamp and I am accompanied by the memsahib, Angela. I used to refer to her as my sergeant major but, as Angela correctly pointed out, officers can't marry NCOs and so it was a nonsense."

All looked around and smiled at each other and either exhaled or coughed in an appreciative way for the mild joke.

"Please do not hesitate to ask any questions or approach us

with any problems. We shall all get to know each other very well over the next few days."

Belchamp had never been in India and perhaps had never served in postings south of Aldershot but he looked the part. Tall, blue-blazered, Royal West Kent regimental tie, Panama hat and the obligatory red face coursed by river deltas of dilated capillaries.

"One very important piece of gen before we go any further. There will be much mounting and dismounting over the next few days and we don't wish to lose anyone when the coach moves off. The natives are friendly but the British Army always recovers its casualties and doesn't leave them on the battlefield. I could just take a roll call at every departure and that is Plan A. It is not really on. I can't treat you all like children on a Sunday School outing to the seaside with the vicar. The foolproof Belchamp method is what I call Plan B. I want all of you to stay in the same seats throughout the expedition. Now look around and identify your neighbours. When I say Plan B look around and make sure your neighbours are all present and correct. If they are not, pipe up and we can send out a search party to find them."

James was relieved that he could stay in his same isolated seat throughout and was only mildly embarrassed that his nearest companions were seated two rows away. He could not escape now. He was committed to spending the next few days in 1940. He began to think more positively. In 1940 he had been eighteen years old, unmarried, no children, with a short or long interesting life ahead of him depending on the lottery of war. Instead of the past fading from full colour to sepia with the passage of years, the reverse was true. On this coach with this group of people, 1964 was turning sepia and 1940 was the reality, at least for those who had been there. Escapism from reality to reality but no worse than that, and James knew that he had survived 1940. He could not be sure that he would see 1965 with such a cool head and optimism.

1921 to August 1938

James Butland was born on November 21ˢᵗ 1921 in the spare bedroom on the premises of Butland, Baker and Confectioner, Marlborough Road, Wealdstone, Middlesex. The war to end all wars had been fought and won. Although unemployment was the reward of many who had survived, most could see a future and perhaps a bright one. Butland's was at the end of a terrace of shops with a large window full of cakes, tarts and bread. It was painted wellington-boot green with bold gold lettering above the window. In the centre of the window display stood a wooden model of the baker's delivery van built to scale. It was painted in the same green and gold livery. Wedged between the wooden shafts at the front of the van was a reproduction of Clare, the old Suffolk Punch mare which had served the family business in Wealdstone since Queen Victoria's days. Clare's neck and body were articulated by leather joints to allow lateral movement. Children, and many adults standing in the shop awaiting attention, could not resist the temptation to coax old Clare's head from side to side and were only mildly disappointed that the leather joints impeded the more natural head dipping of the horse. Her leather neck was fraying with the attention. To the right of the shop door was the gated entrance to the stables where the delivery van and horses stood, bringing the smells of the countryside – horse, sweat and manure – to this Victorian appendage of Harrow-on-the-Hill. Beyond the counter of the shop was a door which led to a sitting room where James's mother seemed to spend most of the day. James's father, also called James, was a master baker and freemason and a man of some substance in the small business circles of Harrow and Wealdstone.

The mainline station of that name was nearby and days and nights were punctuated with steamy eructations from the engines of the London, Midland and Scottish Railway pounding south and north to and from Euston. The population of this new suburb was expanding rapidly with immigrants from the countryside and emigrants from London imbued with post-war reproductive vigour. James, the master baker, was a Suffolk man from a large family employed on the land near Clare. He named the old mare after his birthplace, fettering the past from slipping away into the mists of memory. The combination of large families and agricultural depression in the last decades of the nineteenth century forced James, the younger but more enterprising son, to leave the land and establish a bakery in a thriving community. The Butland family had lived on the Suffolk and Essex border for centuries but there was no prospect for a new bakery in the depleted villages.

His elder brother, Ernest, obtained work as a farm labourer when the season demanded it and joined up with enthusiasm in August 1914 at the prospect of regular employment and adventure. On the day after the declaration of war he walked seventeen miles from Clare to the regimental depot of the Suffolk Regiment at Bury St Edmunds and received the King's Shilling. In May 1915 at the second battle of Ypres his right arm was shattered by machine gun bullets which left him with a flaccid, paralysed limb, heavy and swollen, which chameleon-like alternated between shades of blue and crimson. His family blamed the colour changes on the weather and joked that Ernest's arm was better than any barometer.

During those rare visits to the family roots in Suffolk in the 1920s, James recalled his Uncle Ernest rarely moving from his chair by the fireplace, mourning the useless limb which prevented him from earning a few shillings in the fields. His only frenetic activity was the exercise of one-handed pipe filling, lighting and smoking, which he seemed to accomplish in denial of his disability. Even he was given a white feather during the war for daring to walk the streets in civvies because his right arm, hanging uselessly by his side, was ignored both by the body attached to it and by the torturers.

The baker's wife was a Londoner whose family had moved out of the fetid city for the healthier air of the suburbs. She supported her husband from the room at the back of the shop and had borne him two daughters before the Great War. It seemed indecent to have more children during the war but their son James's arrival in 1921 was welcomed as a symbol of the new world. His father volunteered for active service but his application was rejected as baking was a critical reserved home occupation. This embarrassment gnawed at the family and his brother Ernest never allowed him to forget his good fortune.

James was a generous man who often handed loaves of bread to his poorer customers without charge, especially if their husbands were at the front. After long days in the bakery starting well before dawn he totted up the day's takings, entered them in his copperplate hand in his account book and then walked to the ambulance station at the foot of Harrow Hill, from where he drove ambulances. Sometimes he had no sleep before firing up the bakery ovens for the next day's bread.

James, as a baker's son, developed a heightened sense of smell. Smells, not scenes, are the essential architecture of childhood. Home was the synthesis of newly baked bread, horse manure in the stables and engine breath wafting up from the railway. New mown grass, often fashioned by his father into at least an outline of a steam train's footprint; the frequent arrival of the coal lorry to feed the bakery ovens with dark, greasy, effluent sacks of sweet-smelling coal. James could inhale this miasma with exquisite pleasure all day if allowed. Seaside holidays, usually at Swanage in Dorset, which was warmer than the cold, windswept wastes of the East Anglian coast, which James's father would have preferred, were the indices of childhood time, not calendar years. The annual ritual had a momentum of its own. Two weeks before, his mother would place certain clothes out of bounds.

"You will need them on holiday and I have washed them."

A large trunk and suitcases were carried down from the attic. Some contained holiday plimsolls, inflatable rubber water wings and the bucket and spade. All had retained the sea water tang from last year's holiday. Two days before departure the Carter Paterson van would arrive to collect the family's luggage and would promise to deposit it in the rented house in Swanage coinciding with the family's arrival. The family had no car, the preserve of the aristocracy and the gentry, but would travel by train, which was a premonition of the holiday itself. The coarse, salty air of the sea would penetrate many miles inland and was inhaled through carriage windows long before the sea was visible. Then followed the competition between the younger members to be the "first to see the sea", which was thought to bring good luck to the winner, as well as the taxi ride from the station to the holiday cottage. Days were spent on shingle and sand with alternating ham and cheese sandwiches and Tizer. One often retold family story was the disaster of Mother's wedding ring. It was in 1923 or 1924 that the ring disappeared from the kitchen of the Swanage house.

"I threwed it through the window," James admitted after a day or two of anguish. The whole holiday was spent not at the beach but in the garden sifting every molecule of earth until James's father discovered it on the last day several inches below the surface in a tunnel created by an inquisitive vole. His sisters seemed to live in a separate girls' world but he was content with his own company and with his parents. He did not seek the friendship of children but his parents pressed him to accept invitations from other boys if they were judged to be "nice" and not "rough" or even worse, "common". The tradesmen of the lower middle class had a clear idea of their place in society and most aspired to climb one rung of the ladder through their own efforts and those of their children. They would not attempt two or three rungs as that would have been interpreted as "rising above themselves".

Providing evidence of the puzzling elasticity of time was the perennial sensation of the slow passage of the first week of the holiday with the more rapid acceleration of days in the second. In the final days James would collect colourful stones and shells, and even seaweed, to take home and so prolong the holiday after its end. Once back in Harrow the seaweed had dried and lost its lustre. The stones and shells which had seemed so vibrant with colour when sea-wet had lost their souls and were absorbed into the garden soil. The end of the holiday was always sombre. In reverse order the Carter Paterson van would collect the luggage, indisputable evidence of finality. The same taxi driver, who also drove hearses, would perform the final rites of passage back to the station. James's head would remain fixed outside the train window until he could no longer smell the sea. His mother would tell the perennial story of the little boy leaning out too far whose head was knocked off by a train passing the other way. That would usually force James back onto his seat. One of the cruelties of ageing is the gradual loss of smell which degrades those childhood sensations into memories.

There can be no adult who does not remember the detail of his or her first day at school. Parents prepare their children by describing the new horizons ahead and James anticipated them with restrained enthusiasm. He could read some words but was not expert at shoelaces and required the teacher's help for several days. The little village school, a product of the 1870 Education Act, was gentle and the first day flew by without trauma. The huge surprise to James on the following day was that he had to go to school again. He thought it was a life experience packed into one day and not to be repeated. He learnt to write with a very clear and controlled hand and gratified the teacher's obsession with neatness. Spelling and simple sums were mastered easily. After two terms his teacher pronounced him to be "bright" and, after consultation with his parents, recommended that he should transfer to a private preparatory school with the prospect of his further promotion from the tradesman to the professional class if his brains and his parents' pocket could sustain him.

Dayton Hall preparatory school for boys in Harrow was a solidly middle-class establishment and James's family was firmly at the lower end of the social spectrum at the school. One clear division was between those who ate breakfast, dinner and tea and those who consumed breakfast, lunch and dinner – which was sometimes diluted to supper in households just below the top drawer. James soon learnt to pronounce railway as railway and not row – as in how – way. Two miles was a little too far for a five-year-old to walk to school on his own and so for several years James travelled on the bus while his mother cycled behind to save her fare. She then supervised the crossing of the big road and the last few hundred yards to school. The road was safer on the way home and he could travel without his mother's supervision.

Work and discipline were hard. James was reserved and well behaved but none was immune from the whole form beatings for some minor offence. On a typical day the school master would place the class on its honour to complete a reading, writing or calculating task in monastic silence while he left the classroom for a cigarette or to place a bet on the 2.45 race at Newmarket. On his return, far from rooted to their seats with academic intensity, boys would be celebrating their freedom with a cacophony of laughing, shouting and wrestling which froze into a silent montage as the door opened. The whole condemned class would then form a more or less orderly file to the space in front of the master's desk. Each boy in turn bowed forward. The more theatrical would place the palm of the right hand over the waist and the dorsum of the left on the back as if greeting royalty. A notoriously long and flexible rubber soled gym shoe had been purloined from a boy of pathologically precocious growth some years before and was now stored on the top shelf of the stationery cupboard for performances such as these. One generous swing at the backside and the punishment was complete.

One afternoon, after unwisely backing the outsider, Cox's Bazaar, to win at 7 to 1, Mr Dean lost his whole stake, which represented a sizeable portion of his weekly stipend. Especially angered, he propelled one boy so far forward with the gym shoe that the boy's nose collided with a radiator and mixed blood with the opalescent rusty water beneath it. One Scottish master preferred the weapon of the leather strap or tawse on the outstretched hand. This was, all agreed, more painful and likely to induce a swallowed sob. The schoolboy code of "no blubbing" under any circumstance was therefore maintained. There was more risk from the heavy blackboard rubbers which some hurled with accuracy at their victims. One master, who did not have the skill to coach cricket, broke a window with his misplaced throw. The cost of repair was subtracted from his pay and all in the masters' common room resolved to absolve the boys from punishment who were sitting in front of windows.

Every scrap of food in those post-war days had to be consumed. On cabbage days, at least once a week, the stench of the over-boiled mucinous vegetable would waft round the school during the late morning like a Great War chlorine gas attack and James, who despised cabbage, would experience the nausea and fear that many would have suffered in the trenches. When the dreaded lunch confronted him he would cut off small squares and bury them in potato but would eventually be left with a redoubt of cabbage that he was forced to carry back to the classroom for gradual consumption by the end of school at four o'clock. On one occasion a compassionate sixth-former swooped up the cabbage from James's plate and threw it through the classroom window at the feet of the headmaster. His martyrdom with the cane was never forgotten.

Presiding over the school kitchen was the tiny figure of Miss Copeman, hair netted over an almost bald scalp, with cigarette welded to her lower lip. Mashed potato with a dusting of cigarette ash was her signature dish. Bill Livingstone, the school caretaker, also played his part in the texture of the school. Bill, as known by all staff and pupils, was a short, well-muscled Scot with the impenetrable accent of Glasgow and the gentleness of all truly hard men. His forearms were decorated with tattoos which waxed and waned with the physical exertions imposed on the school's dogsbody. All new boys were warned never to turn their backs on Bill. As a wartime member of a tough Glasgow regiment which had learnt its trade in the Gorbals, it was reputed that he could kill with a single blow. Boys would practise their rabbit punches with the little finger border of the hand to either the back of the neck or where they imagined the kidneys to be located with their hazy knowledge of anatomy.

"This is how Bill killed Germans – with his hand."

They always pulled their chopping gestures for fear of doing genuine harm to their school fellows. Bill took plenty of cheek from the boys young enough to be his grandsons but none overstepped the mark, just in case they pressed the trigger which would force Bill to regress from the gentle caretaker into the bloodthirsty Jock of the trenches.

Dayton Hall was a bizarre experience and pupils at other more conventional schools never trusted the unembellished accounts of Dayton Hall school days. The school was a jumble of Edwardian houses owned by its headmaster, the Reverend Montague Haydon. Tall, with thick black hair flecked with grey, Father Haydon appealed to mothers who admired his uncompromising masculinity and visual appeal, offset by the hint of raffishness imposed by the odours of whisky and tobacco which encased him. The white dog collar and long black cassock, fastened at the front, combined with his black-grey hair and long Roman nose, were reminiscent of a prehistoric badger on its hind legs. Fathers were not so easily convinced by the paradox of testosterone and priestly celibacy. In truth, Mont was wary of women and often uncomfortable with successful men. His dark eyes, protuberant and bull-like, would rotate with barely concealed anger if fathers, with their army service in the Great War so recent, addressed him as Padre rather than his cherished title of Father. His comfort zone was with boys.

Dayton Hall's reputation had grown with an emphasis on hard work and good manners. Father Haydon insisted on less conventional additions to the standard prep school brew. He would often describe the organism as a chapel with a Scout Troop camping in the grounds with a school attached. Mont, who had read history at University College, London, was fired with the Anglo-Catholic doctrines of Newman, Pusey and Keble, and built his ornate chapel within the school, encumbered with plaster statues of Mary, St George and St Francis and the paraphernalia of tabernacles, vestments and incense. The gas clouds of sweet incense, grey with the scent of decay, billowed thickly inside the chapel and, on special holy days like Ash Wednesday, would ghost around the school competing with smelly socks and cabbage stench to give a premonition of Hell rather than Heaven. James was uneasy with the excesses of Anglo-Catholicism but did not fight too hard against them either.

The second priority of this society was the 11th Harrow Scout Troop. Robert Baden Powell founded the movement between the Boer War and the Great War and by the 1920s it was at its peak. Most boys in the school were cubs or scouts and James, after an initial typical reluctance, plunged in and never regretted it. Mont had grown up in rural Buckinghamshire and developed a mission to convert his boys, effectively his family as he remained scrupulously celibate throughout his life, from the conventional Church of England restrained pieties to the melodrama of Anglo-Catholicism. He also wanted to teach the "townies", his favoured term of abuse, how to fend for themselves in the countryside at camps with minimal help from suburban civilisation. Those rancid and oily white sticks called firelighters were excommunicated from 11th Harrow camps. A modest nucleus of newspaper, preferably *The Times*, overlaid by a pyramid of thin sticks, then splinters of axed wood were lit by a maximum of two safety matches. Fires were then scaled up to the specification required for cooking, or on Saturday nights, to the huge fires at the centre of camp life. Specialist cooks could create culinary miracles. James's reputation as a camp cook never recovered from the destruction of a huge leg of lamb. The joint was reverently placed on a roasting plate. The heavy metal bowl was inverted over the joint so that no fire could penetrate the dome. A huge fire was built around the bowl which began to redden as the heat intensified and all looked forward to the lamb cooked to perfection. James could only guess at a cooking time and, when the fire was extinguished and the cooking bowl removed, there remained only a single charred leg bone inside. They dined on cheese and biscuits.

Mont's vocation was to grow "townies", boys with the limited horizons of suburban trade and of the professions, into young men with country skills and deeply spiritual lives. If they were also intellectually distinguished, that was a bonus. The indoctrination with rural skills was an easy task for most were only one or two generations remote from the land. Mont succeeded with most boys though some refused to submit to the ways of Dayton Hall and were ignored. Though socially conservative he truly believed in fundamental scout principles that "a scout is a brother to every other scout" irrespective of country, class or creed. All were exhorted to be unselfish and to spend their lives serving others. The school was at the foot of Harrow-on-the-Hill which was dominated by the great school of Byron, Palmerston and Churchill. No boys from Dayton Hall left for Harrow School, which recruited from distant preparatory schools and from the more elevated strata of society.

James grew very happily at Dayton Hall and absorbed its culture. He was good at work but not too obvious a swot and he was also good at some games. Cricket was an obsession in his last year at the school and he was rewarded with the usual accolades of house captaincy and cricket colours and was promoted to Patrol Leader in the Swift Patrol of the 11ᵗʰ Harrow Scout Troop. His introduction to the nursery slopes of the professional middle class caused some tensions at home. He criticised his parents' limited view of life but it was their vision which had positioned him and he was silently grateful. In later life he regretted the scoring of cheap points off his well-meaning but uneducated mother. She would repeatedly say, "You're as ignorant as you are-eye" in response to his arrogant criticism of some aspect of life at home. Neither James nor his mother had any idea what this phrase meant but she had learnt it many years ago and produced it as her response to his overbearing behaviour. James also snorted at the parting instruction when he was visiting a school friend.

"Remember us to his people."

"Of course they remember you. You met them at the school."

James knew that it was an inherited phrase of tradesmen vernacular but could not resist the put-down. Some members of his family and some neighbours and friends made it clear that he had "risen above himself" and had offended the natural stratification of society, but he could tolerate that. He had a large circle of friends who had learnt, played and camped together. Girls played no part in this society. Sisters, an asexual species, did not count. As early puberty approached the silly jokes identified those who would soon move on to senior schools.

"Look at John. His tie is over his left shoulder. That means he is looking for a prostitute."

No boy of course knew what a prostitute actually offered.

"What did the Chinaman do when his wife died?"

"He went back to Wang-King."

Once again they all laughed without insight. James would willingly have remained in that Dayton Hall womb but he and his contemporaries had reached the weary old age of thirteen and had to move on. It was the unpleasantness and trauma of this new world that made him fear all new transition for the rest of his life.

In the early 1930s, Merchant Taylors' School moved from the City of London to Northwood. This created an opportunity for the boys from Dayton Hall as Northwood was only several stations to the west of Harrow-on-the-Hill on the Metropolitan Railway. After the Common Entrance examination, most boys moved to Merchant Taylors'. It was anticipated that James could win a scholarship which would have reduced the fees to a level which his parents could afford. He was, though, two months too old to qualify for this scholarship and an alternative school was sought. United Colleges School in London was chosen by his Dayton Hall masters, but James, who could offer neither Greek nor calculus, which had been imbibed by the internal candidates from the school's own preparatory department, failed that scholarship examination. The place he was offered without rebate of fees would be less of a financial burden on his parents than if he had attended Merchant Taylors' without a scholarship.

The bicycle ride from home to Dayton Hall had been an enjoyable and social exercise. Boys who lived further away from school chose routes that others would join on the way and James would often cycle through the school gates as part of a convoy. On that first day of term in September 1934 James joined the queue for a bus, with briefcase in one hand and large bag in the other, full of gym and rugby kit. He contemplated the next four or five years with trepidation. He was alone, sitting with his own thoughts on the upper deck of the bus which would take him to Harrow-on-the-Hill station. On the opposite platform, many of his Dayton Hall friends awaited the Metropolitan Line train which would carry them west to Moor Park station, a short walk from Merchant Taylors' School. Again he was alone, awaiting the train which would transport him to London. Initially they would shout at each other across the tracks but then, as the term marched on, they all developed their separate school lives. James watched as the rows of suburban semi-detached houses, often half-timbered in mock-Tudor pastiche, were replaced by grim late-Victorian London terraces. He contrasted his centripetal Metropolitan Line train with the centrifugal version on its journey to Merchant Taylors'. He never recovered that intense happiness and optimism that had characterised Dayton Hall.

He alighted from the train at Finchley Road station, crossing that loathsome, car-fumed carriageway to the road winding up to Hampstead Heath. The huge Edwardian houses, often in roasted red brick with white-yellow stucco, appeared so alien. Halfway up the hill stood United Colleges School with its three large blocks of Edwardian flamboyance hemmed in by the houses and villas of Hampstead society. His new school was a huge cultural shock, with London boys from many exotic backgrounds worlds apart from Anglo-Catholicism and scouts. Many were noisy, argumentative or narcissistic and he did not fit in. Its ethos was utilitarian and secular and James, probably unfairly, considered it devoid of real humanity. It was the antithesis and contradiction of all that Dayton Hall stood for and he never flourished there. Naturally quite shy, though Dayton Hall had achieved a temporary remission from this affliction, James withdrew into himself and frustrated his masters by almost complete silence in classroom discussions and arguments which were the staple diets of London boys. Food at school was poor but then mothers provided breakfast and dinner at home and so lunch was only an interlude in the day rather than an object of pleasure. James would never forget the steamed sponge pudding with lashes of volcanic jam lava which all new boys were trained to call

"Matron's monthly", most not having the remotest idea what it meant.

He compensated for his unhappiness and loss of confidence by studying hard and playing half-hearted rugby and cricket. At United Colleges School playing hard to win was considered to be in rather poor taste. Its teams were points and runs fodder for other schools. James began to envy the beauty of the buildings, vast acres of grounds and playing fields of other schools in contrast to the cramped site in London where he existed. The pink brick and ornate, but sadly eroded, limestone of his school irritated him and increased his antipathy to this alien environment. Merchant Taylors' was where he wanted to be and it was closed to him. It was the first huge disappointment of his life. Only once did he communicate his unhappiness to his parents as this would have constituted base ingratitude. In later life when he spoke more frankly about those unhappy days they expressed surprise and had buried the memory of his confession.

History and literature maintained his relative equilibrium. Mont's history teaching at Dayton Hall was a long didactic progress from the Stone Age until the Napoleonic Wars with traditional obsession with dates and the nuts and bolts to pass the Common Entrance examination to public schools. Interesting details of branch lines of knowledge were reviled as "engine driver's socks" and to be excised. Mont made it clear that he would much rather be on his knees shrouded by incense in the chapel or at the school campsite in Chalfont St Peter than imparting historical knowledge and enlightenment. Naturally Henry VIII's Reformation and the suppression of Catholicism in the sixteenth and seventeenth centuries were painted as disasters for civilisation and were mere footnotes in Mont's historical dialectic. The revival of Anglo-Catholicism in the early nineteenth century had restored the true faith in England.

Dayton Hall was in stark contrast to other preparatory schools in another critical aspect. Those who relished life outside the classroom in the scout troop and the chapel were not cut off from the school after reaching the age of thirteen and moving on to a senior school. With the exception of the minority, whose parents chose boarding schools, scouts continued to be 11th Harrow scouts until their late teens or even twenties. These Friday evening meetings at Dayton Hall were weekly reunions of those still at school with those at a variety of senior schools. In the summer they spent weekends at the Chalfont St Peter camp or fortnights at camps in the West Country, Wales or Yorkshire.

The chapel of St Francis at Dayton Hall continued to be the focus of spiritual life for those who could not bear to cut themselves off from this society. Sunday morning Mass offered the same fellowship as the well-integrated scout troop. For James, this was his family. His sisters were of an older generation and his parents were pleased that he was enjoying a new life outside their family and was gradually loosening the ties with the suburban limits of their own lives. It was not all pleasure. He listened to the stories of his friends now at Merchant Taylors'. Their school lives sounded more vivid and exciting than his own and this eroded the happiness and self-confidence that he had constructed at Dayton Hall. James, a natural conformist but not in religious matters, did make one annual protest. Mont ignored the Church of England *Book of Common Prayer* written by "a heretic called Thomas Cranmer", and chose to use the Catholic Missal. On Good Friday he would intone the prayer, "Let us pray for all heretics and schismatics." The congregation knelt to signify its support of this generous sentiment. James would remain firmly on his feet in full view of most of the congregation but not in view of Mont who was gazing at the High Altar, when not lying prone with outstretched arms and legs at a critical point in the Good Friday Catholic ritual. His arthritic knees imposed an extra penance which, although not quite medieval flagellation, could be turned into a spiritual benefit. Most were ignorant of the meanings of heretic and schismatic. James knew. He had travelled up main lines and branch lines in history that would not have gained Mont's approval.

History at United Colleges School was the enthusiasm of his first form master, Mugsy. His initials were MJGS which had triggered his nickname, probably in his first week as a teacher. He was short, mildly lame and had a face like a Toby Jug which contributed to the affectionate name used by all boys. He had been a Liberal councillor and focused on the eighteenth and nineteenth centuries when liberalism was gradually overcoming the forces of reaction. The study of history was the study of the inexorable triumph of good over evil. The success of the American colonists and the French overthrow of monarchy were presented as the victories of the human spirit, although with regrettable bloodshed. At Dayton Hall these were interpreted as assaults on monarchy, the Church and civilisation. James soon learnt of the flexibility of historical study and the discipline of drawing on facts and evidence to support a case while suppressing contrary evidence. A year or two later he wrote two back-to-back essays on "The English Reformation – right or wrong?" adopting in one the Dayton Hall pro-Catholic line and in the other the Thomas Cromwell pragmatic view of the state. He was awarded alphas for both individually but gamma for the pair as it had signified intellectual dishonesty worthy of a barrister.

It was in 1936 or 1937 that James, with a sudden blinding insight, decided that he must go to Oxford. He was sick of slick London and had developed an unreasonable contempt for the suburban dreariness of Harrow. Oxford was his escape route to a more interesting and provocative life. His parents dutifully drove the Austin 10 up the A40 on many Sundays so that James could visit all of the colleges and choose the most appropriate one for his particular specification. When Magdalen Tower came into view he experienced the same warm sensations which he associated with the sea pheromones of holidays in childhood. On visits in early spring or late autumn, when

Oxford is at its most seductive, the sensations would merge into physical shivers not unrelated to orgasm, sharing the same neurological traffic. His father always parked the car in Merton Street which uncannily seemed to reserve a space for the Oxford aspirant and his parents. Christ Church, Magdalen and New College were large, intimidatingly beautiful and would almost certainly not be interested in him. Balliol was an intellectual tropical house and architecturally dull. James judged that his chances there were thin. Keble, Oxford's incarnation of the Anglo-Catholicism of Mont and Dayton Hall, was enticing but the exuberant late nineteenth-century redbrick Gothicism reminded him of school and was not ancient enough to deserve him. By now almost blind to any worthwhile attribute of his school, which had been founded as recently as 1830, James had acquired a deference to the sheer age of educational institutions. He read Oxford guide books voraciously and became in his rather solitary, obsessive way quite expert on the finer architectural points of each college and its place in the social, educational and sporting pecking order.

The head of history at school was Bingo Darlington and James had grown to love and admire him. Wise, friendly and gentle, Bingo tried to extract the best from all his charges and could even charm the London cynics. Bingo, clean-shaven with a polished bald head, sprouted long ginger hairs from his faded pink cheeks and reminded them all that the age of Dickens was not so remote. His ancient Oxford gown, mutating from academic black to attenuated tobacco-cured green, smelt of the past. A complex musk of library dust and leather-topped desk. Hardly inappropriate for an historian. Bingo simply saved the school in James's eyes from being cast into complete oblivion.

After a final flurry of visits to Oxford, James chose St John's College. The exquisite early seventeenth-century architecture, some said designed or strongly influenced by Inigo Jones, the facing statues of Charles I and Henrietta Maria in Canterbury

Quad, the Garden Front and its mid-size all convinced him that he had chosen well.

"Why St John's, James? Was your father there?" Bingo, a Balliol man, knew full well that no member of his family had been to any university.

"I've visited Oxford many times this year, sir, and quite simply, it's beautiful."

"Very well. An excellent choice. The Head always likes to advise too. You must see him."

The access to the headmaster, Mr Charles Blade-Dawkins, who seemed so cool and remote, was to present oneself before him after morning assembly.

"Sir, Mr Darlington has suggested that I discuss my choice of Oxford college with you. I should like to apply to St John's."

"I shouldn't if I were you. We have no tradition of sending boys to St John's and there are other considerations…"

James broke in. He had anticipated the Head's next point. "St John's has close links with, and closed scholarships for, Merchant Taylors', hasn't it, sir? Both were founded by Sir Thomas White's Elizabethan wealth." He wished to impress the Head with his mature insight.

There was a mutual antipathy between the two schools. It was only in the Merchant Taylors' matches that United boys would actually try to win. And they sometimes did.

"It would probably be a tactical error, Butland. How about Wadham?"

James was aware of a steady stream of boys from his school to Wadham College. The buildings were, like St John's, mainly seventeenth century but more severe and less welcoming. Unusually in Oxford, Wadham had been firmly on the side of the Puritans and an opponent of King Charles. It was almost a Roundheads versus Cavaliers argument and James was currently in a monarchist frame of mind. He wanted to confront the Merchant Taylors' problem as evidence of his strength but he did not feel strong. If he failed it would be almost a replay of the Merchant Taylors' reverse in 1934.

"Thank you, sir, I'll try Wadham." He walked slowly back to Bingo's classroom, convinced that he had failed his first test in the Civil War of the Oxford entrance campaign.

June to August 1938

One evening in early June 1938, James was sitting at his small desk in his bedroom struggling with an outline of an essay on the Risorgimento – the progress of multiple states and monarchies towards a unified Italy. The windows were open and he could see his father bent over the heavy lawnmower urging it towards the pond at the foot of the garden. The reassuring smell of fresh mown grass, reminiscent of breast milk, ascended to the windows and distracted him from the chapter in the huge blue-black volume of the Cambridge Modern History. He would have preferred to read it in bed on his knees but it was too heavy. He would save the thin paper pamphlet essay for bed, accompanied by the large mug of Horlicks which his mother brought him at about ten o'clock each night. The telephone bell broke into his thoughts. He heard his mother's steps on the stairs, much too hurried for the sedate climb with the Horlicks.

"James, Mont wants to speak to you."

She had chosen not to call her son from the foot of the stairs as Mont would have heard and would have considered this poor form.

"I wonder what he wants."

Mont, with his family of ex-pupils who attended school chapel, scout meetings and camps, did not usually telephone. Parents, and even sisters, would probably answer and Mont preferred direct contact with his boys.

"James, Mont here."

"Yes, Mont?"

"Would you like to come to Italy this summer?"

For many years Mont had leased a house in Moggiona, a tiny village high up in the Apennines in Tuscany, and spent a month there in the summer holidays. Each year he invited three members of his Dayton Hall family to accompany him. Mont viewed it as a pilgrimage to the land of St Francis of Assisi whose plaster figure presided over the school chapel dedicated to him. The blood-red paint in the centre of the palms of his outstretched hands, representing the stigmata, gruesomely fascinated the boys. Most accepted the stories of saintly adventures which Mont imparted to each new generation. James had always assumed that his barely concealed scepticism of the tenets of Anglo-Catholicism would exclude this invitation to Italy. The speck-like pebble of his religious feelings would not have disturbed the surface of the pool. Behind the tedious lists of kings and queens, dates and battles which he planted in heads for the Common Entrance exam, Mont was an enthusiastic historian with a deep appreciation of Renaissance art and culture. James would provide historical debate. He hesitated. The expedition would be expensive and his father was already struggling to pay his school fees.

"May I ask my parents, Mont?"

"Yes, of course. But don't worry too much about the money. As good scouts we look after ourselves mainly and don't spend too much."

"Then I should love to come. Thank you very much. As I think I've told you, the Renaissance and Reformation periods are my favourites."

"We'll see plenty of the Renaissance, my boy, but don't count too much on the Reformation."

James grinned. He knew only too well Mont's antipathy to those ghastly Protestants who had driven England away from the true Church. Heretics and schismatics. The flames of the stake were too good for them. He preferred to think of them roasting slowly on a spit in hell for eternity for the crimes they had committed against the Church.

"That's settled then."

In late July, after the end of term, the party gathered at Dayton Hall. Philip Grainger, the son of an eminent surgeon, was one of the minority of Dayton Hall boys who had gone to a boarding school – King's College, Taunton. Mont strongly approved of King's as it was as marinated in Anglo-Catholicism as Dayton Hall. Philip would play the part of devout pilgrim. Roger Trenchard was one of the most pragmatic and practical scouts and an expert on the internal combustion engine. Roger had moved to John Lyon School on Harrow Hill. Harrow School had been founded by John Lyon in the sixteenth century to educate local boys but had long lost its original vocation. In compensation, Roger's school was established in the late nineteenth century as a day school to educate the sons of the more prosperous tradesmen and professionals of Harrow, thus fulfilling John Lyon's intention.

The six parents stood by with their own thoughts. James, Philip and Roger had not travelled abroad before. It was 1938. After the Anschluss between Germany and Austria many thought that war could not be far off. Mont reassured them all that they would travel through France and Switzerland well away from Germany. Although Mussolini and his Fascists were upsetting the essential good nature of the Italians, Mont had never experienced any ill will from the simple people of the Apennines. These tensions added spice to the adventure and all were keen to see the world cut off from England by the Channel. James's mother was the only parent stifling sobs, which stoked the impatience with her which he recognised with the developing insight into his own thoughts.

They packed their tent, supplies and campsite paraphernalia into the old school Bedford van and were off to Folkestone to join the ferry to Boulogne. On the way to their first campsite in France they bought bread, cheese, ham and soup, shyly experimenting with their schoolboy French which, to their surprise, seemed to achieve the desired results. Everything seemed so cheap. James began to feel more relaxed about the costs. Mont slept in his bunk in the van and James and his friends shared the tent. After a breakfast of coffee, bread and jam they were on their way south. It was not long before they saw their first French family in line, relieving themselves by the roadside, and all roared with laughter. Mont and Roger shared the driving and it was late in the evening when they turned into the second campsite in the Vosges Mountains. The high summer breezes could not overcome the foul stench from the holes in the ground which served as latrines. They dined again on soup, bread and cheese, inhaling the aroma from the ripe Camembert competing bravely with the fumes of sewage.

On the third day they drove hard to the Gotthard Pass. The van struggled to climb the steep hairpin bends and soon the radiator was boiling. They were forced to halt every twenty minutes to lift the bonnet and cool the engine. Roger was excitedly throwing cool water over the engine and topping up the radiator. James, with minimal knowledge of physics, was afraid the engine block would crack under the cold shower. Mont sat on his bunk and prayed. Eventually they reached the top of the pass and allowed gravity to lower the van gently onto the Lombardy plain. Their campsite for the night was in a suburb of Milan. There was time to drive into the city and see the Duomo, more like a hedgehog than a cathedral. They felt very conspicuous as fingers pointing like spokes at the centre of a wheel all converged on them with murmurs of "*Inglesi, Inglesi*."

"How do they know we're English?"

Mont marched them rapidly through the streets to Santa Maria delle Grazie as he had planned their first art lesson. In the refectory of the convent adjoining the church they stood in front of Leonardo da Vinci's *The Last Supper*. It was in poor condition but in spite of the damage James could sense the intensity of Jesus and his disciples and the expression of the life force communicated over the centuries.

"You may think this is a fresco – painted onto wet plaster – but it is not. It's tempera on a dry wall and that's why it's in poor condition. You can see the wall is damp and the paint is coming off."

James and Philip listened intently. Roger wanted to be back outside gazing at the Lancias and Alfa Romeos pirouetting along the streets.

The brisk walk through the Milan streets back to the van stretched their rugby skills of swerves and side steps through the dense crowds of Italians chattering and meandering slowly along arm in arm. Philip, destined for medicine after his father's example, observed no pauses for breath and expected them to sink to the ground with oxygen deficiency.

"Why do Italians walk so slowly and drive so fast?"

"The eternal Italian paradox."

"I thought Italians drove on the right side of the road but most seem to spend most of the time on the left side with their cutting corners and crazy overtaking."

Exhausted after their expedition to Milan and too tired to cook their own soup, they dined in the camp restaurant on pasta anointed with a thin meat sauce. Offered Parmesan cheese, the boys urged the waiter to obliterate all signs of the sauce with a pale yellow snow storm. Roger asked for a pizza instead, but Mont vetoed this with an abrupt, "Pizza? Italian peasant food. Certainly not."

James expected to fall asleep immediately but the summer heat as they migrated south seemed to concentrate in the tent. He was distracted by the whine of mosquitoes, though he could not see them and expected to be awoken by bites. The cicadas competed with their single complex note. He could not sleep. Roger snored.

They dozed as the van stuck closely to the right side of the road with the obsession of right-hand driven vehicles in Europe. Mussolini's autostrada was long, hot and almost straight and they were concerned that Roger would be hypnotised by the monotonous rhythm and allow the van to slip off the road. Driving from Milan to Bologna was almost like crossing a featureless sea but as they neared Florence the erect cypress trees on hilltops, the attenuated green tints and the spectrum of every shade of brown and ochre created a new landscape which James had glimpsed in pictures in the National Gallery visited on wet Sundays. He sensed his pulse responding to the stirring of his imagination. Under Mont's orders they skirted around Florence, leaving its treasures for another day, and drove east climbing gradually up into the Apennines. The van, only just recovered from the exertions of the Gotthard Pass, struggled on the tight hairpin bends but did not rebel with a boiling radiator. Over the Casentino they descended in gentle curves down to another plain. A ridge of mountains overhung them on their left and a plain stretched ahead and to the right. Interrupting the horizon, a little hill town arose from the plain with a castle, like a nipple, on its summit.

"Poppi." Mont pointed.

"Poppi, Poppi," they all repeated, rolling the p's because they enjoyed the sound of this well-named place.

"Pull over here, Roger," Mont ordered. "Everyone out."

They were near to a small carved stone by the roadside.

"*Battaglia di Campaldino* 1289," they read.

Mont began his lecture.

"Italy was made up of many states and provinces until the nineteenth century and there were constant feuds and wars. The Guelphs were based in Florence and the Ghibellines in Arezzo to the south and in 1289 each side managed to accumulate about 20,000 men – a huge number for those times when small-scale skirmishes were the pattern. The Ghibellines formed a solid rectangular phalanx somewhere over there but the Guelphs chose a crescent formation so that the points of the crescent engulfed the wings of the Ghibellines and destroyed them. Hannibal was perhaps the first to employ these tactics at the battle of Cannae in 216 BC. The great Dante Alighieri of *Inferno* fame was in the Guelph cavalry which bore the brunt of the attack." They stood gazing at the now empty plain, willing the old flesh of men and horses to rise from the ground, the cries and shouts to repopulate the air and the scents of sweat and blood to fill their nostrils. Many men had died in this place. As at all battlefields, bones stripped of their flesh remain and transmit a signal to those who visit centuries later. They climbed back into the van without speaking. In 1938, war was not so remote a prospect. All three young men imagined themselves as mere bones before too long.

Moggiona, with rays of stone houses clinging to the hillside, looked down on Poppi rising from the plain. On the outskirts of the village there was a small marketplace walled by stacks of cut wood and Mont indicated where the van should be left with the confidence of past visits. The main occupation of the villagers was barrel making and throughout Moggiona lay stacks of wood harvested from the steep slopes.

"The barrels are *bigoni*," Mont explained, "and the makers of the barrels are *bigonai*. The skills are handed down from father to son and no women are involved."

Leaving the marketplace, a small empty street clearly led to the centre of the village. Mont led the way up a steep track off the street and at the head of the track stood a stone farmhouse with an iron-railed balcony on the first floor above the front door. The thick double doors, clearly from the previous century, indicated a house of some provenance. Mont produced a key which seemed too large for any pocket and persuaded one half of the double doors to swing open. Ochre tiles with chips of different hues reflecting the random years since injury covered the wide floor behind the doors and stretched away into rooms to left and right. The stone stairway, rodded but without carpet, faced the entrance. On the walls of the stairwell exuberant flowers had been painted into the plaster in a pastiche of Italian medieval fresco heritage. In response to a telegram from Mont that they were arriving, Margherita had opened the windows and placed flowers on the hall table to chase out the premonition of death and decay of long-empty houses. In spite of the heat of the day the house was cool, protected by wooden shutters.

"My room's the one at the front with the best view of Poppi," Mont declared. "You can work out who sleeps where yourselves."

They ran up the stairs to claim their territory.

The only restaurant in the village, which was owned by Margherita's family, was nearby. They ate breakfast and dinner there to give them most time to explore during the day. The villagers were delighted to see the annual influx of Englishmen and Mont instructed his *giovani* on the most cheery and friendly way to say "*buongiorno*", "*buona sera*", "*grazie*" and "*prego*".

"Important courtesy call tomorrow, chaps. We must call on the Baronessa in Camaldoli. When I introduce you to her you must say '*Piacere, Baronessa.*' It is a polite and elegant way to introduce yourself to someone of quality. It's the equivalent of saying '*Enchanté*' in French."

Baronessa Gabriella Quarles van Ufford was English and lived near Camaldoli with her husband who was a Dutch baron. He held a diplomatic post at the Vatican. They expected a very grand lady but when they parked the boy-battered and dusty van outside a modest villa on the outskirts of Camaldoli, a short, friendly lady came out to meet them.

"Welcome to you all. Welcome to Camaldoli. The Baron's away on business. He will be sorry to miss you."

They entered the villa. Statues of the Virgin Mary and other holy relics filled most surfaces. She attended Mass daily in the church of the Camaldolese monks whose order was an offshoot of the Benedictines. Their monastery dominated the town. She served Vino Santo, a sweet white wine, with lavender-scented biscuits and they chatted about England and politics.

"Mussolini and the Fascists don't bother us up here. Life goes on in Camaldoli as it has for centuries. The Lord will provide."

Conversation slowed and Mont stood up to take his leave.

"Well, Baronessa, many, many thanks. The *giovani* will be getting restless and we are off to La Verna today."

La Verna was the place where St Francis of Assisi received the stigmata. After an attack of spiritual ecstasy, akin to that transition between dreaming and awakening, he found his hands pierced and bleeding as if crucifixion nails had been driven through them. They never healed and were his trademark along with a fetish for birds and animals. Mont assembled his group on a rocky headland jutting out from woods and asked them all to kneel and pray. James and Roger were convinced that they were self-inflicted injuries perpetuated by repeated scratching and dared to offer this explanation during dinner that evening. Mont was angry and stomped off to bed before coffee. Philip sided with him and pleaded with James and Roger to keep their opinions to themselves.

They were better behaved at Assisi, the centre of St Francis's life. They knelt beside a rock which was claimed to be St Francis's pillow and visited the tomb of his female confidante, Santa Clara, who founded the community of nuns called the Poor Clares. She lay prune-like in a glass case and the peasant women encased in black from scalp to foot touched the case and prayed fervently for her intercession. Mont insisted that she had not been embalmed but had been saved from decomposition by her very holiness. James and Roger concentrated hard on the task of facial paralysis in the face of this provocation. The fourteenth-century frescos by Giotto at Assisi, with the most vivid and lifelike faces yet portrayed by an artist, saved the day for James, who was rapidly weaving his new experiences of art into his historical review. On their own that evening James asked his friends: "How can

Mont believe this nonsense?" Roger agreed and Philip would not commit himself.

To James, Florence was "all purple and gold". This phrase, created by the Dutch historian Jacob Huizinga, had colonised his mind since his first foray into Renaissance history the year before. Mont insisted on driving the van from Moggiona to Florence as he declaimed:

"Italian cities are the embodiment of anarchy on earth. No Italian would dare to drive into a van driven by a priest. And, what's more, I know the way to a good car park."

Mont wore his full clerical garb that day with a long black cassock, topped by an only just off-white dog collar, and his comfortable silver-buckled black shoes.

"They never try to cheat me in this. As we walk through the streets you will see how the Italians stand back and give us room. It's like the parting of the Red Sea for Moses."

Beyond Pontassieve they began to see the taller buildings of the city pointing up into the aquamarine sky and to understand why Italian Renaissance skies were more vivid than diluted and attenuated English ones. Brunelleschi's red-brown cathedral dome of perfect proportions was instantly framed against Wren's grey-white St Paul's in James's mind.

"Their colours fit their skies, Mont. Extraordinary. The dome of St Paul's is almost like the upturned half of an anaemic grapefruit. Brunelleschi's, well, its shape does not correspond to any other known living thing – but it simply works. It's a miracle."

They stood for an age gazing at the panels of the heavy bronze doors of the Baptistry carved by Ghiberti. The inside of the Duomo was a disappointment, with the fussy over-embroidery of Catholicism. They split up and explored the cathedral on their own. James found a large memorial to the English condottiero Sir John Hawkwood, who commanded the Florentine army for almost twenty years in the late fourteenth century. He made a promise to himself to find out more about him when he returned to his books in the following term. He could not deny his unfashionable interest in battles and wars, which was treated with disdain by some modern historians who favoured insights into peasant life and social revolution as real history.

"History is a broad church. There's room for every interest and activity."

James mumbled this to himself in front of Hawkwood who would have understood. He commended himself for his open mind. The day swept on. In the busy Piazza della Signoria with its symbols of secular power Mont proved his hypothesis that a priest and his party would not be jostled. Michelangelo's sculpture of David dominated the Piazza with its perfection of form and statement that man can achieve all, perhaps without the help of any god.

"There's just time to see the best pictures in the Uffizi while the Italians are shovelling down their lunch," Mont ordained. The three young men were now hoping that their lunch would prevail but Mont's tactics did not fail them. He chose four pictures. Piero della Francesca's portrait of Federico di Montefeltro: the lateral view of the famous stepped nose contrasted with Mont's convex Roman version. They insisted that Mont should stand with his head aligned with Federico's and Roger extracted his camera to place the contrast on permanent record. An attendant leapt forward with whirling arms and shouted incoherently, which seemed to indicate that cameras were not welcome. Next, Uccello's *Battle of San Romano*. The diagrams rather than lifelike portrayals of white and black horses unnerved and overwhelmed. They thought of Campaldino.

"It's almost modern art with the representations of objects rather than an attempt at lifelike reproductions. The colours are fantastic."

Mont knew that he had scored another bullseye. Then to Botticelli's *Primavera* and *Birth of Venus*. He was not immune to the idea that the *giovani* might appreciate the image of a naked, well-rounded woman with strategically placed hair the colour of ripe hay standing rather improbably in a floating seashell.

"Was it true, Mont, that St Francis loved all that nature could offer?" James whispered *sotto voce*, as no one dared to speak out loud in the presence of such beauty.

"He led the fullest of lives before he was called by God to give up everything. That made it an even bigger sacrifice." Mont spoke with a depth of self-knowledge.

"That's enough for now, chaps. If we spend too long in the presence of such art the mind accommodates and devalues the experience. It's better to leave at the top. Lunch is my treat."

They followed in his wake over the Ponte Vecchio which, all agreed, was spoilt by the street traders and shopkeepers imploring them to buy their cheap leather goods. The River Arno, an impenetrable yellow-brown with a patent acquaintance with sewers, meandered below their feet. Once over the bridge Mont turned left and led them into a restaurant with a terrace covered by a white awning, overlooking the river. The thin meat broth, which they had encountered in Moggiona in less subtle form, was followed by pasta dressed with pesto sauce and then by thin slices of bone-white veal. Two bottles of wine, colourless as water, dry as baked stone, slaked their thirst. They hoped for beer or water but these were not to Mont's taste. Just as he had condemned pizza as Italian peasant food, he considered beer proletarian and water only of use for cleaning one's teeth. James could resuscitate the taste of the Umbrian Orvieto wine for many years by turning his mind to that lunch by the Arno in the summer of 1938. Mont's seminar over lunch on secular Florence, the city state of Machiavelli and realpolitik, and on Renaissance art, turned James's mind to the coming term at school and fed his ambition.

"Truth is beauty. Beauty is truth."

They were all sad to leave Florence and return to Moggiona

for their final evening before returning to England. The long journey was an anticlimax. Mont, a man of tradition and ritual, stocked the van with crates of wine and boxes of cigarettes all hidden in the large box filling the width of the van and sited under his bunk. This was preparation for the annual challenge to avoid paying import duty on his contraband. Before approaching Customs at Folkestone he donned his black cassock and his biretta. He armed himself with a matching black Missal and planted himself on the bunk concealing the booty. When the customs officer inspected the inside of the van Mont was intoning his prayers and would not even lift his eyes to acknowledge his presence.

"It works every year," Mont chuckled as they found the road to London.

September to December 1938

Preparation for the Oxford and Cambridge entrance exams at United Colleges School was excellent. Three historians shared responsibility. Bingo ran intensive tutorials concentrating on the sixteenth and seventeenth centuries. Mugsy, the unashamed Liberal, stretched increasingly elastic minds with the dialectical progression from absolutism, through revolutions to constitutional monarchy and then socialism. A younger historian, fresh from Cambridge, Ian McTavish, Scots by name but really a Yorkshireman and clearly approaching from left field, specialised in the Russian Revolution and dissected essays with forensic relish.

The scholarship exam at the end of November 1938 was held in Oxford, which intimidated and inspired. James wrote furiously on a range of unpredictable topics, choosing to answer three questions in depth in each paper rather than four more superficially. Latin and French translation papers completed the persecution. A week later the five historians from his school, hungry for Oxford, were summoned for interviews: two at Balliol, one at Lincoln, one at Oriel and James at Wadham. He entered the Porters' Lodge and gave his name. No ageing NCO could invest more contempt in the form of address "sir" than Oxford and Cambridge college porters.

"Here is your envelope, sir. It gives details of your interviews and meals. Your rooms are on the second staircase on the right."

"Thank you."

He found his rooms rather cold and drab, not the Oxford

of his dreams. Dolores Ibárruri, La Pasionaria, the Communist heroine of the Spanish Republic, immortalised by poster, frowned down at him as if he were a disciple of Franco. A simple gas fire and an uncomfortable bed.

"*Ils ne passeront pas!*"

"She would not be so passionate if she had to sleep in this igloo."

"First interview with Dr Smith and Dr Carter at two o'clock today. Interviews tomorrow at Exeter College and also at Keble and Pembroke, both to be held at Keble," he mumbled to himself. "Surprise, surprise, maybe they want me after all." He had become increasingly gloomy about his chances of success.

As he turned into the staircase for his first interview at Wadham the ample Warden, Maurice Bowra, filled the available space. James pressed his back against the wall and gave way with a courteous, "Good afternoon, sir." His features were widely known. He swept by, glancing but not smiling at the terrified aspirant for admission to his college. James, after prising his back from the wall gripping him like a magnet, broke the spell and lunged towards the door fearing that he might be late. An open outer door competed for his knock with a closed inner door but only momentarily. He struck the inner door more firmly than he had intended but then thought that he must create a strong impression.

"Ah, Mr Butland, come in and sit down. You wrote some interesting answers."

"Thank you, sir."

He seemed to be saying that too often. It sounded oily and formulaic. His hands sweated and his face reddened, his response to stress.

"'The Renaissance was a fabric of purple and gold...' you wrote."

"Yes, sir. A phrase borrowed from Huizinga."

"You seem to present an emotional response to the Renaissance rather than a hard-hearted northern European one."

"I spent the summer in Tuscany with friends. It was the perfect synthesis of Renaissance history and art each feeding off the other. In the Uffizi we saw Piero's Federico of Urbino who is considered to be Machiavelli's model of the perfect prince. He combined the finest art and the finest governance. An example of ultimate civilisation. I agree, sir, that it is possible to be infatuated with the Renaissance unlike, for example, Cromwell's Republic or Tudor government reforms. It is one of a range of responses that I have to historical events. In Italy we visited the battlefield of Campaldino where Dante had fought. I confess that I actually enjoy detailed accounts of Wellington's battles though these are not fashionable historical study at present."

"Quite. Our venerable Warden Bowra perennially advises his pupils to travel below the wine line. The experience clears foggy English minds and loosens inhibitions. You seem to have anticipated his advice, Mr Butland."

James had heard much of Maurice Bowra, who not only prodded his pupils towards the Mediterranean sun but also praised the Oxford sun that rises over Wadham and sets over Worcester.

"Now, let's change the scenery from Renaissance purple and gold to soot and coal. What do you know about the Industrial Revolution, Mr Butland?"

"Perhaps there was no Industrial Revolution. Industrial and economic development had been a gradual process since the Middle Ages. Max Weber in his *The Protestant Ethic and the Spirit of Capitalism* argued that the system of capitalism had been made possible by the Protestant mindset and by Calvinism in particular. Professor Tawney in his *Religion and the Rise of Capitalism* identified transition from feudalism to capitalism in the decades leading up to the Civil War. John Nef in his *History of the British Coal Industry*, published several years ago, identified the origins of what he called a 'proto Industrial Revolution' in the early sixteenth century. I think I would prefer to describe the eighteenth and nineteenth centuries as the acceleration of industrial evolution rather than revolution."

"You're well informed, Mr Butland. I assume you have read these works?"

Deciding that honesty and integrity would be more highly regarded than bravado, James replied, "I have read Tawney's book, sir, and dipped into the others."

"Very wise of you, my boy."

The historical banter continued over many subjects and centuries. James thought it was all going rather well. He spoke in a far more exuberant way than normal as he thought it was part of the expected Oxford performance. His school fellows, if they were able to listen, would have been shocked by this reformed character. His escape route from his background was in reach. He was enjoying himself. It was a taste of what was to come.

"Thank you, Mr Butland. We shall inform you of our conclusion during the next two weeks."

"Thank you, sir."

Once again it sounded rather Uriah Heepish and lugubrious. He must practise.

James returned to his rooms and had some hours to spend before dinner in Hall. He decided to visit old Oxford haunts and thought that he knew the city as well as any undergraduate from his weekend expeditions with his parents. He walked along Broad Street and past the Martyrs' Memorial to St John's. Many aspiring undergraduates were idly standing or wandering, some chatting with others. They did not seem better bets than him and he silently cursed his headmaster for warning him off this Cavalier college. Worcester College had also appealed and he walked purposefully off to compare it. The classical proscenium entrance gave no clue to the scene within. Down the left side stood a medieval terrace pierced by passageways and on the right an elevated Georgian façade proclaiming its superiority over the Gothic. He walked down by the medieval terrace and, confident from previous visits with his parents, stepped through the last tunnel into the finest garden in Oxford. Meandering past the lake, disturbed only by ducks, he could not stop thinking about *A Midsummer Night's Dream*. He began to wonder whether he had chosen well.

Dinner at Wadham. At 7.30 the bell summoned the collection of Wadham aspirants and a minority of undergraduates who had remained after the end of term. He joined a group who all seemed to be alone – the majority. Only a few had come from the same school and were chatting loudly and overconfidently with those whom they probably loathed. The talk was desultory.

"Where are you at school?"

"Was your father at Wadham?"

One other "man", the Oxford word for not only undergraduates but schoolboys, had been interviewed for history and they compared topics. James slept well and enjoyed his generous breakfast. The college scouts were middle-aged and quite elderly men whose "sirs" were more friendly and genuine than those of the porters. Even James could tolerate cabbage now without retching.

To Exeter College. An elderly ordained clerical gentleman clearly disliked his answers on the Reformation probably because of doctrinal disgust but Exeter did award an exhibition to one of his school friends who would have preferred Balliol. No chance of Exeter, then. James was relieved as three years' purgatory with the cleric would have been sour.

At Keble, James was on top form. It was a performance, an act of melodrama and once again antithetical to his school demeanour. Perhaps this was his true demeanour, not the repressed suburban boy intimidated by the Hampstead would-be intellectuals who were mostly second and third rate. Oxford would be his catharsis, his escape from London oppression: 1789, 1830, 1848 and 1917 all in one.

His Pembroke interview was with a very junior fellow, hardly older than James himself, but probably a post-doctoral researcher who asked, "What would you like to discuss?" This rather disconcerted him, but only briefly.

"We could discuss Munich."

"Yes. What do you think of Munich, Mr Butland?"

Chamberlain had only just averted war by making huge concessions to Hitler on the future of Czechoslovakia. *That's not history, it's politics*, James reflected without speaking.

"We may be at war with Germany by this time next year."

"I think I agree with you, Mr Butland. Have you been following our own recent by-election in Oxford which has been widely reported in the newspapers?"

"Indeed I have, sir. I understand the Master of Balliol, A.D. Lindsay, stood as an 'Independent Progressive' candidate bitterly opposed to the Conservative candidate and Mr Chamberlain. He had the support of the Labour party and the Liberals and of many Conservatives who find Munich repugnant. He lost but halved the Conservative majority."

"Yes, indeed. Before you leave Oxford go and see Picasso's *Guernica* which is on loan to the Ashmolean."

"Thank you, I shall."

It was rather tame and he regretted the lack of academic sabre rattling that he had enjoyed at Wadham and Keble. He walked to the Ashmolean Museum in a stupor. He could not hear his footsteps on the pavement. James stood before the *Guernica*, Picasso's abstract nightmare of the destruction of the small Spanish town by German bombers in April 1937 in the Spanish Civil War. British government reports had predicted that 600,000 would be killed by bombs in the first few months of a future war with Germany. Guernicas would be as commonplace as thunderstorms.

He continued to Oxford Station and caught the next Paddington train. Circle Line to Baker Street and the next Metropolitan Line back to… Harrow. As the train stopped at Finchley Road, where he would usually alight for school, he was relieved that he did not, on this day, have to get off for the climb towards Hampstead Heath. Oxford seemed so far away. About a week later, just before Christmas 1938, the envelope with an Oxford post mark arrived.

Wadham College
Oxford
17th December 1938

Dear Sir,

I am glad to tell you that you have been elected to a Woodward Scholarship in History at this College to the value of £40 per annum to read History beginning in October, 1939. We should be grateful if you would let us know as soon as possible whether you intend to accept our offer.

Yours faithfully,
C. M. Bowra
WARDEN

James's mother almost collapsed with excitement and grasped him with a fervent hug which rather shocked him. Over the next few days he received letters of congratulations from his headmaster and from Bingo Darlington. When other masters expressed doubts about him, Bingo had always expressed confidence in his ability. James treasured his letter.

Dear James,

I cannot be satisfied by congratulating you merely on the phone. What a triumph for you! It is, you know, and with all your modesty you must recognise it. I am enormously pleased, and delighted. Con-millions-of-gratulations. You deserve it all right; and now to enjoy a most happy Christmas.
Yours,
Jim Darlington

Two of his school friends had won awards at Exeter and Oriel. Two others were unsuccessful, certainly not less talented than the Oxford three, but victims of interview chemistry. James's father wrote a letter of thanks to his headmaster and informed him that, with immediate effect, James had left school.

January 1939 to May 1940

At United Colleges School, as at most independent private schools and some grammar schools, there was an Officers' Training Corps. James enjoyed the organised discipline and conformity which seemed so paradoxical at that school. It was almost the 11th Harrow Scout Troop with guns, marching and drill. The rough khaki uniforms with puttees reminded them of the experiences of their fathers and uncles only two decades before. To learn how to look after and fire a rifle was a counterpoint to the academic gymnastics in the classroom and James enjoyed the rifle range. He was a good shot and the school had a good shooting reputation and had even won the Public Schools' Cup at Bisley several years before. James was awarded a lance corporal's stripe and learned to give orders to his subordinates in a calm and understated manner which he had learnt as a patrol leader in the 11th Harrow. During 1938 the prospect of war with Germany was real though his sights were on Oxford and not on Berlin.

Having left school behind them, James and some of his friends decided to join a Territorial Army battalion in early 1939. The choice lay between one of the local Middlesex Regiment battalions or the more interesting London battalions, the Queen Victoria's Rifles or Queen's Westminster Rifles. James and his friends joined the QVR, the 7th volunteer battalion of the King's Royal Rifle Corps or 60th Rifles, an old and distinguished Rifle regiment who considered themselves superior to the Guards. The Commanding Officer was Lt Colonel John Ellison-

Macartney, who was also the Bursar of Queen Mary College in the University of London. The battalion was well educated and motivated with a high percentage of professional men in its ranks. It had been raised in the 1860s when threats to Britain from the Continent were perceived and it had performed very well in the Great War. Riflemen marched more rapidly and were better shots than the rest of the British Army and considered themselves an elite.

The company of the QVR which James and his school friends had joined was based in West Hampstead and, coincidentally, used the grounds of United Colleges School for their drill. In the spring of 1939 they became a mobile motorcycle battalion and assumed that they would specialise in a reconnaissance role in the event of war, which was looking increasingly likely. In August 1939 the battalion was mobilised and ordered to a camp in Kent. After the outbreak of war the British Expeditionary Force or BEF crossed to France to form a continuous line of defence with the French to meet the expected German invasion.

James received his mobilisation orders and wrote to the senior tutor of Wadham informing him that he would be unable to go up in October 1939 as planned. He received a reply by return of post reassuring him that his scholarship would await him "at the end of the present emergency". With only the briefest of shudders did he reflect that he might not be around to accept it. Since September 1939 there had been many changes of personnel in the QVR. Many NCOs had been posted for officer training and some men who were skilled tradesmen were forced to leave the QVR and return to their essential reserved occupations.

The QVR spent the first winter of the war at Paddock Wood near Tonbridge in Kent. As a rifle battalion they were part of 30th Infantry Brigade commanded by Brigadier Claude Nicholson. In practice, they were not trained infantrymen but were a light mobile reconnaissance force relying on motorcycles. In April

1940 the QVR were prepared to join the forces for the expedition to Norway but this order was cancelled and they returned to home defence duties. The battalion comprised 566 officers and men. On May 18th 1940 they were suddenly deprived of their twenty-two scout cars, which were required by other units.

Motorcycle battalions in 1940 had much less punch than regular rifle battalions like the King's Royal Rifle Corps and the Rifle Brigade. Each QVR company had only ten Bren guns and five Boys anti-tank rifles. One third of the men had only revolvers and were not issued with rifles as they were classified as cavalry. Their experience of firing Bren guns was minimal and only selected riflemen had fired a few rounds with their anti-tank rifles. They had two-inch mortars but were equipped with only smoke bombs. Lieutenant Colonel Ellison-Macartney was ordered to stand by and prepare for overseas duty. Hours later, definite orders were received.

Here is a message for you. Eastern Command to 1QVR. Battalion will move in two parties to Port Vic for embarkation. First party will leave by train from Ashford at 0515 hours and second party at 0545 hours tomorrow morning. Load all equipment in trucks at Ashford.

Port Vic was code for Dover but no one had informed them of this translation. Two other orders disconcerted the officers. They were instructed to leave behind their motor transport and were informed that 800 seats were available for them on the trains. Clearly the War Office believed that the QVR was a fully equipped rifle battalion and not a motorcycle battalion of under 600 men. In the heat of the crisis they had been selected for a role for which they had neither trained nor were equipped. This staff work blunder was critical. They had only a few night hours to strike camp and prepare for embarkation. Men were unable to contact their families. The train to convey them from Ashford to Dover went to the wrong station but eventually halted at Dover. Gunfire from France could be heard. Light drizzle further dampened their spirits. Their morose anxiety changed to anger when they found that the ship to transport them across the Channel, City of Canterbury, did have room for the motorcycles and sidecars after all. They had been left behind at Paddock Wood. The men could have easily ridden them to Dover but instead marched many miles with heavy equipment. This was manhandled from the station to the quay in torrential rain. When the loading was complete many men were given only a sausage roll, chocolates and tea.

Some troops at Dover had just returned from France and the QVR were dismayed to hear:

"Most of the movement today seems to be in the opposite direction to you."

Ellison-Macartney opened his sealed orders: "…a few German tanks have broken through to the Channel ports… the QVR are to proceed to Calais and take the necessary steps to secure the town."

He was reassured that the remainder of the 30th Infantry Brigade would follow in a few days. The War Office had assumed wrongly that the QVR were part of the Brigade with the first battalion of the Rifle Brigade and the second battalion of the King's Royal Rifle Corps and not part of the weakly equipped and inexperienced First London Motor Division which was not expected to provide a front line infantry role. Without their motorcycles, sidecars, and their wireless trucks, Ellison-Macartney realised that he would have no effective communications with HQ and other units. In desperation he telephoned Ashford, ordering as many motorcycles as possible to be ridden to Dover immediately, but they had not arrived when City of Canterbury had left for Calais.

The sea was calm and the rain lifted. One officer was reading Richard II and opened it at random. His eyes fell on the passage describing the banishment of Thomas Mowbray, Duke of Norfolk and declaimed to his fellow soldiers: "The hopeless words of never to return breathe I against thee upon pain of life." At this stage of the voyage they were still able to conjure a nervous laugh.

Gradually the outline of Calais with the prominent clock tower appeared. A coaster had been sunk alongside the quay. Houses were burning and there was a large hole in the roof of the Gare Maritime. City of Canterbury docked, but unloading was delayed as a train blocked the whole length of the siding so that all baggage had to be carried by the soldiers to the road. Three cranes were lying idle as there were no crane drivers. Before unloading was complete, British and French wounded were carried up the same gangways, causing chaos.

The QVR, the only organised infantry battalion in Calais, were directed to block the six principal roads into the town. The perimeter they were ordered to defend was enormous for a battalion without transport and of which only two-thirds had rifles. Positions were hastily chosen from maps. They could dig no trenches as picks and shovels had been left in their vehicles in Kent. "A" Company covered the bridges dividing Calais Nord from Calais Saint-Pierre. "B" Company had the longest march to block the coast road to the west to Sangatte and to cover the shore for three miles. "C" Company covered the eastern approaches to Calais along a road running parallel to the eastern ramparts and also had a three-mile stretch of beach to defend to prevent German aircraft landing at low tide.

James, with some of his school friends, was in "D" Company. They marched over three miles from the docks to cover roads from the south. His platoon took up a position on the Guînes road just south of Les Fontinettes. An abandoned ten-ton lorry was pressed into service as a partial road block.

Throughout the nights of 22nd and 23rd May and the whole of the following day all approaches from the south and west were congested with French soldiers fleeing from the Germans. Nothing had prepared the riflemen ordered to defend their precarious position. Instead of using all their senses to spot Germans infiltrating from the south, they were overwhelmed by refugees seeking safety in Calais. Old men and women, conscripted to help the younger members of their families, pushed prams and hand carts piled high with their most prized possessions. Mothers carried babies in their arms and fathers carried older children on their shoulders. Some children preserved their joy and sense of adventure, running ahead to play with their friends and back again to the security of their families. Most tramped on with drooping shoulders and masked faces too distressed to recall the happy past and to contemplate the bleak future. The riflemen were then ordered to turn back the refugees and all French and Belgian troops who had discarded their rifles. This provoked such an outpouring of grief that James and his fellows began to feel as wretched as the civilians who begged them to relent. Then someone spotted tanks on the edge of the forest to the southeast. These were joined by German reconnaissance planes and suddenly the refugees vanished into unnoticed ditches. Many had already been strafed by the guns of the Stukas and ME 109s on the roads and had learnt the cruel lesson.

This was the first sight of German ground forces by D Company. They disappeared back into the forest in the face of French artillery fire. By midday on 23rd May the remainder of 30th Infantry Brigade arrived at Calais. The 1st Battalion of the Rifle Brigade and 2nd Battalion King's Royal Rifle Corps, first rate regular soldiers, were ordered to hold the inner perimeter formed by the ramparts and moat of the old town, a front of about eight miles. The QVR continued to hold the outer perimeter as long as possible. When this became untenable they fell back and reinforced the battalion of regular soldiers in their strong defensive positions. In the early hours of 24th May, Brigadier

Claude Nicholson, who commanded all British troops in Calais, was informed by London that evacuation of the garrison had been decided in principle, and probably that night. All fighting personnel were to remain at their posts but "useless mouths" – non-combatants and wounded – were to be evacuated at once. These marched or were carried onto the ship which was still unloading ammunition, vehicles and tanks. As a consequence, most of these were never unloaded and were returned to Dover with the evacuees.

Shortly before midnight a further message was received from the War Office.

In spite of policy of evacuation given you this morning, British forces in your area now under command of General Fagalde (French) who has ordered no, repeat no, evacuation. This means you must comply for sake of Allied solidarity.

The order was to hold on as long as possible. The defenders of Calais had understood their role to protect the flank of Dunkirk but this order ripped the legs from under them. They were now condemned to play a minor part in a scheme to impress the French that they would not be completely deserted by their Allies. D Company of the QVR was ordered to withdraw to the line of the ramparts and reinforce the line held by the regular soldiers. James had not yet fired his rifle. They took up positions along the railway embankment adjacent to the bridge over the Canal de Calais.

The sound of small arms gunfire was on all sides and it was not long before they would be in action. The platoon, still in darkness, sited its Bren gun with a clear field of fire over the bridge and along the canal running to left and right for several hundred yards. The road to the southeast across the bridge would be an obvious approach route for German troops. The QVR felt exposed but had been reassured that they would be reinforced and all were clinging onto the belief that they would eventually withdraw back to the quay and be evacuated to England when further defence was impossible.

The QVR were inexperienced but keen to show that they could fight as well as the regulars of the KRRC alongside them. James lay prone next to David Hotson, a friend from school days who had enlisted on the same day. He had won a history exhibition at Exeter College, Oxford.

"How long do you think we shall be here, David?"

"You've heard that the BEF is falling back on Dunkirk. We are too few to make much difference, surely. They'll take us off in a day or two."

"Oxford seems far off now, doesn't it? Do you think this will all be over in time for us to go up next year?"

"I don't know. It's possible that Churchill and Halifax will make an armistice leaving the Continent to the Germans and our island to float between the Channel, the North Sea and the Atlantic."

It was still dark on the morning of the 25th and soon it would be a good time for an attack. Their eyes darted left and right, searching, searching for the field grey uniforms. It was reassuring to see the bridge and the canal; easier to defend, they reassured themselves, than a flat field or copse. They could see other QVR and KRRC platoons on both flanks and relaxed a little. All was silent except for distant gunfire, probably up the coast. No one spoke.

Their steel helmets incinerated their scalps until sweat was pouring down their faces and into their eyes. Their platoon officer, second lieutenant Geoffrey Barnes, informed them that 10th Panzer Division had advanced from southwest to northeast across the front, threatening Calais from the east and preventing any link between Calais and Dunkirk. It made sense and they were relieved that no tanks were visible on the road facing them across the canal. They had no artillery and could not defend against tanks with rifles and Bren guns. They could hold infantry in their position. It had been like an exercise so far. They had not yet been tested. It could not last.

"I can see something moving on the other side of the canal."

"Probably Marcel crawling home from his girlfriend's bed back to his fat madame."

"Face your front!"

It was Sergeant Jenkins. They all stared into the darkness with only the first evidence of the day to come and all strained ears. The loud silence of the graveyard at night. The salty mist puffed a few feet over the canal. A dog barked once several hundred yards away in the town. The fast heavy hammer blows in his ears and chest and sweaty fingers holding his rifle reminded James of the terror minutes before he turned over his first paper in the Oxford scholarship exam. Although sweating, he felt cold and shivered for several seconds uncontrollably. A platoon on the right fired a flare and in the cemetery light, grey crouching figures well spread out were approaching the bridge on the other side of the canal. They huddled as near to the buildings on either side of the road as they could.

"Open fire! Fire at will!"

The recall of that first shot in anger never left James. He calmly chose a large NCO about twenty yards beyond the bridge. He took careful rifle range aim, and fired. The grey NCO immediately grabbed his left arm, dropping his rifle, and knelt down on one knee. The Bren gun opened up and Germans were sinking down like deflating balloons. Some stirred with random movements of arm or leg. Others lay very still. James pointed his sights slightly to the left of the NCO just in case his rifle was firing a little to the right and smoothly squeezed the trigger again. The NCO, already kneeling, toppled backwards, his legs ungainly flexed at the knees and under him. He lay very still, with no puppet movement of limb. James had no remorse. He realised immediately that he was enjoying this moment of killing much better than taking a crucial wicket or opening the Oxford envelope.

The glassy daylight of the flare had now gone and the Germans were running back down the road, leaving about twenty of their comrades on the approach to the bridge. None had crossed. The survivors would report that the canal bridge was strongly held by the QVR, although they would not know the identity of their opponents. James lay prone on the dry soil with index finger resting on the trigger, massaging it gently, gently to reassure himself that it was in exactly the same place, ready for the next squeeze. His mouth was dry and the thumping in his head and chest had gone and the sweat had evaporated with the arrival of the day.

The platoon relaxed a little with tea, which arrived from somewhere, and thick bully-beef sandwiches were passed around. They lay shoulder to shoulder gaining strength from each other and enjoyed new confidence that they could hold this position for as long as was required of them. James thought of his Uncle Ernest at Ypres in 1915 and of unknown ancestors holding the line on other battlefields in other wars. They were all one, generation after generation supporting those who follow. There was no shortage of wars to keep the flames alive.

The scruffy street over the canal began to reassure rather than threaten them. No civilians. They had entombed themselves in cellars or had slipped out of Calais to stay with friends or relatives in the villages. Dogs had not divined the rules and trotted along the street, keeping close to walls, only sidestepping occasionally to follow a scent. The German dead remained and the dogs often left the security of their walls to sniff the bodies but did not linger long. One dog sniffed rather longer than most and James and his friends hoped that he would salute the corpse with his rear leg. The dog left the body in peace and sought the sterility of the wall.

As the day lengthened there was gunfire to both left and

right but no further attempts by the Germans down at the Rue Madeleine opposite the bridge. They needed bridges to cross the network of waterways but clearly had not identified James's bridge as critical. The QVR gained confidence and began to stand up rather than crawl to stretch stiff limbs and empty bladders. The weather was hot for May and the men were allowed to remove tunics. They knew little of what was happening at other points of the perimeter. Perhaps they did not even care. Their focus was their bridge, their canal and their arc of enemy-infested town. With a modest lift in spirits came rumours of the major reinforcement of Calais. Nicholson's three battalions could be a bridgehead and the base for a major counter-attack to cut off the Germans in a pocket stretching from Calais to Dunkirk. It was beginning to seem too easy.

In the early evening lower pitched noises were heard faraway which could be interpreted as heavy vehicles and possibly tanks. Nearer to them came the crump of many boots marching in step and then their disintegration into a random cacophony of men running. From the far end of the broad street of the Rue Madeleine, stretching away from the bridge, two light tanks approached. Men were running from doorway to doorway and slipping down side streets before reappearing with new courage. The QVR had some Boys antitank rifles but no artillery support. The small force of British tanks remained to defend the port itself. James saw smoke from the nearest German tank barrel, followed a split second later by a cough and then the shell exploded fifty yards behind the platoon. It sucked the men towards it and then let go with a brief vertigo that bullied ears for a few seconds. Then silence.

"Is everyone all right?" Lieutenant Barnes shouted.

"We're fine, sir."

The platoon awaited the next shell which was likely to be corrected in range. Two tanks fired together but both shots fell short, one landing in the street near the canal and the other in the canal itself in a fountain of water. James saw the plume of water hanging almost lifelessly in the air before it subsided into the flat canal. The grey figures crouched behind the tanks. Some were elbowed out from the dead ground and jumped back into semi-safety, but they all came on.

"Face your front!" Sergeant Jenkins yelled. A superfluous order of course as every QVR eye was welded to the scene ahead. The cold sweat, dry mouth, pounding head and bowel writhing returned. A dog retreated at a fast trot into a side road.

James felt around the smooth trigger as if it were a firm nipple, though he had never had this tactile experience. It was soft yet hard, not as smooth as he had once thought when introduced to his rifle. The trigger's subtle pits and contours only revealed themselves to him in this intensity of sensations.

"Good luck, James," David whispered from his right.

"And to you too, old chum."

"Hold your fire until I give the order."

Was that Sergeant Jenkins or Lieutenant Barnes? Their voices had climbed an octave and were indistinguishable. They wanted the men to experience that self-confidence of discipline and belief that they could not miss their targets when the time came. Further tank shells burst behind them but were ignored. The German gunners dared not fall short when their own men were only fifty yards from the bridge.

"Fire!"

James felt his right shoulder jerk backwards with his first shot. The first shot always seemed to hurt the most. After that, the shoulder became anaesthetised to the punch.

"Choose your targets and fire at will."

The Germans were now packed too tightly to take individual aim at them. James fired into the mass, knowing that every bullet was striking home. Bren guns fired short bursts. The approach to the bridge was paved by German bodies. In the previous attack James had not been aware of any return of fire by the Germans, but now it was different. The call for stretcher bearers was all around him. The surge to the bridge was ebbing away as the bodies proved not a physical barrier to their comrades still alive but a barrier to their courage. The QVR maintained their intense rate of fire. Once again it was possible to choose targets and James selected one of a pair of soldiers dragging away a wounded officer. He had already discovered his preference for shots to the left rather than to the right, which he did not understand, but this newfound instinct chose the left-hand retreating German. He chose the left shoulder blade as his aiming point and fired. The victim fell forwards heavily, dropping his rifle from his left hand and his officer from his right. The other soldier could no longer help the officer alone and he too dropped him and ran. *Perhaps I killed two Germans with a single shot*, James mused. He was learning of a new facet to his character and felt no regret, only exultation.

The platoon had suffered casualties: two probably dead and several others wounded. Another attack would surely be pressed before the evening.

"We can't hold if they attack again with more tanks."

Lieutenant Barnes was working his way around his platoon.

"You all did bloody well. Keep holding on. We can see them off again if they dare come."

The officer was excited, breathless, proud of his men. He had seen no action himself before and was relieved that he had come through so far.

"They're coming again."

It was Sergeant Jenkins in a bass baritone this time.

"The Boche don't give up that easily. They just hit harder. But we can take it."

The QVR were in a strong position but clearly could not hold much longer without more men and heavier guns. James heard Lieutenant Barnes speaking to the battalion HQ on the wireless.

"Do you want us to try and hold, sir, or can we pull back?"

"We hold, Sergeant."

"Very good, sir."

They did not come again that night. The Germans had taken many casualties and soon an officer and two soldiers, one carrying a white flag and the other a red cross, emerged from a side street on the right-hand side of the road.

"English soldiers – we ask for a truce to remove our dead and wounded."

"Go ahead. You have five minutes," Barnes replied.

He knew they would make careful reconnaissance of the QVR positions during the lull. He would move his Brens and anti-tank rifles after they had gone.

They took turns to doze off but never relaxed. Spirits always fell with the darkness and rose with the dawn although threats were reciprocal. They all kept their thoughts to themselves but all were now hoping for the order to withdraw to Calais Nord, to the station and the port for evacuation. The rumours of heavy reinforcements had subsided as no replacements or relief came. With a steady rate of casualties they were thinning out without the spirit-gripping reassurance of shoulder-to-shoulder fighting.

D Company was ordered to withdraw to the old ramparts and they moved off with only desultory fire to speed their movement. They took position near an old bastion on the south of Calais Saint-Pierre. A company of the KRRC were nearby. The close proximity of regular soldiers rebuilt their confidence and of course they were nearer to the sea.

"Stand to."

The order came from the KRRC but it spread rapidly between all officers and NCOs of the QVR. From the south, a group of Stukas swept in like carrion and began to bomb the ancient walls. They all pressed their bodies as closely to the old cool stone as possible. The Stuka sirens which had terrorised civilian refugees in France and Belgium sounded ridiculous to the defenders of

Calais. No bombs fell close to James's position but there were casualties in the ranks of the KRRC.

As soon as the Stukas had cleared the skies, artillery from the southwest started its barrage and the old walls which had stood for three hundred years began to crumble. This was much worse than assault by troops. There was nowhere to return fire. No soft flesh at which to aim. The act of firing the rifle brought strength and reassurance. Passive waiting for a shell to explode and dissolve human bodies was degrading. Shells killed more men than machine guns. They all knew that from the Great War. James began to shiver from listening to his own thoughts. The bombardment halted. He had survived this too. *If fighting is no worse than this, it won't be too bad. I can survive.*

"Face your front!"

This time it was Sergeant Jenkins. This was it. Tanks. Soldiers on the move in well-spaced groups. Mortars fired from our own side with that beguiling and unearthly plop.

"Fire at will!"

Once again it was not the firing range discipline of target selection which James had enjoyed in the first action, the synthesis of intellect, senses and skill. This was just firing as rapidly as possible into the mass of advancing Germans. You could not miss but this less focused game did not bring the same visceral reward.

James felt as if he had been punched in the right side of the head. He stopped firing and looked to his right to see if he had been struck by an elbow or rifle butt by a clumsy neighbour. David was on his right. They had become a team; almost twins. They had never felt as close at school but this was a different planet. He could not have imagined the blow. But perhaps he had. It did not hurt. He felt water running down his face and into his eye. It was not water. It was warm and when his fingertips dipped into it they were bloody.

I am fine.

His head began to thump but he was alert. His helmet must have slipped back or been pierced by a bullet or piece of shrapnel. He continued to fire but he was shooting too high and could not seem able to correct the shot.

This is bloody silly.

His rate of fire reduced as his right hand kept dabbing his head to see if the flow of blood was continuing. It seemed to stop but felt very sticky and around his eye there was a thick dry paste.

I must be all right.

The Germans were once again falling back after taking heavy losses. So many of them lay still in the posture of boneless dolls. James felt no pity for them. The throbbing continued and he felt faint and nauseous.

"Butland, go to the Regimental Aid Post."

"Yes, sir."

"You've all done very well, men, and seen them off again. Stay calm. Fire low."

Men, James thought. *We're only boys on an OTC field day, or Oxford undergraduates promoted to men by sarcastic college porters. We're not really here at all. There's been some mistake. We've stumbled into some sort of play or film set. It all seems so unreal, so remote.*

He lay still, unable to absorb all the sensory inputs of the last few days. He was dreaming. It was just like that no man's land between deep sleep and awakening when reality and unreality had merged and become one.

"Butland, I told you to go to the RAP. Move."

Where was the RAP? He stumbled off, gripping his rifle firmly in his right hand, dabbing his head with his left hand. It still thumped but did not hurt very much. David found James's field dressing and applied it inexpertly.

"Off you go, old chum. I'll see you on the quay when we get off today or tonight."

"Can you tell me where the RAP is?"

He kept asking as he stumbled back from their line, politely and perhaps too formally, but he did not want to make too much fuss.

"Keep going that way, chum."

James walked in circles, directed by over-helpful soldiers who did not seem to be QVR. It seemed like the hunt for the mythical sky-hook at his first camp. There was no such object but it was part of the initiation and harmless fun for the old lags. Most were sitting, lying or lurching about, recovering in their own way from the action of only a few minutes before. He was soon in the network of alleys and streets in the south of Calais Saint-Pierre and walked on with no clear plan or direction. James recognised a street down which they had marched from the port several days ago. He decided to walk in the opposite direction which would navigate him towards the port. The RAP was likely to be north rather than south of the action, he reasoned. He pressed against the wall as the drone of aeroplanes distracted him.

They don't sound like Stukas. More like lawnmowers.

He then saw three stubby aeroplanes with large fixed wheels and long bat-like wings.

They're Lysanders dropping supplies to our boys.

He started to wave both arms at them in relief but then felt deflated. He stood almost to attention with his rifle in the air. When they had flown away he resumed his walk in a daze of unreality.

What drew him off this route down a narrow street to the left, he would never know. It opened into a little square and in the far corner of the square was a house. It was guarded by large metal gates, solid in the lower storey and topped with spiked railings running off to both sides. Unmown lawns squeezed the gravel path to the front door. A large monkey-puzzle tree hid the view of the right side of the house. James could never walk past this Chilean tree without stopping and admiring it, wanting to touch the round, green spiky limbs. It reminded him of home. They always seemed so exotic, so confident, so foreign, but exerted a gravity field that he could not resist. At the gate James saw a brass plate.

Dr Jacques Hugo MD
Médecin et Accoucheur

A doctor's surgery. This would do. He must have missed the RAP. The doctor would patch him up and he would be able to return to his platoon. All was silent in this square, though there was distant gun fire which seemed blunted and unthreatening.

He approached the front door and pulled the bell. It clanged joyfully and then subsided to silence. No one came. He rang again, twice, and then light footsteps came from inside. The door opened six inches and a young woman of perhaps twenty-two or twenty-three curled round the door. *Not very French-looking*, James thought. Her face was round with very pale skin and Pre-Raphaelite auburn hair. Her eyebrows were so pale, not red, that they were invisible. Her mouth was open and one hand pressed over it. He could not see the rest of her body behind the door but knew that she was tall and thin.

"*Pardon, mademoiselle, mais les Allemands sont fusillés moi. Est-ce-que le médecin est ici?*"

"You are English," the woman replied with obvious relief. "I thought you might be the Germans. Come in. My father, the doctor, is not here. He was called up into the army at the beginning of the war and is somewhere down south. But I can help you. I am a medical student at the University of Lille. I returned home when the university closed down with the German invasion."

"I am sorry. I am intruding. If the doctor is not here I must go and find our own RAP – Regimental Aid Post – I was trying to find it but must have missed it."

"Come in. I can dress your wound. If you need something more clever then we can find your British Army doctors."

"But what about your mother, your family?"

"My mother is dead. She died before the war. My brother is in the army. When I pass my exams I hope to join my father's practice here. Many women like a woman doctor."

"Thank you. Thank you, mademoiselle. What is your name?"

"Agnès Hugo."

He noted her pronunciation as "An-yes" in French, more elegant than the English equivalent.

"I am James Butland."

He followed her down the hall, through a waiting room area for the patients and into the surgery. It was neat, tidy and smelt of carbolic acid soap.

"Sit here, Monsieur Butland."

She began to clean his head with cotton wool soaked in disinfectant. She then shaved the area around the wound with a razor and cleaned it again.

She's clearly done this before, James thought but dared not speak during the procedure.

"It's a nasty cut by the bullet, Monsieur. You are so lucky that it split the skin and then flew off. It needs stitches. I have no local anaesthetic but have forceps, needles and silk and I can suture it."

James understood how near he had been to death. One inch one way and he would have lost skull bone and leaked brains. One inch the other way and he would still be lying with his fellows in the bastion. *Soldiering is a lottery*, he mused.

"Yes, please, mademoiselle. I'm feeling a little faint and sick. Can I hold a bowl just in case?"

"Of course."

She started work. The needle burnt a little as it punctured his skin but then it just tugged. He watched her fingers moving neatly and economically. No unnecessary motions. Each new stitch felt different. She sutured for about twenty minutes and then applied a lint dressing soaked in ammonia. She bandaged his head so that he would look like every other injured soldier acting in a play. He began to feel very sick and swayed a little in the chair.

"You are concussed, James. That is why you missed the Aid Post."

She called me James. How very odd.

"I must leave and return to my platoon. They will wonder what has happened to me. They may think I've deserted."

"There's plenty of time for that. I'll help you to bed for an hour or two. Then you will feel stronger."

He tried to stand, instructing his muscles in his calves, thighs and spine to obey his orders in turn, but his legs felt lifeless, dangling uselessly from his body. But they moved. Disobediently and in a rather awkward sequence, but they moved. Agnès held his arm and led him back to the hall.

"You will feel better if you climb the stairs and sleep."

He did not resist and by the top of the long, straight staircase his limbs had learnt what to do and did not seem to need conscious orders. They entered a bedroom at the rear of the house. James fleetingly saw the garden, an expanded version of the small enclosure fronting the square. Formal lawns, gravel paths and another monkey-puzzle tree at the end of the central gravel path marking the boundary.

"I feel so tired. I shall make a terrible mess of your bed." His khaki blouse and trousers were spattered with mud and blood.

"You must sleep. When you have slept we can find your friends again. You are concussed," Agnès repeated.

"Then I must be if you say so, Docteur – I am sorry – Docteuse."

She eased him out of his blouse. His thick army-issue vest underneath seemed clean, sparing him embarrassment. She removed his boots as he sat lifelessly on the side of the bed like a small child manipulated by its mother. She reached for the buttons of his trousers and deftly disengaged them. She strongly but softly pushed him back onto his bed and he responded by lifting his thighs so that she could slip off his trousers with the minimum of effort.

"It's the first thing we learn in casualty at the hospital," she lied.

James now lay on the bed and remembered no more. When he awoke it was dusk. He must have slept for the whole day. What day was it – the 26th or 27th? He had lost track. He could hear rifle and machine gun fire from many directions but it did not seem too near. He dozed off to sleep. Surfacing again, he looked around him. A glass and water jug were nearby. There was already water in the glass. He was glad as he did not feel that he had the reserves to pour from the jug himself.

He emptied the glass. He found he could lift the jug with two hands and refilled the glass with only a few dribbles of water onto the little table. He wanted to pee. He leant over the side of the bed and found a chamber pot. He placed it on the floor as he could not trust himself to hold onto it standing. He knelt and felt the warm flow and the reassuring circular motion in the pot. Clockwise or anti-clockwise? He could not remember which was which and which laws of physics applied in France. He slid the pot slowly with both hands under the bed so that he would not tread in it later or worse, upset it.

He slept again. It was light when he awoke. Footsteps, footsteps outside the door. Germans? He was relieved to see it was Agnès with some coffee in a large bowl and some pastries. She wore a long, white, straight nightdress with a high neck encircled by green flowered embroidery. Her long, straight, red-brown hair hung down to her shoulders. She smelt of that carbolic acid perfume which pervaded the surgery downstairs and scented the ground floor.

"Good morning, James. Are you feeling better?"

"Yes thank you, Agnès. May I call you Agnès?"

"Yes, of course. Mademoiselle is much too large a word for an Englishman."

"My head doesn't hurt and I seem to be thinking straight now. Any news of the fighting?"

"I don't know. I'll try to find out later. It's been quite quiet around here. I'm not a very good nurse but you must bathe. The atmosphere in this room is like a barracks."

"I am sorry, Agnès. My last shower was about a week ago."

"Don't worry. I have tried to sponge the blood and dirt out of your uniform so that you will look smart when you rejoin your friends."

Agnès squatted down and found the chamber pot. She carried it out of the room and down the corridor. She returned.

"I'm sorry you have to do that, Agnès. I seem to be saying sorry for everything. You were not expecting a visitor, a refugee, one rather lame English soldier?"

"*C'est la guerre.* Everyone's response to everything now."

"Tell me about yourself."

"I have always wanted to be a doctor like my father. I saw him help so many people, not just with drugs and instruments but just sitting there listening to them, holding their hands, propping them up when life was not kind to them. Every day is different. My father is not only respected but loved by so many of his patients. There are very few women doctors but my father was at the University of Lille in the same class as the Professor of Medicine. He convinced him that I was a man – steady, conscientious, hard-working and a good scientist. To be truthful, I have never felt like a scientist but I do enjoy gaining the confidence of patients and observing the effects of the treatments we give them. I know that I shall be a useful member of the community and I also know about myself that I need to be needed."

"Selfish selflessness," James murmured. *That's what makes doctors tick*, he thought to himself.

"What do you do in England, James? Have you always been a soldier?"

"No, no, not at all. I should now be in the middle of Trinity

Term at Oxford in my first year reading history. A world away from all of this."

"How old are you, James?"

"Eighteen."

"Only eighteen. I am twenty-one with three more years' experience of the world. We grow up very fast in medicine. We have a very clear and conceited idea of our role in society with none of the uncertainties of youth. Well, not as many as others, I suppose."

Agnès left the room, having exposed almost too much of herself to this English boy. Once more on his own, James thought again of his platoon and the QVR. They might have found out that he did not reach the RAP. They might have posted him missing presumed dead in some Calais street. Even now his parents may have received such a telegram. He must go and find his platoon, or if not his platoon, any British unit in Calais.

He left the bedroom dressed only in vest and long pants and found the staircase. He found Agnès in the kitchen preparing lunch.

"I must go, Agnès. You have been so kind and I am so grateful for all your help. My platoon will think I am dead. May I have the rest of my uniform?"

She left the kitchen and returned with his uniform. He dressed quickly and walked down the corridor to the front door. His rifle stood upright against the wall, accusing him of lack of military commitment in the last day or two. He did not recall placing it there but he was relieved to see it. A rifleman without his rifle could be accused of desertion.

"Where will you go?"

"I shall retrace my steps and try and find the bastion which we were holding."

"Eat your lunch first. You don't know when you will eat again."

James hesitated, thinking that he must now leave this heaven, remote from the war, but followed Agnès through the hall to the kitchen without further resistance. They sat at the kitchen table. A large bowl of mushroom soup, fresh bread and butter. He ate hungrily, not speaking but planning his reluctant escape from this flash of what life should be without the war. They walked slowly to the front door. Agnès opened it and looked out into the square. It was empty and she could hear no movement beyond the square.

"Thank you again, Agnès. For everything."

They shook hands with firm grips and a single up stroke and down stroke. The pumping action of English handshakes seemed empty and inappropriate. James hurried off, looking around him into the square, and made for the street in the far corner from which he had entered. He brushed his right hand on the railings of the other houses in a semblance of keeping cover and was soon on the street which he was sure led to the bastion. No. It was further on, another turning before reaching the right street. He hesitated as he reached each new corner and stopped and peered around. No reason to be excessively brave or foolish. It was unrealistic to think that the QVR would be in the same position from which he had left. He had lost a night and a day. They could have been reinforced and counterattacked and be back at the canal bridge.

He froze at the next corner. Near to a bastion – was it his bastion? – were about thirty German soldiers relaxing in the sun. He could walk up to them and ask where the QVR had gone. Perhaps not. James reasoned that they had either been overwhelmed and captured or had withdrawn back to the port. Perhaps they had been evacuated and he had been left behind? He must head north to the port and hope that he could reach the British lines if they still existed. He decided to once again retrace his steps and find his way back to the square where Agnès lived. She should be able to find out where the British were without arousing too much suspicion. The streets seemed so quiet and so empty. A short distance from the turning to Agnès's square he saw another large group of German soldiers near to another bridge over a canal or river. He sprang into a doorway. He was trapped. He could not go forwards or backwards. Clearly the battle had moved on without him and the Germans seemed to be in control of all Calais. He pressed himself hard against the door for about ten minutes, trying to make some plan. He could surrender. This war was going to last a long time, or perhaps Churchill would conclude an armistice. Or, he could be in a prison camp for years but, at least, alive.

The objective that consumed him and allowed no other useful thought was to make his way back to Agnès. At her house he would have time to think and make plans. After some minutes he plucked up courage to leave the security of his doorway. Secure, at least, until a German patrol marched by and out of sight. He walked slowly but purposefully down the street and found the turning to Agnès's square without encountering more Germans. James ran across the square to the front door. He pulled the chain. No delay this time. Agnès had opened the door almost before the bell rang as she had heard the running boots in the square and saw James from an upstairs window.

"Come in quickly. German patrols have been in the square. You must not be seen."

"If the Germans find me here, you could be shot."

This was the first time that this thought had occurred to him. How selfish and stupid of him to return to Agnès.

"I must give myself up."

"No. You must not. We shall find a way to return you to the British area. There is still some shooting around the Citadel and the port. The British are still there. My neighbour has family who live there and I spoke to her only half an hour ago."

James now realised that he had not been walking around in a silent world for the past hour. There had been plenty of gunfire but he had blotted it out and existed in his own unconscious world. He had ignored the planes dropping bombs in the port area and to the west around the Citadel.

"I shall go out myself and see what is happening. You go to your room and stay there till I return."

James could think of no other option. His war so far had not been a glorious one. He had shot a few Germans but had managed to lose himself and to become detached from his unit. He lay on the bed and fell asleep. It was late evening when Agnès returned and entered the room.

"James. It is all over. There are Germans everywhere between here and the port. There is no way through. The British have surrendered."

"Then I must give myself up."

"No. There is another way. Can you sail small boats?"

"I have crewed in sailing dinghies a few times and have a rough idea."

"My father has a small boat with a motor and a sail at the end of Blériot-Plage near Sangatte, only a short distance from Calais. If it is still there you could get back to England in it."

James was horrified at first thought but it was only twenty miles or so across the Channel and he could hardly get lost.

"Okay, if you think it is possible."

"We'll discuss it over dinner."

Agnès prepared more soup, a casserole, and there was cheese. She found a bottle of Bordeaux from her father's cellar and they finished it. It was almost midnight. They had not discussed the project which seemed impossible. James thought that she had changed her mind and that she had come to terms with his surrender. They climbed the stairs. James went into his room and undressed. He poured water from the large jug into the bowl. There was a flannel and soap. For the first time he noticed a full-length mirror on the opposite side of the room. He washed the barrack fumes from his body as thoroughly as he could. He dried himself and could see his penis hanging at an angle of 45 degrees like a railway signal with too much slack. He climbed into bed and surveyed the contours of his life at eighteen. The war, the QVR, Oxford and perhaps medicine. If he remained alive, he should do something useful like medicine and not frig about with dilettante subjects like history. He would think about it. He had always liked to plan the future, even if he had no future. James dozed with scenes from school, the army, the trips to Oxford with his parents and now the war.

He jolted back into wakefulness. Soft footsteps on the landing. It must be Agnès on some errand before going to bed. He watched the handle of the door turning very slowly. It was like a slow-motion film or a dream where you can only run painfully slowly when chased. As the catch released the door it opened a little and hesitated. Agnès stood in the doorway. The long white shift nightdress. The red-brown shoulder-length hair. When he had seen her the previous night he had been unaware of her breasts lifting the nightdress from its vertical plane. A darker area between her thighs which then cleared and obscured as she moved towards the bed. He pushed out his left arm, inviting her to compress it with her body. She was soft and warm. James removed his vest but was still imprisoned in his long pants. He did not know what to do next and lay almost to attention. His right arm moved across her and his hand rested in the small of her back as she faced him lying on her side. He moved his hand up her back to her hair. Agnès turned on her back, releasing his right arm but straining his left shoulder. James turned to kiss her, extracting his battered left arm. The heavy bedclothes, too much for summer, oppressed him and he threw them back down the bed. In the same movement he was lifting her nightdress with both hands and she was tugging down the ridiculous long underpants.

"Not yet, James."

Agnès lay on top of him, compressing him and allowing no

movement. She then lifted her pelvis and manoeuvred herself gently so that his level of consciousness was dissolved. He shuddered and she slowed down to a catatonia which they held for long minutes. They fell asleep.

James awoke with a sense of panic as from a nightmare. For a few seconds he could not remember where he was. It was not his room in Harrow. The windows had changed. The colours were wrong. Then he remembered. He was not alone. Agnès. No regrets, only concern and love for this French woman who had cared for him, risked her life for him, and wanted him. As so many of his type – formal, over-educated, middle-class, predictable men – he had considered that women had an innate physical reluctance that had to be nurtured, cajoled and overcome by... he had no idea. The war seemed so far away but they were both in the eye of the storm.

He must leave. Agnès did not stir. It was light and quiet outside. The square seemed out of bounds to soldiers and to the war. But not to him and Agnès. During the night he had moved away from her, seeking his own space. He had never shared a bed with anyone before and it seemed strange. He turned over and placed his right hand where her left breast might be. She was lying flat on her back and breathing so lightly that he had to watch closely and reassure himself that she was alive. Agnès smiled without opening her eyes. James was relieved. He expected her to be dismayed and regretful. Yet she had come to him in his room in her house.

"Agnès, I must go."

"Not yet. Hold me." James was now vividly aware of their predicament and with every second he expected the square to erupt with lorries and boots. Agnès, from lifelessness, jumped from the bed and almost ran to the door and downstairs. The random notes of plates and cutlery. She soon returned with coffee bowls, bread and jam. They ate but did not speak, exchanging eyes and smiles.

"I don't think that you should attempt to leave for a few days, or even a week or two. The Germans will be busy rounding up stragglers and then they will relax and it should be easier for you to escape."

June 1940

The following days passed very slowly. A German van with a loudspeaker did crawl into the square announcing that Calais had fallen and that all British and French troops had been killed or captured. Their French accent was crude and corrupted mellifluence into coarseness but the message was clear.

"All Frenchmen and women should report any escaped French and British soldiers immediately to the German authorities. Anyone harbouring escaped soldiers will be shot."

The house had a cellar of two rooms divided by a door. James and Agnès emptied a heavy dresser so that it could be moved across the dividing door, obscuring it from sight. They decided that James would hide in the far room and that Agnès would use the dresser to block the door. It needed all her strength to open and close James's tomb. He lived in darkness and used a torch sparingly as there were no replacement batteries. He slept on the floor on thick rugs. Agnès would bring food at regular intervals but they did not make love again. The danger of their position suppressed desire.

After a few days Agnès decided that she must find her father's boat. She cycled to avoid questioning on the bus by her father's patients and acquaintances. James was terrified when she left, not because he was unable to leave his cellar prison without her help – although it was a nasty thought – but because he was afraid that she would be captured and shot.

As Agnès cycled off she felt vibrant and alive and wondered why other French men and women seemed so forlorn. They had all shrunk six inches in a matter of days. She could not understand why Germans in lorries shouted at her in a friendly way but she was never stopped. The long sandy beach of Blériot-Plage stretched away, drawing her gaze to the chalk cliffs of Sangatte to the west and to their geological cousins ghosted in haze across the Channel. She checked her pocket and found the keys to the boathouse which stood at the end of the beach nestled under the cliffs ascending to Sangatte. Agnès cycled furiously along the path behind the beach and prayed that the boat would be safely inside and not looted. The boathouse was concealed until she rounded the bend leading up to the cliff. She shouted with excitement as she saw the vivid, deep blue vertical planks, freshly painted in 1939, deserted by the sea as the tide was out. As she approached, she did not dare to believe that it was undamaged after months of war. She turned the key in the padlock of the door facing the path and resigned herself to the prospect of no boat inside. But it was there, resting on its side, oblivious to the war. It was about eighteen feet in length with two sails, a jib and a mainsail and an outboard motor. It was also painted boathouse blue. Her father had painted the name of the boat in careful, stencilled yellow letters on both sides near the bow and on the stern – *Agnès*.

Silly, sentimental old Father. Where is he now? Is he still alive? She had heard no news about him since the beginning of May.

There was petrol in two large cans by the wall. Both full. It was a good omen. She longed to watch the sea surging up the beach, trying to suck the boathouse down into the depths at high tide but there was no time now for this visceral pleasure. The doors which permitted the sea to flow underneath them at high tide and float the sleeping boat were locked by another padlock. She unlocked and then locked it again and returned to the end of the boathouse nearest to the path. She stood still, listening, heard nothing and locked the doors behind her. It would not be long before the Germans explored their new territory and plundered everything of value. Agnès cycled back to Calais.

James had been anxious all day about her. As the day wore on he convinced himself that she would not return. Perhaps she had even decided to sail the boat to England herself while she had the chance. He cursed himself for his evil thoughts.

"Yes, I might die here in this cellar without food and water," he spoke out loud, testing his power of speech in the vacuum of solitude.

"Would I want to live without her?" which posed a heavier question when spoken than just thought about. Odd. He had never felt like that before, not even about his sisters and parents. Although it was a morbid thought it exhilarated him. He dozed and tried to read a Guy de Maupassant story which Agnès had left for him. The struggle of translating from French soon overcame him. The ugly creak of the dresser and light woke him. Agnès almost extinguished it as she slid through the narrow gap. They gripped each other with a fervour that neither of them had exerted nor experienced before.

"I think you should go tomorrow, James. The boat is ready and it cannot be long before the Germans start scouting around in that area."

"Agnès, are you coming too? Come to England with me."

They had not discussed this before and James had not dared to raise it.

"No. I must complete my studies in Lille. The university will reopen soon. Life must go on in France even if France is dead. England will soon make peace with Germany and we should be allowed to return to some sort of normal life. Just like after the 1870 war. We can visit each other by the ferry. Perhaps I shall become an Englishwoman or you a Frenchman. This will not be the end for us. I know it."

James longed to stay in Calais and allow the war to pass them by. He too thought that an armistice would be arranged, probably leaving continental Europe to be run by the Germans. Britain would be allowed to control the seas and maintain its empire of trading nations. Life would not change very much. James spent the night in his prison cellar and Agnès in her own bed. He did not sleep.

He was relieved when Agnès pushed the dresser, bringing his coffee, bread and jam with the morning. James dressed in his uniform and covered it with a mixture of clothes from Agnès's father and brother on top so that he could avoid being shot as a spy if captured. She had prepared a basket of food and drink for his voyage. This was the worst day of all. They had planned that he would sail in darkness and so they had a whole day to consume with little to do. They could both see a future together but so many obstacles reared up to batter down their vision.

They gathered their strength for the early evening. James's legs tottered from disuse as he climbed up from the cellar into the house, but they soon began to function again. They cycled off together. It was twice the effort to cycle with so many clothes but he managed to keep up. There were no checkpoints. It was too soon in the occupation for a tight security system and that evening many French men and women were walking and cycling as if the war had petered out. Their spirits rose. They had entombed themselves far too long.

It was about nine o'clock when they arrived at the boathouse, now lapped by the high tide. James did not want to sail in complete darkness as he did not trust his sense of direction and the boat had no compass. His previous sailing experience had only been along the coast and into river mouths. Dusk combined with sea mist was his best chance. The wind was a gentle south-westerly, which was ideal.

Agnès explained the quirks of the boat and packed the food and drink securely on the deck, giving instructions of how and when to eat it as if James were her son off on a school expedition. He rehearsed the address and the telephone number of the doctor's house, not daring to write them down. He wanted Agnès to come with him and thought that her defences would crumble under sustained assault. She had sailed with her father and knew the boat. She could even do engine first aid if necessary. James hated engines.

"What would I do in England, James? I could not continue my medical studies. I would be a burden to your family who don't even know me. It is better that we part now and start all over again together when the war is over."

He knew that she was logical and correct but she was already an addiction which he had no will or wish to give up.

At about half past nine Agnès unlocked the padlock on the door facing the sea. The engine started after only two pulls. She set the jib sail for him. James did not plan to use the mainsail as he did not trust his skills and it would make the boat more conspicuous. They touched, hugged and kissed until they were breathless. James felt a deep sob arising from somewhere deep in his chest and a surge in his eyes but managed to conceal them with a cough. Agnès's eyes flooded but she did not cry and she dissipated her tears with a conscious, random darting of her eyes. James realised for the first time that they were green and not blue. She jumped off the boat and onto the decking which ran along both sides of the boathouse and pushed the boat off.

"James, *au revoir*. Come back soon."

"*Au revoir*, Agnès. Thank you. Thank you for everything."

He was now crying freely without embarrassment. He was on his own. He had relied utterly on Agnès since losing contact with the QVR. He had allowed her to do all the thinking and make all the decisions. He had been a passive recipient of all of her good sense.

James now returned to the war. He realised that there was a strong chance of capture by a naval patrol but there was no choice. To stay in France equalled prison. At least he now had a slim chance of escape. The wind and the current would push him northeast so that he could even miss Dover in the darkness.

He sensed rather than saw the cliffs and he steered northwest to allow for plenty of error. The sea was calm and there was a kind mist already obscuring the detail of the French coast. He turned back. He had not dared to turn back before. Agnès was still just visible standing on the side decking in the boathouse hidden from the path. He waved frantically with high windmilling swings of his right arm while holding the tiller with his left. She then closed the boathouse doors on the seaward side. Seconds later she reappeared sitting on her bicycle. He kept turning his gaze from the direction of the Dover cliffs to the French coast until even he could no longer convince himself that Agnès was still there. He tried to imprint his last sight of her in his long-term memory so that he could summon it up during long, sleepless nights for years to come if necessary. James succeeded. For the rest of his life he could replay these images as if filmed. Others would join them in later life.

The sea was calm and blue-black with a faint pink sky in the west. If patrol boats approached from the east he would be silhouetted but not if they came from the west. The Dover cliffs were now just visible rather than imagined but seemed no closer than ten minutes before. The engine sputtered at a reassuringly regular rate and the sea slapped happily against the bows. The jib sail played its part too, with the breeze just leaning on it rather than beating it. He scanned in all directions for other vessels. None so far. The English coast began to grow a body with individual limbs rather than an amorphous background border to the sea in the foreground. Two aircraft were flying west to east, parallel to the English shore. He – unreasonably – assumed they were friendly and his confidence began to stiffen. He could just about tolerate capture by a German sea patrol but machine gunning by a bored German pilot was less appealing.

It was now almost completely dark but the June dusk was slow to die away. James estimated that he was about halfway to England, judging by the land in front and behind him. The coast ran to both left and right and now he knew he could not miss. He dozed as he sat by the tiller. He had emptied the second can of petrol and hoped that he would have enough to cross. If not, he would have to try and set the mainsail recalling Agnès's instructions. He could now see the port of Dover even in the blackout and steered towards it.

Agnès. In so few days she had become part of him, part of his life, a given rather than an option. He prayed that she had returned safely to Calais and was not in a cell awaiting interrogation for cycling after the curfew. He imagined her in Dr Hugo's house preparing her soup and cheese in the kitchen looking out at the monkey-puzzle tree thinking about the unexpected and uninvited Englishman. "That was a warm, pleasant English interlude," she would say to herself. "Now back to real life. Medicine and my patients." James dearly hoped that he was more than that. His gloomy ramblings vanished and he dozed off into a light sleep, still gripping the tiller firmly.

He shuddered back to life with the noise of an engine from a patrol boat and the glare of a search light.

"Ahoy, there. Identify yourself."

"Lance Corporal James Butland, Queen Victoria's Rifles, escaping from Calais."

"Steer towards the light."

James obeyed, relieved that his inquisitor was clearly English. A rope line was thrown down to him and he was ordered to attach it to the bows of his boat.

"We'll tow you in, soldier."

The boats were soon in the outer harbour and he was towed expertly to the quay alongside an iron ladder. He tied up his boat to the rungs and began to climb. A naval officer on the quay asked, "Are you alone?"

"Yes, just me, sir. I became separated from my unit when I was wounded. I stayed with a French family." He was afraid to say French woman. "They lent me their boat and I've made it."

Funny word, "lent", which usually denotes a gift with every expectation of returning it. He had no intention of sailing it back, at least not in the near future. But who knows? Perhaps after the war he could sail it back. He could imagine Agnès waving and signalling him into the boathouse with appropriate gesticulations. No. She wasn't like that. Not like the continental stereotypes. She was economical with movements. Each action had a clear purpose. No extraneous nonsense. Focused.

"Well done, soldier. Which unit did you say you are?"

"QVR. Queen Victoria's Rifles. We were with the 60th and the Rifle Brigade at Calais."

"We know. You all had a tough time over there. You were lucky to escape. There was no evacuation like at Dunkirk and all of your chums will be POWs if they are still alive. We'll look after your boat. Don't you worry."

"Thank you. I should like to give it back to the French family one day."

James was led to a car and driven up to the barracks in the castle. He climbed out at the guardroom and was gently guided inside by a friendly corporal.

"QVR, you say. Territorials. You've done great, mate. Who's your next of kin? You'll have been posted missing."

James wanted to say Agnès Hugo but instead said:

"Mr and Mrs James Butland, 24 College Avenue, Harrow Weald, Middlesex." They had moved away from the bakery in the more prosperous 1930s when they thought they could at last afford a house and the Austin 10.

"We'll let them know you're safe. Now, Fred here will take you along somewhere nice and quiet where you can sleep. I expect they'll ask you loads of questions in the morning but you're bound to get some leave."

James was exhausted and rolled onto an iron bedstead covered by a blanket in a room full of men asleep. In exercises with the QVR he had always slept in tents rather than barracks and now the stench of unwashed bodies and cigarettes nauseated him. He slept and did not dream.

On the following morning an officer in Intelligence asked him to recall all events from landing at Calais to arrival at Dover. He described the landing and the march to their positions at the canal bridge. He described the attacks which they fought off and the withdrawal to the bastion. The head wound and his confusion and loss of memory. Not utterly accurate but it eased the explanation of how he had ended up with a French doctor's family rather than at an RAP. He had tried on several occasions to find other British troops, only to run into German patrols. The family nursed him back to health and gave him their boat for his escape. He considered giving a false address for the Hugo family in case of a leak falling into German hands but decided to speak the truth.

"Docteur Jacques Hugo, Calais Saint-Pierre."

"You've put up a damned good show, Butland. Managing to escape like that was bloody marvellous. They might even give you a medal."

James did not want a medal. He wanted to be back in Calais with Agnès, dreaming about their future.

"I expect you would like some leave?"

"Yes please, sir. I don't know what will happen to me as the QVR no longer exists. They will all be dead or prisoners."

"Don't worry about that now. Go home to your family. I'll make enquiries and we'll let you know in a few days."

He was given a railway warrant to Harrow and Wealdstone station and he was allowed to send a telegram to his parents informing them that he was on his way home. Dover to London Bridge. Northern Line to King's Cross. Circle Line to Paddington. Then the familiar line to Harrow and Wealdstone station.

James could not connect the experiences of the last few days in France with the experience now of sitting in a suburban train chugging between repetitive Victorian terraces. He was not living the one, same life. He had been leading two utterly different lives with no links between them. Harrow-on-the-Hill on his left, topped by the church spire. It hadn't changed. Why should it change? Should not old, familiar sites change because we are changed and because the world has changed? The train pulled in to Harrow and Wealdstone station, the square gabled tower badged by its clock, as much an icon for the suburb as Big Ben is for Westminster.

The same ticket collector collected tickets as he had done throughout James's lifetime. Never looking up. Making no human connection with the passengers. The two newspaper sellers were at their usual patch outside the station. One was very short, sitting hunchbacked with cigarette defying gravity as he shouted the unintelligible, "You, yeart, de-dert!" The other taller, always standing. Less mangled, alternating with his companion, "Light stop."

What do these almost animal noises mean?

James could never relate these two meaningless exclamations to the *Evening Standard* and *Evening News,* for those they were selling. Or was it the reverse, the *News* advertisement followed by the *Standard*? He recalled how other phrases devoid of meaning had inserted themselves into the vernacular. His mother sometimes chided him with "Gert yer." He could never translate it into anything intelligible. Nor could she. These sounds were imprinted in his head from childhood and the two old men were station fixtures like the clock tower. When one died years later he was not replaced and the other soon gave up, having lost his unrelated twin.

He walked up the High Street past the library and the adjoining police station at the end of Grant Road. The air-raid warning siren was on the top of the police station but it was silent today. He passed the Great War Memorial Clock Tower with names of the fallen on all four sides. James could see no vacant spaces for the names of the dead in this war but, of course, 1914–1918 was the war to end all wars. He supposed the Mayor and Council would come up with something. There would be room for new stone plaques to be fixed to the four walls. He began to convince himself that he could see his own name there, foretelling the future. He imagined his parents standing stiffly at a civilian version of attention, tightly gripping each other's hand, tightening facial muscles to avoid "giving way" at annual Armistice Day ceremonies. They would get over it. But leaving Agnès behind, that would be intolerable.

The Art Deco cinema was the next landmark on the left. The rows of suburban terraces, semi-detached and detached houses queued up as this was boom territory between the end of the nineteenth century and the 1930s. Nothing had changed. Were they all ignoring what was happening in France? James enjoyed the walk from the station to Harrow Weald, looking around him with new attention to the people and buildings that he knew well. He turned into College Avenue and walked steadily to his own house just beyond the doctor's house which was another genuflection to Art Deco. His parents were overjoyed. They had received his telegram but until then had feared the worst.

"Missing," his father kept repeating, "presumed dead. We thought we would never see you again, James. We hoped you might be a prisoner but we almost dared not to hope."

James said little. He had never spoken freely to his parents, confiding his innermost thoughts to himself. He ate, slept and read books. He tried to read new books but could not concentrate and keep a story in his head. He then returned to old favourites through which he could navigate without too much effort. Thomas Hardy was best. About two weeks later a telegram from the War Office arrived.

"Report to KRRC Depot, Winchester, as soon as possible. Railway warrant to follow."

It arrived on the next day. His mother had done her best

to clean and press his uniform. He had lost his rifle. Agnès had promised to bury it in the garden. No one confronted him with this fundamental dereliction of duty. His parents walked with him down to Harrow and Wealdstone station.

"They should have given you a longer leave, James, after all you've been through." His mother switched her attention from her son to her husband. "James has done his bit already. What will they do with him next?"

"The Nazis will be planning their invasion now. We'll need every man we can get." His father spoke quietly.

The newspaper sellers were still there, accompanying the day. He hoped that he would return safely to hear them again. James kissed his mother and shook hands with his father. The ticket collector punched his railway warrant.

After a whole day of navigating the railways of London and the south James arrived in Winchester and reported to the depot of the King's Royal Rifle Corps, the 60th Rifles. The QVR was a territorial battalion of the KRRC although James had never visited the Winchester depot before. He described his experiences in France again to a major who seemed to be genuinely interested and impressed.

"Butland, you QVR men are really part of us. All riflemen together. There is a second battalion of the QVR being formed and they will need you. Your own performance at Calais, escaping in a boat and all that, was outstanding. I see that you've been educated at United Colleges School, quite a respectable establishment, and that you were due to go up to Oxford in thirty-nine were it not for this little inconvenience. We've lined up a spell at Sandhurst for you and after that you will receive the King's commission. Will that meet with your approval?"

"Thank you very much, sir. I hoped for a commission in the QVR before Calais but things moved rather too quickly for that."

"Just so. Present yourself at Sandhurst on the day after tomorrow. They'll be expecting you. I am sure I don't need to

90

tell an intelligent chap like you that we are expecting Jerry to attempt an invasion and we'll be in the front line when he comes. You have a month or two to become an officer and a gentleman but perhaps not even as long as that if Jerry comes sooner."

"Yes, sir. Thank you, sir."

July 1940 to July 1941

Sandhurst and other Officer Training Units were converting schoolboys, undergraduates and NCOs into green officers with understated desperation. James, with his OTC background at school and brief intense experiences in France, was "leadership material" but needed polishing. About half of his new intake had been in France but none in Calais. The sacrifice of the three rifle battalions had not brought credit to Churchill's government. All understood that they should have been evacuated. Admiral Bertram Ramsay at Dover, who organised the evacuation of Dunkirk with exemplary courage and efficiency, had been keen to evacuate the Calais garrison after they had been isolated from Dunkirk but Churchill decided that the French could only be pacified if at least one garrison fought to the last man and last bullet. The third bridgehead at Boulogne had been evacuated after only brief resistance. Churchill regretted this premature evacuation and resolved that Calais would stand and fight. Ramsay sent destroyers into Calais throughout that critical week to evacuate the riflemen but had direct orders from Churchill to evacuate only the wounded.

James was proud that the QVR were given equal billing with the two elite regular rifle battalions. His fellow officer cadets were keen to hear about Calais and James leaked just enough to gain the respect of his group without blowing his trumpet. The course lasted six weeks and invasion was expected before the autumn of 1940 and deteriorating weather. Fighter Command was denying the Luftwaffe command of the skies over the invasion beaches and the Royal Navy had undoubted command of the seas. At this stage of the war it was not clearly foreseen that ships were vulnerable to air attack and that the Navy would have been unable to save Britain if the Germans controlled the air.

At the end of the course at Sandhurst James was commissioned as Second Lieutenant in the 2nd battalion of the QVR which had been recruited rapidly after the destruction of the 1st at Calais. It was important to keep the name and spirit of the regiment alive but the QVR was sent on a round of camps in England and Scotland effectively in reserve for the coming invasion. From Sandhurst he was posted to the battalion which was encamped in the grounds of Abington Hall about six miles southeast of Cambridge. He enjoyed training his platoon in the use of the rifle, the Bren gun, grenades, map reading and all of the duties of the infantryman. Night exercises over fields in the mainly flat countryside were followed by assaults on the chalk ridges of the Gog Magog Hills, as the obvious position of strategic strength in the district. The nearest the battalion came to action in 1940 was when a German bomber, lazily discharging its load somewhere in the vicinity of Cambridge, scored a random but direct hit on the tiny bridge over the stream dividing Great from Little Abington, leading to debates in the villages about which one of them was cut off. Certainly, villagers had been impressed by the assumed skill of German airmen who, having noted the great strategic importance of this bridge, were able to target it from a great height.

From Great Abington the 2nd QVR were posted to coastal defence duties in Norfolk at Titchwell. The long flat sands were an ideal invasion beach and the battalion worked rapidly with civilian contractors, building pill boxes and other concrete defensive works to face the enemy. Intelligence sources had provided no assistance to the defenders in the identification of the site of the invasion. The flat beaches of East Anglia had to be as secure as the other obvious beaches of Kent and Sussex.

A military hospital was established on the beach at Titchwell and James had to visit one of his men who had broken his leg in an exercise. The pungent smell of carbolic acid as he entered immediately thrust him back to May of that year and the dressing of his own wound by Agnès in the doctor's surgery in Calais. He absorbed the discipline of long rows of hospital beds, the faux-formality of the nurses and doctors and the unequivocal role of these men and women in helping others. He thought about that prism of insight he had experienced in Calais when he allowed his mind to demote the study of history to an intellectual whim rather than a subject of worth. Agnès's calm confidence in her role in life had even begun to sow the seed of medicine in his own mind. Agnès. He thought of her every day, though she was now so inaccessible to him.

As he stood gazing out over the North Sea his mind turned to the bastion in Calais. It was a different life; a part played by someone else, not by him. He did not deserve her. He had deserted her and left her with the Jerries. Perhaps she was back in Lille at the medical school. That should be relatively safe and would keep her busy. She would not have too much time to think of him. He would have relished letting her know that he had made it. For all Agnès knew, he might be in a POW camp in Germany with the other survivors from Calais who had been marched off after the surrender. James wanted to let her know that she had at least helped one man to escape and fight on.

At Titchwell, officers were billeted in houses along the coast. As well as continuing infantry training, they constructed thick barbed-wire fences and engineers laid mine fields, carefully mapped, interspersed with the concrete gun emplacements and anti-aircraft positions. James was popular with his platoon, who were impressed with their officer "who was a hero at Calais". He gave clear and precise orders in a low voice with a friendly timbre and an invariable smile that endeared him to his men and fellow officers.

There was no invasion, at least not in 1940. There was a

rumour of a small-scale landing at Shingle Street down the coast in Suffolk. Eyewitnesses reported bodies in Nazi uniforms bobbing in the surf. To avoid public concern, it had never reached the newspapers and the myth had probably been created to keep everyone, soldiers and civilians, on their toes. James even allowed himself to be bored with so little to do. There were exercises and more exercises at company, battalion and divisional level. His platoon and company did well. The officers began to resuscitate their usual peace-time pursuits. Never attracted to riding and hunting, which amused some officers, James took up golf at Brancaster, nearby. In those brief winter days a round or two passed otherwise empty hours.

The QVR settled down to winter on the Norfolk coast as no one expected the Germans to attempt invasion now before spring 1941 at the earliest. For his Calais exploits James was awarded the Military Medal. His only thought was that Agnès deserved it more than he. He tried to add up the time that he had spent firing at the enemy in Calais but it did not amount to much. It was the romance of the single-handed crossing of the Channel which had impressed his superiors. But Agnès planted him in the boat, almost held her hand over his on the tiller and pushed him off in the right direction like a father with his son on a boating pool. He did not deserve it. In those idle days he began to think again about life after the war. History at Oxford? He could not see that he now had the motivation to put in the hours studying such a useless subject. Medicine? Doctoring like Agnès? Perhaps in a practice with Agnès in London where there would always be a French or cosmopolitan population who would be attracted to the French lady doctor. Children? No. That really was a thought too far but perhaps they would come along. They had made love only once but it had created a bond that could never be broken. James could not really define love as his life experiences were so thin but the constant thought of Agnès fired his bitter resentment of the war which walled him off from his world. His parents were proud of the Military Medal and wrote to his headmaster so that the decoration could be publicised at school. He recalled that during the Great War schools almost competed for the honour of decorations won and numbers killed as if war was an extension of the rugby or cricket field.

No, that was an unworthy and malicious thought.

The Norfolk coast was cold and bleak that winter. Local society was friendly and hospitable, entertaining the officers and offering recreations.

"This is Lieutenant Butland. He's a Suffolk man but we won't hold that against him."

"Not really. My father was born near Clare but I was born and brought up in London."

He usually did not mention Harrow because it always brought the next inevitable question:

"Were you at Harrow School like Winston Churchill?"

It killed all conversations. The farmers and middle-classes of Norfolk had daughters who relished the wider spectrum of manhood which had invaded their rural idyll. They were invited to mess parties and enjoyed trips to the cinema for the constant unrationed diet of Pathé News and patriotic films. James invited two or three girls on these expeditions but could never, or *would* never, summon up the courage to kiss them. He felt unavailable and they soon lost interest in him. Sunday lunches in large farmhouses were less threatening and more convivial. Brancaster Golf Club became a focus of energy and exercise although he never transferred his skills as a marksman to hitting a golf ball in the direction intended.

He could not stop thinking about medicine. *After the war.* There was a war to win – or lose – first but he began to anticipate Oxford and how he would spend his three years there. History was interesting but it could never now be a motivating life force for him. Agnès had that calm, confident certainty of her role in life that he envied and that envy burned more strongly the longer their lives were separated. It had been the main reason, probably the only reason, why she had not left Calais with him. Medicine was stronger than love. "Selfish selflessness," he repeated to himself, and sometimes spoke it out loud as the thought carried more force. He hoped no one had heard him. After the war he would become a doctor. He needed a life plan, a structure that would drive him on. He had been a weak and uninterested scientist at school because he had been brainwashed by the standard prep school fare of Latin, French, History, English Literature and Maths from a very early age. The traditional model of a cultured British education had delayed the teaching of science until about the age of fourteen, which placed it at a huge disadvantage for all but a small minority who fell under the spell of experiments and pieces of kit when they eventually encountered them. James and many of his intelligent contemporaries could not dissociate physics and chemistry from the "oily rag" spectrum of endeavour. They felt superior to scientists, whose intellects had been stunted by playing too often with Meccano and chemistry sets as children. Bizarre, fanciful speculations about Shakespeare's mentality and elegant linguistic gymnastics, or Elizabethan religious contradictions, were more conducive intellectual pursuits. He would learn science if he must and if he was motivated and worked hard. Motivation was the keystone and science was the means to an end. He knew that he loved Agnes. He would grow closer to her by sharing her profession. He envied her certainties. His path was clear.

James began to buy books on biology and chemistry but drew the line at the impenetrable black arts of physics which he had loathed at school. He appreciated that his understanding of the human body was minimal and began to resent the huge lacunae in his expensive education. One afternoon, gazing out over the North Sea, James recalled that, not so long ago, he had believed that the buttocks acted as the storage system for the products of intestinal digestion. It had seemed logical.

In the spring and summer of 1941 there was again the raised expectation of invasion. It was difficult to maintain his platoon at the peak of efficiency and blood-hot fever pitch which was easy to conjure up in the autumn of 1940. Although it remained unspoken, the threat of invasion, whether across Titchwell sands or Dungeness shingle, ended with Hitler's decision to invade the Soviet Union in May 1941. He would not divide his forces across two fronts although he did send a small but powerful force to North Africa. Rumours of a move from coastal defence duties in England to North Africa ebbed and flowed throughout 1941 in the messes of East Anglia. Wavell's army had destroyed the Italians but when on the verge of complete victory in Africa he had been convinced by Churchill to divide his forces and support the defence of Greece. Rommel's Afrika Korps completely reversed the gains achieved by Wavell and threatened Egypt and the Suez Canal until late 1942. Rumours about reinforcing Hong Kong or Singapore to meet the increasing threat from Japan competed but the QVR remained on coastal defence, convinced that the war was ignoring their skills and commitment. James, who had some experience of action, did not suffer as severely as others who had seen none. If he was honest with himself he wanted to see no more action, to survive this war, to study medicine and resume life with Agnès. During periods of leave with his family, his father sensed that all was not well.

"You seem bored, James. Missing action?"

"Yes, Father. I feel that we are wasted guarding sandcastles in Norfolk. I know we can't deplete England of all its troops but surely we could be useful in Africa or the Far East?"

His parents were relieved that their son was relatively safe but commiserated with him. James was not a natural soldier. Not many of the participants in the Second World War were. After the initial clash of regulars and territorial volunteers with the enemy in 1940, the army evolved into a citizen army of conscripts, many of whom were less committed risk takers than the 1940 cohort.

He was too quiet and reserved to compete with the other officers in the mess, with their verbal or physical excesses.

"Butland is the studious type, Oxford and all that."

He was popular with his men, always using the verbal techniques of respect and even affection. When he gave orders they did not seem like orders but he was obeyed without question. Company exercises were followed by battalion and divisional exercises linking infantry with armour and artillery so that these unemployed troops would have something to boast about to their families and girlfriends.

James had never been an easy sleeper and sleep became more difficult. He had no pictures of Agnès in his wallet to share with inquisitive friends and he did not confide much about his Calais days. He felt ashamed that following a minor wound he had opted out and almost deserted his QVR comrades when they still had more days to fight and risk their lives. He had taken the softer option. When lying awake he could smell her and feel her hair. He would fall asleep easily but would awake an hour or two later with negative thoughts bursting through. So tired during the frequent lazy days he could not repress fits of yawning in battalion briefings. His colonel summoned him after one session.

"You slept through most of my lecture, Butland."

"I'm very sorry, sir. I'm kept awake all night by… well, I just can't sleep. The RAF bomber boys don't help very much."

Bomber Command was developing the night bombing campaign over Germany and their route out over the North Sea seemed to funnel over the QVR's billets.

"Go and see the MO, my boy. He'll give you some knockout drops. That should help."

"Very good, sir."

"It's clearly stress and strain, old chap," the RAMC doctor reflected. "I know you saw action in France and I know that you would like to go back and have another go at Jerry. It's a great strain just sitting on our arses here. We see more of the war at the pictures than in our little corner of England. You're frustrated. You feel guilty, and how difficult it is to keep your men on their toes. Truth is, most of them would rather be here saving their skins than grappling with ugly Jerries in the desert. Stands to reason. Relax a little. Enjoy yourself while you have the chance. Your time will come again before too long."

"You might be right, sir."

James knew this was wrong. He was given a combination of potassium bromide mixture and barbiturates which gave him a profound hangover.

"Have you something less strong, sir? It's like drinking industrial French cognac without any of the pleasure."

"What did you do before the war, Butland?"

"I was about to go up to Oxford to read history in October 1939."

"Interesting. Let's hope it won't be too long before you can."

"No. I want to read medicine when this lot's over."

"Really? Medical family?"

"No, sir. But I got to know a doctor a year or two back and this utterly convinced me that this is my future. A vocation, if you like. I can't analyse it but I only know that I must do it. I'm not a religious sort of chap but I suppose a sudden will to believe in God is a similar process. No logic in it. Only passive inevitability. An irresistible force making the decision for you. Brains are only a box of chemicals and if the right sequence of reactions is triggered, there's not much alternative. That's how I see it."

James did not reveal that it had been Agnès who triggered the chemical chain reaction. Any sane advisor would have blamed a late adolescent infatuation for a life-changing decision and would have mistrusted it. Loving a doctor was not equivalent to loving medicine.

"How do you suggest I go about it? What should I do next, sir?"

"I can't see there is very much you can do until the war is

over. Oxford, you say. Have you asked your college types whether they might allow you to study medicine instead of history after the war?"

"No, I haven't, but it's a great idea. I'll write immediately."

James slept more soundly without the bribery of pills but he then developed shimmering at the periphery of his vision followed by thumping headaches. He sometimes vomited and for several days found it difficult to perform his duties.

"It sounds like migraine, but just to make sure I'll arrange for you to see Major Stern at the Eastern General Hospital in Cambridge. He was a Harley Street neurologist before the war." In his referral letter he briefed Stern on James's medical ambitions.

James motored over to Cambridge to consult Major Stern, who performed an obsessively detailed medical assessment.

"I'm sure it's migraine, Butland. It can start at any age and some say attacks can be brought on by stress."

"I am having a very comfortable war, sir, in coastal defence. I haven't set eyes on Jerry since May 1940."

"At least you were over there at the beginning. Most soldiers have never left these shores. They will be either delighted at their good fortune or frustrated at their failure, so far, to be put to the test of their courage. You're in neither group."

"I don't know what to think, sir. I was thrown into the deep end with the QVR with very little training and managed to learn to swim a few strokes. Since then I've never been allowed in the paddling pool."

"I hear you want to join our exclusive club after the war."

"Oh, medicine. Yes. I'm utterly set on it."

"You were about to go up to Oxford to read history?"

"Yes, sir."

"You'll have a bit of a struggle with the science. I was in the same boat myself. I was in Classical Sixth at school when I began to think about doctoring. I managed to convince the Dean of

St Thomas's that I was in earnest and there I was in the First MB class, studying physics, chemistry and biology. I hated it but squeezed through. It was a piece of cake after that if I put in the hours with the books and the bodies."

"Do you think they might have me?"

"I see no reason why not with your track record. I'll write to the Dean and put in a good word for you."

"I say, sir, thank you. Not just for the migraine but for your advice. I think I'm really getting somewhere now."

August 1941 to November 1942

Queen Victoria's Rifles
Battalion Headquarters
Weybourne Camp
Norfolk
15th August 1941

The Senior Tutor
Wadham College
Oxford

Dear Sir,

Your records will show that I was elected to the Woodward Scholarship in History at Wadham in December 1938 with plans to go up to Oxford in October 1939. The "present emergency" interrupted those plans but you kindly offered to delay my scholarship until after the war. I must inform you that I have decided not to read history but to read medicine instead. I appreciate that my science background is thin but I have been informed that if I complete the First MB course in London, this should equip me to start reading medicine at Oxford. Please let me know if this plan of action meets with your approval. Of course I cannot predict when I shall be discharged from the army but I should like to establish the principle if possible.

Yours faithfully,
James Butland
Second Lieutenant
2nd Battalion
Queen Victoria's Rifles

Wadham College
Oxford
1st September 1941

Dear Butland,

Thank you for your letter of 15th August. I note that you have had a conversion (Pauline?) from History to Medicine. I have consulted our fellows in History and Animal Physiology who would be most affected by this change of heart. We do not consider that you are at present in optimal circumstances to reach such a major decision. Your war experiences will have brought you into contact with all manner of tragedies and we can understand that your mind has been moulded towards serving your fellow men in this most obvious way. I commend your thoroughly laudable motive. However, at Oxford you need a first-rate scientific brain to cope with the demanding course in Animal Physiology and then in Clinical Medicine and we are not convinced that this is your particular talent. Make no decision now. You are most welcome at Wadham when our country and your military masters decide they can succeed without you. Have you considered PPE, Jurisprudence or English if History no longer exerts its charms for you? Please keep me informed as your plans develop.

Yours sincerely,
Ian Dombey
Senior Tutor

James was bitterly disappointed. His early life on the fringes of London had primed him for escape to Oxford, from mediocrity to the exotic. Grossly unfair to his family but nevertheless true.

They had encouraged him to seek more distant horizons. They had facilitated it. What was his first priority in life? Oxford first and medicine second or the reverse? Agnès was there with him. Standing at his shoulder, she would know what he should do. Medicine, and he must give up Oxford. The next step was to follow Major Stern's advice and apply to St Thomas's, one of the two medieval medical foundations in London, which appealed to the historian still within him. He asked Major Stern to write in support of his application and he composed a letter to the Dean of St Thomas's, setting out his case for admission as a medical student when the war permitted. He detailed his school and military career and emphasised that his motivation had been tested by his willingness to forego his scholarship at Oxford in favour of medicine.

From the Dean's Office
St Thomas's Hospital Medical School
London
SE1
1st October 1941

Dear Butland,

Thank you for your most interesting letter of application for the First MB course at St Thomas's. Major Stern also expressed his support for your case. I fully understand that none of us can predict when you will be released from the army but please be assured that we shall admit you as soon as you are permitted to join us. Please keep us informed.

Yours sincerely,
Robert Bevin FRCS

James flushed. The die was cast. He was so keen to tell Agnès but that was impossible. During long sleepless nights, which continued but less frequently than before, he tortured himself that she might be dead or now in love with a Lille medical student or that she now considered him to be only a brief infatuation. He forced himself to dwell on other subjects – his men, his family or recent news of the war.

James's war continued on his Norfolk beach with coastal defence. The threat of invasion had diminished when Hitler directed his armies away from the Channel and the North Sea in June 1941 when he invaded the Soviet Union. The pessimists predicted that the Soviet Union, which had struggled to defeat modest Finland, would soon collapse. This would allow Hitler to turn back again to invade Britain and thus finish the war. Britain was fighting hard in North Africa against the Italians and the Germans and the RAF was gaining rapidly in strength with huge resources devoted to the creation of the heavy bomber force that would deliver hammer blows to the German homeland. The Royal Navy and the Merchant Navy were fighting desperately in the North Atlantic to maintain essential supplies from Canada and the United States.

Coastal defence. Battalion exercises in East Anglia and on training grounds around the country, assaulting or defending ground. Interminable weapons practice so that every gun could be dismantled and reassembled by blindfolded soldiers. On a good day combined exercises with tanks. Mine laying on beaches. Taking up mines and laying them again. James visited the military hospital at Weybourne Camp which was busy with infections and minor injuries and occasionally the medical officers would allow him to join rounds as he was a potential medical student. He noted down the diagnoses of the patients he had seen although the diseases held little significance for him. He hoped they would mean something to him when he encountered them again.

Agnès. In those long tedious days of 1942 his mind often turned to her. It was now two years since their days together and there was no sign of an end to this long, dreary war. The 2nd

Battalion of the QVR were now being stripped for replacements in other units and James decided that he would apply for a posting to another regiment. Lieutenant Colonel Masters did not try to dissuade him.

"I fully understand, Butland. It seems unlikely that the QVR will suddenly be posted to North Africa for some excitement."

Masters broke eye contact and shuffled the papers on his desk.

"Truth is, most of the chaps are relieved that they might spend the rest of the war on coastal defence. They can visit the old woman and kids on leave every so often and we have to admit we're pretty safe here."

James realised the Colonel really was one of those with no ambitions higher than coastal defence and then he knew he must go if he could.

"What did you do in the war, Daddy?"

"I guarded sand castles on a beach in Norfolk."

That would not stir many hearts of the generation to come and even James could not rely on his Calais exploits forever. Most had already forgotten about the stand now and could only remember Dunkirk.

The King's Royal Rifle Corps, the parent regiment of the QVR, and the Rifle Brigade were rival regiments but strong allies and both were convinced that they topped the more fashionable Brigade of Guards. The Rifle Brigade was forming a 10th battalion, mainly recruited from East London, and was looking for officers. James applied for transfer from the QVR, was accepted and promoted to lieutenant. He was not sorry to leave the grey seas and sand and shingle beaches of Norfolk. The pretence that these beaches were the new front line after the fall of France could not be sustained indefinitely. He was aware that his departure challenged the officers and men who remained on their Norfolk beach, watching the tides completing their twice-daily complacent routine with only mild expressions of irritation when the wind blew. Some, like Colonel Masters, almost avoided him, while others clearly considered him a fool to give up his gentle, well fed and secure present life.

James was posted to the Rifle Brigade depot in Winchester where he was inducted into the history and traditions of the distinguished rifle regiments, who were proud of their rapid marching and marksmanship. He had discovered that he had a good eye and could shoot straight and usually challenged for the lead in competitions. His experiences in Calais, at least those he was prepared to discuss, set him in good stead with his fellow officers and men. Some of the recruits, mostly undereducated in the East End, could barely read and write. Their lives, clearly focused on their families, girlfriends and West Ham Football Club, were more limited than those in the typical QVR ranks. Yet, they threw themselves into their new lives with enthusiasm and their identity with the Rifle Brigade was woven into their old loyalties to their particular part of the East End.

The Battle School system of training was now the method of turning civilians into soldiers. The battalion, having learnt to march and shoot to the grudging satisfaction of their NCOs, joined exercise after exercise. James could sense the growing skills of his men which brought confidence that they could match anything that the enemy might throw at them. Salisbury Plain became as familiar as Epping Forest. Gradually the routine of assault courses – scrambling over walls, leaping across streams, crawling along tunnels roofed by huge tarpaulins – was mixed with all arms exercises, using live ammunition which sometimes struck flesh and bone. Platoons were even driven to abattoirs so that they could eat their lunch amid the sights and smells of dead severed flesh. Those with some experience of action reflected that this theatre did not include the mingled smells of cordite and human meat half-cooked by the explosion of shells. These war games never incorporated the ultimate stench of men incinerated in tanks which Germans, with more sense of humour than usually credited to them, called "Tommy cookers".

In the summer of 1942 the battalion was posted to the west of Scotland for an exercise involving a seaborne assault on one of those long beaches of off-white sand which always seemed so out of place in this far northern country. James's company embarked in assault craft and were expected to land on and capture the beach and dunes in the face of small arms fire whistling above their heads. Behind the dunes, field guns and tanks were defending, sending high fountains of water into the sky only just behind them. As they waded ashore without much confidence in the precision and accuracy of the enemy, which was trying to frighten them without killing them, a flight of Hurricanes swept in from the west, strafing the columns of angry water. For reasons which James could not understand this was more terrifying than his actual experiences under fire in Calais two years before. Either his 1940 courage had deserted him in the two years of coastal defence sloth or he was beginning to realise that one's life on a battlefield, real or synthetic, was at the mercy of random selection for life or death. This comforted some and tortured others. James found, as the war stretched out and as the accumulated exposure to violence increased, he could accept the incalculable risk of his own death and excised it from his thoughts and dreams.

As 1942 ebbed away, 10th Rifle Brigade began to speculate that they too had been forgotten. James even heard a rumour that, like 2nd QVR, they might be due for a stint on coastal defence. They hoped for a posting to Montgomery's Eighth Army in North Africa but would settle for Burma with less enthusiasm. James began to consider whether his decision to apply for a posting to 10th Rifle Brigade had been the right one.

December 1942 to
September 1943

In November 1942 Operation Torch was launched. Franklin D Roosevelt's Americans, who had recovered from the shock of the initial Japanese victories in the East and the Pacific, were gradually gaining confidence. With their immense military and naval resources they were now keen to match themselves against the Germans in Europe. Churchill diverted them from their favoured plan to make a direct assault on France, predicting that they would be annihilated on French beaches. He convinced them that exploiting recent success in the Western Desert and bringing the whole of North Africa under Allied control would be the wisest move of military chess. Torch comprised landings of American troops at Casablanca in Morocco and Oran in Algeria and of British troops at Algiers. The plan was to overcome the Vichy French control of Morocco, Algeria and Tunisia and to convince the French to join the Allies. German and Italian forces were concentrated in Libya up to the Egyptian border but Montgomery's Eighth Army won the decisive Battle of Alamein in October and November 1942. With the Americans and British advancing from the West and the British from the East, the enemy would be bottled up and destroyed in Tunisia.

In December 1942, 10th Rifle Brigade, settling down to winter in their Winchester barracks, suddenly knew that they were off on their travels. It was announced that they were to parade before King George VI, who liked to inspect every battalion before posting overseas. James was shocked to see how ill the King looked. His face had been rouged to give him colour but it was a poor disguise. They boarded ship in Liverpool on Christmas Eve but had no idea of their destination. Bets were evenly split between North Africa and Burma which involved a long voyage down to Cape Town and then north through the Indian Ocean.

"Where do you think we are going, Tom?" James asked his sergeant out of hearing of the rest of his platoon. Tom Woods was a regular soldier but not disappointed in his wartime officer who seemed to be shaping up and holding his own with the regular officers posted to the new battalion. Tom, who had grown up in a village near Winchester, joined the army at sixteen and was now twenty-six. His London recruits with a leavening of regular soldiers were more pliable than he had anticipated. The platoon and company were working well.

"I put my money on joining First Army in North Africa, sir. That'll suit us just fine."

"I hope you're right, Tom. I don't fancy Burma. I'd rather be back on coastal defence."

"The boys are ready to show what they're made of now."

"Yes, you're right. It'll be a bit different from Calais. And I'm sure you'd like another crack at them after Dunkirk."

Tom Woods had been evacuated only a day before the final withdrawal. James chided him with his cruise back in a destroyer compared with his own escape in Agnès's little boat.

Two days out of Liverpool they were informed that they were sailing to Algiers as reinforcements for General Anderson's First Army. The journey from England to Algiers was about 1500 miles. Many troop ships were converted pre-war liners. Officers were awakened by stewards with tea. Waiters posted printed dinner menus outside the officers' restaurant. They were escorted by destroyers which suddenly veered off to port or starboard on walls of water with their funnels dipping almost to the sea. At night the soldiers could hear distant explosions.

Below the water line in the troop holds, they felt vulnerable in "Torpedo Heaven" but there were no sinkings in the convoy as it ploughed through the Bay of Biscay. The days were spent in briefings about North Africa.

"Never smoke or spit in front of a mosque."

"When you see grown men walking hand in hand, ignore it. They are not queer."

American soldiers were told to regard the North Africans as if they were the "First Families of Virginia in bathrobes".

There were lectures on health and in particular on the dangers of VD, and the medical officers always included short arm inspections when checking for hernias – "Cough harder!"

James never forgot his first sight of Gibraltar to port on a rare sunny day. Many days in Biscay had been rough with the large drums for seasick soldiers sliding across the decks, splashing their contents in synchrony with the swelling seas.

Gibraltar, "Tuxford" in British code books, was a lump of rock three miles long by one mile wide, controlling access to the Mediterranean, bristling with guns set in the Jurassic limestone. James mused on the possible link between Gibraltar and Tuxford, an obscure village in Nottinghamshire. Probably some Intelligence Corps type wanted to advertise his own home town. He may even have won a bet in the village pub on the strength of it. The great stone edifice of Gibraltar had been honeycombed by thirty miles of tunnels concealing colonies of worker bees toiling in the war effort. To everyone's disappointment the soldiers were not allowed ashore but from the decks there was so much to see. The Rock dwarfed the ships. Cruisers, destroyers and smaller crafts were fitted into the wharves and jetties like jigsaw pieces. The aerodrome pointed out to sea, extended by the spoils excavated from the tunnels, and there was a constant traffic of planes, British or American, landing or taking off. The heavier ones lumbered along, only lifting off just before the runway ended, creating much concern until all realised that the delay on the ground was calculated rather than enforced. To the south the pink mountains of North Africa across the Straits were easily visible. The warm sense of the vast continent almost reached the senses of the soldiers glued to the rails of their ships. They too would soon be over there, inhaling the thicker air of another world so far from the East End.

The interlude of Gibraltar was soon over. The convoy left at night and by sunrise the Rock was no longer in sight. The voyage to Algiers was more hazardous than the route south from England to Gibraltar. About two days out from Gibraltar, James and Tom were leaning over the rails at night, discussing the morale of the platoon, when the adjacent ship in the convoy was lifted out of the water by a lightning flash across the sky which soon subsided to an inferno of flames and smoke as the ship listed towards the onlookers. Screaming men were racing up and down the decks trying to make sense of it. Armoured cars, lorries and stores began to slide across the decks, imperceptibly at first and then gathering momentum to burst over the side into the sea. The ship lost way and began to fall back behind James's ship, being overtaken on both port and starboard by other ships in the convoy. James and Tom stood still, saying nothing save a whispered, "Oh Christ, torpedo." Both knew that their ship could be only seconds away from the same fate. But no other ships were lost that night. The destroyers plunged around like a pack of fox hounds, radars seeking for a sense of their prey. No other submarine tried its luck.

They docked in Algiers on the 3rd January 1943 and all troops, pleased to reclaim control of their legs on firm African soil, disembarked. For most of James's platoon this was their first experience of overseas. Many later recalled the smell rather than the sights of Algiers, a combination of oranges and donkey bedding, of rough Algerian wine and local cigarettes, soon christened Dung d'Algerie. Arab boys, conforming to stereotype, really did jump around in front of the pale soldiers fresh from an

English winter, offering, "Hey, Tommy, jig jig, m'amselle, dix francs."

Most men, immune to the threats of hellfire from priests and padres since adolescence, were deterred by the medical officers' lurid descriptions of the risks to one's wedding tackle incurred in brothels and specifically African brothels. There was, however, one in the Kasbah in the old town of Algiers which was considered a rite of passage before moving off to the front. Other ranks were banned from visiting it but James and some of the other officers decided to widen their horizons. They were not after what Montgomery called "horizontal exercise" but had heard of the exhibition that was also on offer. Madame, having taken a hundred francs each, led them to a small room with a padded bench around the walls and a large bed-sized cushion in the middle. They had been warned by the old hands that one or more of them might be selected from the audience to assist in the proceedings which stretched the fevered imagination of their fate. Two ugly and rather fat naked women appeared. One strapped on a dildo and demonstrated with a broken English commentary the love making attributes of different nationalities. Clearly the Germans were the worst with a highly regimented, violent unsmiling tempo just short of rape. The Italians were best with a long, languid, unpredictable repertoire, with smiles on all sides. The British had to be enticed from their beer and cigarettes for a brief, perfunctory coupling. James's party left feeling sordid and shamefaced.

There was an epidemic of pilfering by the "wogs" of everything not locked up or screwed down.

"If they could carry it away they would steal the air from our tyres," claimed Tom.

After one week of acclimatisation in Algiers, the battalion embarked by train on a two-day journey to the front, facing Tunis. The narrow gauge boxcars inscribed HOMMES 40 CHEVAUX 8 in the approved French manner puffed so slowly uphill that soldiers often jumped off to walk alongside, brewing their tea in the hot water from the engine. They were pleased to leave the train and alighted at a village halt in a marketplace where skinned goat carcasses dripping blood reminded them of the abattoirs in England. They saw old buses propelled by charcoal engines lashed to the bumper and stirred by the driver with a poker and thought that this was their transport. It was now late evening and to everyone's surprise in this chaotic dream a line of British army lorries, six feet apart, awaited them for the final part of the journey to the front. Two German ME109s, known as Gert and Daisy after the two Cockney comediennes, regularly patrolled the route and so the trip along Messerschmitt Alley was usually undertaken at night. The convoy climbed a mountain pass with sheer drops on either side which then levelled out onto cultivated plateaus with the stink of human waste used as fertiliser.

"Every village smells like something dead."

Eventually they arrived at their allotted area near to the front at Sedjenane. They stiffened as they saw artillery flashes in the night sky followed seconds later by rumbles which suggested that the guns were some miles off. James's platoon was directed to a low rise and he set the men to work, digging in on the reverse slope. Each two-man trench was dug to the regulation six feet deep, six feet long and three feet wide. It was cold and wet and after a hard night of excavating heavy thick clay the men were exhausted, sodden and covered with mud.

After spending two days and nights in their trenches, expecting a German attack, the battalion was drawn into reserve, several miles behind the line. The old routines of training and drilling with long periods of boredom returned. Many grappled with the two conflicting emotions: first, relief that their lives were not in danger and second, shallowly buried shame that others were fighting and dying not so far away when they had not as much as fired their rifles in anger so far in North Africa. Those who had already seen some action in this war experienced only the first reaction, as they knew their time would come again to test themselves.

Tunisia's mountain spine, the Grande Dorsale, aligned roughly north and south. There were three passes through the spine, Sbiba, Thala and Kasserine, giving access to the eastern plane held by the Germans and crowned by Tunis itself. In mid-February 1943, 10th Rifle Brigade were roused one night and ordered south. At 5.30 am they set off in trucks in rain as the light appeared from the east. They were relieved that the low cloud and mist would protect them from enemy airplanes. After a day's uncomfortable drive they reached Thala, their objective, and were told that there was a flap on. General Erwin Rommel who had outwitted the British army in Libya and Egypt throughout 1941 and 1942 until bludgeoned into retreat by overwhelming force at Alamein, was now in Tunisia trying to conjure victory by skilful manoeuvres in the face of the gradual accumulation of strength of British and American forces to the west. The American troops, still inexperienced in the face of the Germans, had overextended themselves. Rommel, concentrating his forces, including two panzer divisions, attacked through the Kasserine Pass, sweeping the Americans aside and inflicting a major defeat. If Rommel could burst through and then drive north towards the sea behind the Allied Front, he could even cut off the Allies from their line of communications to the west. This recalled the German thrust in May 1940 in France, which left the French and British armies to extricate themselves from Dunkirk.

The 10th Rifle Brigade were rushed to a new defence line south of Thala. At first light, on the 21st February, they left their trucks and dug in on small hillocks on either side of the valley road. A and D Companies were ahead, with B and C Companies behind. They were supported by artillery and mortars and James realised that this time there would be no withdrawal into reserve before the enemy approached. It was raining and bitterly cold. They had had no proper sleep for two nights. The ground was hard and stony and they were unable to dig trenches and felt vulnerable. Brigadier Cameron Nicholson, commanding the British component of the defence, visited them that day and expressed contempt for their poor shallow trenches, mumbling under his breath but still audibly that they had no conception of what was coming to them.

Funny, thought James. *Our brigadier at Calais was Nicholson. Claude, not Cameron.*

"I seemed to be destined to participate in heroic defences in hell holes under the command of different species of Nicholson."

He spoke this aloud to himself but Tom Woods heard.

"War is full of coincidences, sir. They're reassuring, usually. They make a sort of pattern as if it is all planned for us already. Nonsense, of course."

"You're quite a philosopher, Tom."

James often spoke to his sergeant as a friend in tight spots, forsaking the military formality of Sergeant Woods.

He realised how much he owed him and how he relied on him to keep the platoon afloat and confident in themselves.

After Brigadier Nicholson's withering remarks they resumed digging their trenches but they were only two feet deep before they hit solid rock. There had been no time to prepare minefields in front of their positions. His men were lying in shallow trenches watching, waiting. They all knew the German technique of driving tanks over trenches then spinning round to crush the men below.

"They won't even have to spin if they reach us," James mused.

In mid-afternoon Allied vehicles, mostly American, starting screaming past them nose to tail, clearly in full retreat. James knew that there were many Allied troops between them and the Germans and that they were in reserve, backstops for the real action well ahead. An American jeep with two men, towing a 37mm gun, pulled over.

"Are you stopping here?"

"Yes."

"Then I guess we had better stop too."

They set up their gun in front of the platoon.

When the evening light was fading fast a British Valentine tank approached A Company 400 yards ahead of James's platoon in C Company. Soldiers without hats lay smoking on the tank. In better light they might have seen APPLE SAMMY stencilled on the Valentine's flank but they would probably have been none the wiser. How were they to know that Apple Sammy had been captured by the Germans at Tebourba three months before?

"Keep away from my bloody trench," a rifleman shouted. "You're knocking it in." Then the Germans on the captured British tank jumped off and fell on the defenders.

"Surrender! The panzers are here."

It was now clear that three German Mark IV panzers were close behind. A Company soon recovered its balance and opened intense fire but many surrendered and were rushed back as prisoners. One of the tanks fired and exploded the mortar ammunition truck nearby. The tanks then threw their gears into reverse and disappeared into the night.

James and the rest of C Company to the rear froze and awaited their turn. This was more like Calais. Waiting. Waiting. Fingers massaging triggers, varying pressures well short of that required to fire. James, disdaining his officer's pistol which was only useful in very close contact, had acquired a spare Lee Enfield rifle and felt closer to his men with their shared weapon. For half an hour after the first German tanks approached nothing happened, their positions shrouded in eerie stillness. Perhaps they had beaten them off for the night? Everyone knew the Germans did not like night fighting.

Tom Woods heard them first. The distant squeaking of tank tracks in the cemetery black ahead of them. James felt the old sensations of dry mouth, pumping temples and chest.

"Yes, Tom. They're coming."

"Face your front!" Tom's Hampshire voice filled the valley.

"If you'd been a Cockney like the rest of them, you'd have said 'yer front', Tom."

James muttered this very quietly, only to himself this time.

Suddenly there were revving engines and German voices shouting. James was surprised at so many Very flares like phosphorescent fireworks revealing the positions of the panzers.

"Open fire!"

Rifles, Bren guns and mortars opened up and soon one tank was hit nearby and set on fire. The screams of one of the crew seemed unending. These merged with the screams of the American gun crew who had volunteered to stay and help as their gun was overrun by another tank. In spite of the wall of sound of shells, mortars, machine gun and the isolated cracks of rifles, the sounds of dying men seemed to rise above all and were recalled when all else was forgotten.

Ahead of him, A and D Companies had disappeared. James tried to press himself down in his shallow trench, numb, beyond terror, watching himself firing his rifle with detachment. He later dreamed that he was floating above his trench, watching himself firing desperately at the enemy all around him. Then almost as suddenly as the firing had begun, it stopped. He was alive without a scratch. He could see no trace of his platoon. They must all be dead.

I'm the only one left.

"Tom!"

He cried for Tom as others cried for their mother. The name did not leave his lips. Just a few yards away a small group of Germans were sitting smoking. James inched away and eventually reached the curve of a hill. For the first time in what seemed like hours but was only minutes, he felt confident enough to stand up and walk away. The moon had risen. He reached the plateau and ran into an Arab shepherd and his goats. James offered him a cigarette and they sat together in the still moonlit night, smoking and not attempting to speak to each other. The inferno one mile away seemed to be on another planet. In the distance there was the pink glow of burning vehicles creating a sequence of small false dawns.

Raising his hand to the shepherd he asked, "Thala?" The shepherd indicated the rough direction. James stumbled off and after another mile he began to run into British soldiers, many of them familiar faces from 10th Rifle Brigade. C Company had come off best. Most of the others had been taken prisoner or killed. He learnt that a battery of Royal Artillery 25-pounders had put in a tremendous fire and had knocked out many German tanks which had then withdrawn. An officer from another company, who always seemed to know everything, told him that they had held up Rommel's 10th Panzer Division.

10th Panzer? We last ran into them at Calais, James mused. *How do all these coincidences occur?*

He was not thinking straight. He was led away to a rest area and tea and stew were forced into his static hands. The cooks moulded his fingers around the tin mug and mess tin so that they would not fall through his grasp.

He soon fell asleep. When he awoke a familiar grinning face stood over him.

"Glad to see you're still with us, sir. The lads thought you'd bought it. I steered them back. It was clear we were overwhelmed. It was that or surrendering and I was damned if I would do that and spend the rest of the war in a POW camp."

"Tom, you old bugger."

He slept again, slipping off into that exhausted oblivion which cannot be so different from dying. He dreamed of the bodies of his men lying on the recent battlefield. He dreamed of the Arabs stripping the bodies of the spreadeagled dead, shockingly white.

The Greeks had a name for it – necrosylia.

After the Kasserine episode, 10th Rifle Brigade was once

again drawn into reserve and awaited reinforcements from England. More of the story emerged over the next few weeks and James began to feel that his platoon had done well in spite of its inexperience. The old feelings of survivor guilt, which had tortured his nights since Calais, ate away at him. Most of his battalion had been captured. American and British artillery had concentrated in a three-mile arc and rained shells on Rommel's forces. Instead of counterattacking, low on ammunition, fuel and rations and with evidence of converging Allied reinforcements, he had decided to retreat.

Thala proved the high water mark of the Axis forces in North Africa. Over the next month the prospect of imminent Allied victory in Tunisia grew. Once again James had survived when most of his fellows had been killed or captured.

There was one more challenge for James and his Company before the final victory in Tunisia in May 1943. The area around Longstop Hill and Medjez el Bab were crucial to the approach to Tunis. Intelligence had determined that von Arnim in charge of all Axis forces in Tunisia would try one final desperate counterattack to disrupt the Allied advance. C Company was selected to set up a forward observation post in a farm overlooking the plain from which the German counterattack would be mounted. As Major Hall briefed his junior officers on the operation, James, for the first time in the war, began to feel that his chances of survival were poor. Concealment and secrecy were crucial. The Company would therefore approach the farm on foot, without transport.

It was a warm evening, scented with spring flowers, when they formed up behind a hill out of the sight of the enemy. The Royal Artillery captain, whose role it would be to direct fire onto the advancing German forces, arrived in a jeep with his radio equipment. He looked familiar. He climbed out of his seat and approached the waiting infantry men.

"Captain Martin Willis. I'm your artillery spotter for this

jaunt. This is Lance Corporal Ellis who twiddles the knobs on the radio."

Major Hall returned his salute and shook hands.

"This is Lieutenant James Butland."

James saluted and shook hands. "I think we're old acquaintances. Were you at Dayton Hall in Harrow?"

"Yes. Indeed I was. And then Merchant Taylors'."

The old school wound itched, though James illogically now felt more confident about the project. Such thin connections to other human beings fighting alongside somehow stretched his courage. They marched off through rough scrub and thin forest country, climbing about 500 feet before reaching the brow of a long escarpment. They scrambled the last few yards on hands and knees, not knowing what might lie ahead. The farm stood nearby, commanding an excellent view of the plain stretching away towards Tunis and the sea. A water tower dominated the area, surrounded by white-walled farm buildings enclosing a flat compound.

"There's our cushy billet for the next few days, chaps."

Major Hall tapped his map although there was no other farm or building for miles around.

"It looks unoccupied."

"Sergeant Woods."

"Sir."

"Take some of your chaps and make sure the farm is unoccupied before we expose ourselves."

"Yes, sir."

Tom Woods and three other members of the platoon edged forward, well spread out, and approached the farm from the four points of the compass, seeking cover where they could, although there was none. The farm was unoccupied.

Captain Willis climbed the ladder to the top of the water tower, and descended two steps at a time, impatient to describe what he had seen.

"I can see everything. Just over that hill about five miles away there are about 200 Jerry tanks and hundreds of tents for infantry. Intelligence was right for once. They're sitting ducks."

"I'm going back up again to call up our battery of 25-pounders to get going this morning."

The sun was now fully up but it was too early for the intense heat of noon. It was not long before they heard the heavy crumps of their own guns from the west followed by the sound of shells passing over their heads, not unlike the sensation of fast trains passing through stations. Then, in the distance, a sequence of explosions. From the ground they could hear Captain Willis transmitting orders to modify the direction and ranges of the shells so that they would pinpoint the German positions.

James felt superfluous. He and his men rested in the gentle sunlight trying to spot the shells arching over their heads, sensing the rippling of air pressure but seeing nothing. It was unlikely that the Germans would send out a patrol in their direction before evening but they all knew it would come. Occasionally enemy aircraft would fly over but they all lay low out of sight, giving no evidence of their positions. They hoped that the Germans would blame their shelling on Allied air reconnaissance. As the day gradually wore on and as the light was diluted by dusk Willis shouted down from the water tower.

"Three Jerry armoured cars approaching!"

The Company had dug trenches outside the farmyard walls as forward posts and, as the armoured cars were almost on them, let fly with Bren gun fire, mortars and anti-tank rifles. Two of the armoured cars blew up and the third turned full circle, driving away at top speed to carry news of the observation post causing such damage.

"Now they know we're here. We'll be for it tomorrow."

Major Hall requested permission to withdraw that night but was refused.

"You are just too damned useful up there to withdraw, Hall.

You must hang on and hold out. I'll send up some anti-tank mines tonight which should help you cope with the armour if they try to winkle you out tomorrow."

True to his word, two lorry loads of mines arrived an hour later with ten reinforcements fresh from Algiers. Their faces pale from England rather than fear were ghostly in moonlight, but they were afraid too. They all shared that fear.

James offered to lay the new minefield.

"I spent far too many hours planting these things on Norfolk beaches, sir. It will be just like old times on coastal defence."

He spoke with a flippancy which he did not feel but at least he had a job to do which would help the night move on and allow him little time to think about the next day. The rock-spattered sandy plain rolled away to the east and seemed as peaceful as the sea off those Norfolk beaches. After many hours of darkness they had managed to lay the mines in a wide arc around the farmhouse and then they settled down to wait.

"Tom, here we are again, waiting for the Jerries to come. This always seems to be our war. We've become defence experts, never attackers."

"You're right, sir. Comfort yourself with the fact that you're more likely to live defending than attacking. We should be pleased."

"Of course, Tom. Will you stay in the army after the war?"

"I'm a regular, sir. The army's my life. I couldn't do anything else. Of course you'll be off doctoring, sir, won't you?"

Tom knew James's plans and loved him for it. Neither wished to acknowledge their mutual dependency and sheer friendship, so inhibited by the relationship of officer to NCO. James felt closer to Tom than to his fellow officers and this reinforced his duty of obligation to his fellows that was at the heart of his decision to become a doctor.

He was sitting and dozing behind the white wall of the farmyard when suddenly the two men were picked up and dropped again by the impact of a shell thirty yards away, which they had not heard. Their ears hummed with the monotonal sound of a swarm of bees. Deafened, their shouts were wordless with writhing lips. The bombardment was furious for five minutes and then Willis called down from his eyrie.

"Tanks and infantry, about 600 yards away. I'll try and bring down some of our stuff on them."

James was never clear whether it was friendly fire from British guns falling short of their target on their own position in the farmyard or whether German artillery or tanks had located them. Tom was conscious, eyes searching the sky for some interpretation of the holocaust. His eyelids flickered, flickered to dam back the blood that was trying to drown them. He was lying in an expanding pool, fed by the pumping artery from his severed thigh. James saw that his right arm had flown away but could not understand why the stump was not contributing much to the lake of blood in which Tom lay. The film had stuck in a single frame. All were paralysed in a staged montage of photographic intensity. This exposure joined others in the past and anticipated others to come in his unquenchable memory. It was his voice that restarted the cine film of time and action.

"Tom! You're hurt. Don't move." Later James often summoned up these absurd words which, by emotional reflex, always brought tears throughout his life. He gripped the pumping femoral artery, trying to make a tourniquet of his hand, but he seemed so weak, so clumsy that he could not maintain his hold on the ragged flesh. He saw the pool of blood was already coagulating in the growing heat of the day. Tom was still conscious, his lips flailing as fast as his eyelids in his will to speak. His remaining left arm jerked at James and his hand found James's right hand slippery with blood.

"James."

He had never addressed his officer like this before. He said no more. His face slowed down from furious activity to a walking pace and then to a calm stillness, reflecting the colour change from red to the waxy yellow of the recently dead.

"Oh, Tom, you old bugger."

It was then that he realised he had not escaped injury himself. Solemnly covering each eye with his hand he found that he could only see with his left.

It's blood just blocking off the right one.

He was aware of pain in his chest and back. He coughed and could not comprehend why bright red blood was fired onto the ground next to Tom's magenta pool. His head ached. He tried to stand but could not, pitching over onto his left side as his left leg refused to support him. He could recall no more until later that day or perhaps even the next day. He was lying on a stretcher in an ambulance truck rocking across the bumpy scrub with pain that was present but somehow distant and unthreatening. Morphine, he concluded.

This time I shall reach the regimental aid post. No more stumbling through the streets of Calais. No Agnès to patch me up.

Agnès.

He realised that he had not thought of her for days, perhaps weeks, and this distressed him. She seemed so far away in space and in time. Perhaps she never existed outside his imagination. He could not be sure as he jolted across the desert.

"I must give it some thought," he said loudly.

"Yes, do, chum," mumbled the wounded soldier from the stretcher above him.

He had no idea how seriously wounded he might be. He knew that a shell fragment tearing through his femoral artery would have killed him. Like Tom. He did not feel faint from blood loss.

At the RAP the doctor explored his wounds and speculated that no shell splinters had been left inside. All had probably scythed through soft tissues and left his body. His right eye looked a mess but precise diagnosis was beyond him. They had never taught him much about eyes in medical school. He had been on a rugger tour during the attachment to the Eye Clinic. He continued to cough up blood. There were entry and exit wounds in his chest, indicating that his right lung had been skewered. He felt short of breath and the doctor felt that his punctured lung had partially collapsed.

"Algiers base hospital for you, Lieutenant."

James dreaded the journey which he knew would take two or three days. Stretcher-bearers transferred him from ambulance to ambulance and then to a hospital train. He would never forget the stench of blood, sweat and faeces sometimes lightened by the intrusion of wild flowers and orange groves. He would try to hang on to these pleasures, forcing them to overlay the perfumes of death and decay.

He spent the next four months in hospital in Algiers. He felt lucky to have survived Tunisia, if indeed he did survive. With no recovery, the right eye was removed. He had two operations on his chest to remove shell splinters which had not managed to burst through his chest after all. These operations were complicated by empyema, pus collections in the chest cavity, which had to be drained painfully by large needles. This was more painful than the original injury. The surgeon thoughtfully presented the bottled shell fragments to James as a souvenir. They later resided at the back of the bottom drawer of his desk. He developed a superstition that if he lost them, he would die. Perhaps they would find their way somehow back into his chest and kill him.

By the end of 1943 he was feeling much stronger, but then his old sleeping difficulties returned. The vicious nightmares began to take hold of him – of Tom, of Agnès's death so that he would be incarcerated in the Calais cellar with no hope of escape, of... cruel horrors still awaiting him. He could not work out the details of these but he knew that they would be even more destructive than their predecessors. He dreaded going to bed. The migraines returned with a new intensity. He developed spontaneous tremors in his right hand, the hand that tried to staunch Tom's blood, which he tried to control with the other hand. This in turn took up the uncontrollable muscle spasms. James knew all about shell shock from the accounts of the Great War.

I'm not much of a soldier, or a man. I deserted my men in Calais. I was in a complete funk at Thala. Terrified. I suppose I fired back that night. I can't even remember. And then I deserted Tom and the others at the farmhouse. They're all dead and I'm alive. Why am I still in one piece? It doesn't seem right.

The war was getting on fine without him. Sicily had fallen. Italy had surrendered. The battalion was fighting on against the Germans in Italy without him.

They probably don't even remember I existed.

"It's time I stopped killing. It's time I stopped killing. It's time I stopped killing."

He spoke this clearly out loud to no one in particular one day in the grounds of the hospital. The medical board which had to decide his fate reached its conclusion.

"Physically he's almost back to normal, short of an eye, but mentally he's shot to pieces. Full of survivor guilt. He sees himself as something of a coward though, by all accounts, he should be MC and Bar by now after what he's been through. St Thomas's has promised him a place as a medical student when the army's finished with him. I think we should make this happen now."

The RAMC lieutenant colonel in his late fifties and keen himself to return to civilian life at his old hospital spoke convincingly, and the medical board supported his conclusions. They agreed that he would be better employed as a medical student than as a battered, one-eyed infantry officer. James's colonel did not offer much resistance and allowed him indefinite leave of absence which could be terminated in an emergency. In other words, if he ran out of junior officers, James could be recalled later in the war.

October 1943 to
September 1944

The voyage home from Algiers was grey. James, once again, was flattened by letting down his fellow soldiers – the old nagging fear reaching back to Calais that he had found an easy way out. Outwardly he seemed physically fit with only a subtle lack of fluency in his walking that caused him to hesitate before striding out. He then compensated by striding too hard, causing a little quiver as he walked. He did not discuss his injuries with his travelling companions, implying that they were too severe for him to be posted back to his battalion in Italy. The black patch worn over his right eye offered an extra barrier to those who wanted to become friends. They docked at Gibraltar and his ship was delayed there for a week while a convoy back to Britain could be assembled. James formed no alliances with other officers but spent the days walking the streets of Gibraltar, drinking coffee at pavement cafés and climbing the Rock three days running to help regain his physical strength. As he gazed over the Straits towards North Africa his mind was full of Calais, two utterly different worlds both divided by a narrow plateau of water.

"It's three years since we last met, Agnès," he spoke out loud. No one else was near to question his sanity so he could create a dialogue without embarrassment.

"James, how are you? I think of you every day and wonder what you are doing. Are you in England or somewhere overseas? Maybe North Africa or the Far East. Perhaps you are dead. I have heard nothing from you since 1940. Sometimes, I hear, messages arrive from England about Frenchmen who followed de Gaulle there after France died. But no message from you. I must press on here. I am now a qualified doctor and working from dawn to dusk – and then from dusk to morning – on the wards of my hospital in Lille. Do send some message, some sign, James, that you are alive and that you still want me."

This reply from Agnès sounded just like a wireless broadcast.

"Agnès, of course I want you. I love you. I only want the war to end so that I can return to Calais and see you again. You know it's impossible now."

"I understand, James. You come when you are able and we can resuscitate our lives."

"Yes, Agnès. The war is turning now. It won't last much longer. By the way, I'm going to medical school soon if they will have me. You see what you have done? Pulled the rug out from under the feet of the embryo historian and replaced it with a life of medical hard labour."

James walked down the long road, clear in his mind but unable to make plans for the future when the world was so confused.

On the following day the ship resumed its passage to England. It was difficult to relax and all eyes were alert for evidence of U-boats. These infested the Bay of Biscay, snapping out from their bases at La Rochelle, Lorient and Brest, but the journey was uneventful. The ship docked at bomb-scarred Plymouth and soon James was in a compartment on the London train. He did not try to strike up a conversation with the other officers in his compartment and they left him alone to his own solitary thoughts. Morose sort of chap, they must have thought of him, James speculated, and they were not wrong. He should have felt elated to be back in England with a new life in medicine ahead of him but he could not summon up any shafts of light. The fields so green, so comfortably moist, so content. James dozed and looked forward to his dinner. He could always eat, whatever his state of mind, and it bracketed the journey.

Paddington. Well-known territory. Harrow and Wealdstone station. Why does nothing change when the whole world is changing? He was soon with his parents, overjoyed at the return of their son, punctured but alive.

"Father, I'm going to write to St Thomas's tomorrow and ask when I can start First MB in October."

"Whatever will make you happy, son. What will Wadham think about all of this?"

"Not very much. They can't see an historian somersaulting into a doctor."

Almost by return of post a letter arrived from Mr Bevin at St Thomas's.

From the Dean's Office
St Thomas's Hospital Medical School
London
SE1
7th October 1943

Dear Butland,

I am delighted to receive your letter and am very pleased that you have made an excellent recovery from your wounds and that you would like to join us on the First MB course. I much look forward to welcoming you to St Thomas's.

Yours sincerely,
Robert Bevin, FRCS

In late October 1943 James packed two large suitcases and made his way to St Thomas's on the Embankment opposite the Houses of Parliament. Moorfields Eye Hospital had fitted a glass replica of his intact eye and he was still learning how to retain it and how to ignore the subtle reaction of others to his face. The row of red-white Victorian pavilions had been interrupted by bomb damage but much of the work of the hospital continued though some had been evacuated to Hydestile in Surrey.

James was billeted in St Thomas's House which accommodated the medical students and he set to work on the physics, chemistry and biology which would equip him to start real medicine. It was hard but he learnt by heart without any real understanding. There were not many students as most had been conscripted. The few who tried to keep the medical school alive all had some reason why they were there and not in the services. James repeated his well-rehearsed story that his injuries did not allow him to remain in the Rifle Brigade and that the Army had decided that he was able to serve his country better by studying medicine. It was difficult to raise rugby and cricket teams but they did their best to keep the old traditions alive. There were hospital hops and parties, and in the unspoken background, a shared feeling that the war was going well and that Great Britain should end up on the winning side. James decided to make one more attempt to be accepted as a medical student at Oxford, reassuring the senior tutor that it was likely that he would pass First MB in May 1944. He would then be able to hold his own with the other new medical students going up in October 1944.

From the Senior Tutor
Wadham College
Oxford
1st December 1943

Dear Butland,

We rejoice that you have achieved your ambition to read medicine but regret that we are only able to hold open your place and scholarship at Wadham if you choose to give up medicine and return to history or another of the arts schools of your choice.

Yours sincerely,

Ian Dombey

He was not surprised to read this rejection which closed off Oxford as an option. He could imagine completing the whole course at St Thomas's but then in a sudden, stark insight, Cambridge became a thought that would not disappear. He had last visited Cambridge during leave from his Norfolk coastal defence duties in late 1940. Wartime Cambridge was cold and drab and he predictably could not compare it with the majesty of warm, yellow-brown Oxford stone. Still, if Cambridge would take him, it would do. He carefully constructed an exploratory letter which he sent to the Tutor for Admissions at every college.

St Thomas's Hospital Medical School

London

SE1

15th December 1943

Dear Sir,

Please forgive this enquiry if it is of no interest to you but if you would allow me to set out my current situation I should be most grateful. In December 1938 I was elected to an Open Scholarship in History at Wadham College, Oxford but was unable to go up in October 1939 for obvious reasons. I had joined the Queen Victoria's Rifles in early 1939 and was most fortunate to escape from France in a small boat after the surrender at Calais. I was later commissioned in the Rifle Brigade but was wounded in Tunisia in May 1943 and I was considered medically unfit to return to full duties.

It was as early as 1940 that I decided to study Medicine rather than History but Wadham will not allow me to take this unusual step. I have proved my commitment to Medicine by undertaking the London First MB course at St Thomas's Hospital and by relinquishing my Oxford scholarship. Clearly I could continue the course at St

Thomas's but then I realised that I could perhaps apply to Cambridge for Natural Sciences Tripos with a view to returning to St Thomas's for the clinical course in October 1947. May I therefore request that you consider my application for admission in October 1944.

I should inform you that I have sent an identical letter to every college in Cambridge because I have no other method of determining which college might be prepared to consider my application. I am most grateful to you for your attention to my request.

Yours faithfully,
James Butland
Lieutenant, Rifle Brigade and medical student

Over the next few weeks multiple letters of courteous rejection collected in his pigeon hole at St Thomas's House. He had not discussed his plans with anyone but others had spotted the obvious Cambridge postmarks and ribbed him about them.

"Thought you were an Oxford man, James."

"I thought so too but they've changed their mind."

James had almost given up the Cambridge idea but then a letter arrived from Magdalene College.

From the Master
Magdalene College
Cambridge
9th January 1944

Dear Butland,

I am interested in your letter. Please come and discuss it. Telephone my secretary and we can arrange a suitable date.

Yours sincerely,

Walter Hammerton

About two weeks later he caught the train from Liverpool Street Station to Cambridge and then walked the two miles from the station to Magdalene. It was a bright day in late January when he made his way over Magdalene Bridge. He was thirty minutes early. He leant over the bridge staring at the Cam silently moulding its course so unlike the noisy, irritable seashore. The pink Tudor brick of Magdalene faced him and he contrasted it with the yellow-brown Stuart stone of Wadham. Wadham stone always seemed so disciplined and formal. Magdalene brick was more human and forgiving. He had never visited Magdalene before. His one or perhaps two visits to Cambridge with his parents years before had followed the obvious route along the Backs, encompassing Queens', King's, Clare, Trinity and St John's. He had admired them but did not ever believe that he could learn to love them. James dared not hope that the Master of Magdalene would offer him a place. He probably wanted to examine this odd species of mind-changing turncoat as an intellectual exercise.

At the Porters' Lodge he asked for directions to the Master's Lodge. He entered First Court and turned left through the passageway by the Chapel and knocked firmly on the door. Mr Hammerton opened the door himself and ushered James into his study. He did not know what to expect. He recalled his historical interrogations in Oxford and half expected some replay of that intellectual sparring. Mr Hammerton asked him questions about his school. As a past headmaster of Rugby himself, he knew Mr Blade-Hawkins, the head of United Colleges School. He gently probed James's mind and tried to establish the depth of his decisions and whether he was sane. After a very gentle discussion James was directed to the Director of Studies in Medicine, Dr Bernard Statham, an organic chemist intensely interested in medicine and perhaps even a frustrated doctor himself. James did his best to convince him that he would work hard to compensate for his scientific deficiencies and he was then directed back to the

Master's Lodge. The Master welcomed him back warmly and sent him on his way with the promise of a decision soon.

Within a week a letter from the Master arrived offering him a place in October 1944 subject to his passing the London First MB. He passed, though his 51% in Physics, with a pass mark of 50%, suggested that either God or the Dean or possibly both were on his side.

James was sorry to leave St Thomas's. It had provided his passport into medicine when the idea seemed impractical and hopeless. Facing the Houses of Parliament across the Thames it was convinced of its divine right to rule the profession. Many thought that it justified its existence more clearly than its famous neighbour. James, who was not required to enter the hospital itself for his First MB studies, chose to walk down the main corridor of the hospital in his white coat, inhaling the exciting pheromones of disinfectant and sheer sterility. They reminded him illogically of the pungent incense in Dayton Hall chapel a decade before. He smelt the atmosphere, the ethos of the medical profession of those days. Pretending to be a clinical student, he sometimes entered the observation domes overlooking the operations undertaken in the theatres below. On one occasion he was alone, watching a rather dramatic thoracic operation with exposure of the heart and lungs when the surgeon beckoned to him and invited him to change into scrubs and watch the operation more closely within the theatre. He ducked and beat a hasty retreat as he would have had to confess that he was only a First MB student, hardly a medical student at all. He never dared to speak to a Nightingale, a nurse trained in Florence Nightingale's School of Nursing at St Thomas's, as they were terrifying. They were also self-confident, so military in their bearing that he, a mere veteran of Calais and Tunisia, could not hope to hold his own. And so he bid farewell to those redbrick Victorian blocks on the Thames, fully expecting to return in three years for his clinical studies.

October 1944 to
September 1947

It had all happened so fast. He had been an Oxford man or at least had done everything possible from his mid-teens to be admitted to Oxford. In the space of three months he had rejected his acquired birth right and was entering the Porters' Lodge of Magdalene College, Cambridge. He was not a callow eighteen-year-old fresh from school and so the terrors and uncertainties were not so vivid but he still had to find his feet. He gave his nàme to the head porter, who called him "sir" but delivered without the sarcasm of the porters at Wadham in 1938. Of course, his Rifle Brigade soldiers had immunised him to the form of address of "sir" long ago.

"Ah, yes, Mr Butland, Mallory Court 6."

He carried his suitcases to his set on the opposite side of Magdalene Street and lowered himself onto the seat next to his desk overlooking the Court with a view of St John's College Chapel. He did not unpack but went off to explore. He did not know Cambridge. It was a foreign land and he felt an imposter, an Oxford spy in the very heart of this ancient enemy. He studied the exuberant red brick of the Lutyens Building for which he knew of no convincing counterpart in Oxford. He stood by the river, which marked the far boundary of the Court which he had observed when sitting at his desk. Those taking the last opportunity of the season to punt were behaving like young undergraduates although they seemed older. He retraced his steps across Magdalene Street, past the Porters' Lodge and into First Court, a relaxed pink brick Tudor enclosure.

"Stop thinking about Oxford."

He spoke aloud, as he would so often when making a decisive statement that he wanted to etch into his mind for future review. A passing undergraduate looked rather oddly at him. James usually whispered when others were within hearing but he had failed to spot the intruder on this occasion. The Hall and Chapel were understated and more modest than those at Wadham where he had admired the hammer beam-roofed hall, one of Oxford's best kept secrets. Facing him in Second Court was the Pepys Building which he saw for the first time. Clearly a late seventeenth-century façade faced with elegant stone with an enclosed arched cloister. When he had visited the Master for his interview he dared not explore the college as a prospective undergraduate as rejection would have been even more painful. But Pepys Building was visual mandragora which he could conjure up in his mind's eye for the rest of his life. He followed the central path towards the middle of Pepys and then skirted round to the left into the college garden. He had been a connoisseur of Oxford college gardens, often measuring the value of the college to him by the beauty of its surroundings. Magdalene's Fellows' Garden – though all members of the College could enter it – was the usual sequence of lawns, tall trees, shrubs and flowers but had the virtue of a long river front. Buried in the shrubbery were the gravestones of long forgotten Masters' dogs. Clearly Magdalene was a kind, gentle and relaxed place and would meet James's deepest wishes without doubt or regret.

Magdalene had other huge advantages. It was small, with a century or two of undergraduates, and it was not obsessed with the pursuit of academic excellence and distinction to the exclusion of humanity. With his vestigial grasp of science that would not be a disadvantage. The undergraduates were an odd group of those who had somehow not been ingested by the war and the flood of older ex-servicemen would not really come until 1946. Before Hall on that first evening of Full Term the medical students were summoned to the rooms of Dr Statham to meet each other. There were four of them and in that first Michaelmas Term they developed the tight and discreet bonds of those who knew their life destiny which contrasted them with most undergraduates.

Oxford was soon forgotten. James worked hard and held his own in spite of his scientific ineptitude. He spent his first year terrified that he would fail Tripos and be sent down, thus betraying the trust of the Master's judgment. He did not know how to measure his performance against others. Even science exams in Cambridge relied on essay-writing techniques and all of his literary and historical skills were employed to conceal his lack of science.

The medical students often walked together in the late afternoons after lectures and practicals and before evening supervisions which preceded dinner in Hall. Their route was consistent. Through Mallory Court and into St John's, a mix of exuberant Gothick leading to the Bridge of Sighs, a Victorian vision of Venice, and on to the older pink brick of sixteenth-century St John's. The leitmotif of Cambridge is Tudor pink brick which contrasts with Oxford's yellow-brown Cotswold stone.

Out of St John's, turning back over another St John's Bridge to the path along the river. The Wren Library of Trinity, not red bricked but grey stoned like St Paul's Cathedral, dominating this stretch of the Cam. Clare, Trinity Hall, King's to the left mesmerising the senses with sheer perfection and overwhelming any Oxford comparisons. James often recalled that during his blunderbuss Cambridge application to all colleges he hoped that Clare might accept him. The origins of the college were in the little Suffolk town of Clare from which his father had moved at the beginning of the century. Clare had not taken the bait. Down to the Mathematical Bridge at Queens' and retracing their steps either by the longer route in and out of the colleges or, if time were short, back along the road bordering the Backs or through the narrow streets of Cambridge itself.

James was deeply grateful to Magdalene. At United Colleges School where sporting enthusiasms were unfashionable, rugby and cricket were chapters of loss, but Magdalene won its matches. Carefully secreting his glass eye in a bowl of water in his rooms, he played the best rugby of his life in spite of his narrowed visual field. If he had not been compelled to work so hard at his medical studies, he would have pulled out all the stops for a Blue. To his genuine amazement he gained an Upper Second in the first part of his Tripos. He began to relax and knew that he would qualify as a doctor if he continued to work hard. Cambridge became his new addiction.

The war ended in the summer of 1945 at the end of his first year. The Rifle Brigade had never summoned him back to the battalion in spite of severe manpower shortages as the war dragged on. James often assumed that he had been forgotten, left off some list. His soldiering days were over. During the autumn of 1945 he wrote a letter to Agnès at her Calais address but received no reply. He clearly was no longer part of her life. She had perhaps married another doctor in Lille and decided that it was for the best if she did not fan old flames. May 1940 was so long ago. In early December he chose a Christmas card depicting King's College and the Backs and posted it to Agnès with a letter imploring her to reply so that he could measure her enthusiasm for a reunion.

Early in the New Year, as he entered the Porters' Lodge at Magdalene one Siberian Cambridge day, he could see his Christmas card sprouting from his pigeon hole. Across Agnès's address in heavy black diagonal crayon was inscribed: "Return to Sender. Must have gone away. Current address unknown." He stood in the Lodge reading and rereading the words, speculating that Agnès may have been killed in the heavy Allied bombing of Calais in the spring and summer of 1944, which had completed the destruction started by the Germans in 1940. He could do no more. With the seasonal optimism of the spring of 1946 he considered an expedition to France to track down Agnès but could not bring himself to act on this impulse. If she had survived, she would be constructing a new life, he reasoned, and would not welcome the intruder who had forced his way into her house that May of defeat six years before.

There was one other reason. At St Thomas's James had been in awe of the nursing staff, who seemed to be so confident and dismissive of mere students, especially wet behind the ears First MB students. At a rugby club hop he had chatted to one nurse called Alice, who seemed to like him. It was generally agreed that nurses were only interested in clinical medical students as they were hunting for husbands and a delay of six years or more was one sacrifice too many. Alice Dent wrote to him at Magdalene and invited herself for the weekend in the spring of 1946. How did she know that he was at Magdalene? Female intelligence services were stronger than most men appreciated. As he had had no contact with her since 1944 he was perplexed but was prepared to be friendly. He booked her into a pub with some small rooms up Castle Hill and arranged to meet her at the station with no absence of awkwardness on both sides.

"Hello, Alice. How nice of you to contact me after so long. How are you? How's St Thomas's?"

"I so much enjoyed that evening we spent together at the rugger club hop. I thought that we got on so well. I was really disappointed when you made no effort to contact me again."

"I'm sorry, Alice. The truth is that I met a French girl in the early part of the war and I always thought that we would get together again when it was all over. Silly, really. I tried to contact her at the end of the war but she never replied to my letters. So it's all over."

They walked around Cambridge for two days and he enjoyed

showing Alice his favourite haunts. Women were not allowed to dine in college and so they ate at modest little restaurants like the Gardenia in Rose Crescent where large helpings of inexpensive moussaka were popular with students in those still rationed days. Through Alice, James was introduced to the nursing set at St Thomas's and he would visit at weekends and in vacations, sleeping illicitly on the floor of the nurses' home or in Lambeth flats where nurses and students were allowed to live outside the hospital. They felt relaxed together and he grew to be fond of Alice but never reached that brief peak of love that Agnès had offered him in 1940. Of course the shared danger in Calais in the intensity of war inflamed their senses but it was a far cry from the threadbare placidity of 1946. He had decided that Agnès clearly did not want him but Alice did.

The pattern of his second year in Cambridge followed that of the first. The confidence that he gained from his Upper Second made him study even harder. In the second year they studied pathology which was almost real medicine compared with the anatomy, physiology and biochemistry of the first. James found this easier and more interesting.

Increasingly he would spend some weekends during term in London with Alice. In the vacations when he still lodged with his parents in Harrow he was a frequent visitor to St Thomas's. He met old acquaintances and anticipated his return to the hospital with eagerness. At the end of his second year he was again awarded an Upper Second but Dr Statham confided to him that he had been very close to a First. This knowledge caused a sharp burning in his chest and an enthusiasm for success in medicine that proved to him, if he still needed proof, that his decision to relinquish Oxford history had been sound. He even considered writing to the Senior Tutor at Wadham and boasting of his success at Cambridge. Historians could become doctors, and good ones.

His tutor was a medieval historian and at the beginning and

end of each term, James presented himself gowned in front of Mr Stennett to review his progress.

"Why don't you read History Part I in your final year, Butland?"

Cambridge was unique in British medical schools in the flexibility of the third year. The tools to equip medical students for clinical medical studies were packed into the first two years, allowing a free choice of study in the third. Mr Stennett, at the beginning of James's first year, had confessed that he had been sent James's scholarship papers from Wadham and had been impressed.

"Why not give up butterfly collecting or medicine, whatever you call it, and try history for one year before you sell your soul to the smells and degradation of your chosen path in life? Prodigal son and all that. I should like to teach a bright young historian. We're a little short of those at present."

James countered:

"Sir, I'm enjoying medicine immensely and feel comfortable with my rather abrupt conversion. Thank you for your encouragement but I dare not read history again. What's more, I'm terrified that I may enjoy it too much. It would be a real danger and potentially destructive."

"You may be right. I do understand but to lose such a natural and talented historian, to let him slip through my fingers, is difficult. You have my very best wishes, my boy."

"Thank you very much, sir. If I work hard and choose pharmacology and experimental psychology in the third year I think I might get a First. I only just missed one this year."

"I'm aware of that. You could have a First in history if you applied yourself."

"Mr Stennett, I know that I shall work hard because if I do not I shall make a real mess of it as I am not a natural scientist. I just don't think that I could now summon up the energy to work so hard in history for the sheer love of it. Motivation drives me to work hard in medicine. I dare not return to history."

"Well at least I tried. Off you go, my boy, and have a good vacation."

The third and final year in Cambridge was not a success. Against his own prediction he despised experimental psychology and pharmacology was not much better. His life-long addiction to hard academic graft deserted him and he began to miss lectures and practicals and did not spend evenings filling in the gaps from books. James was vividly aware that this was his final year in Cambridge and that he must compensate by plunging into other pursuits. He could play more rugby and cricket and row but he could not summon the enthusiasm to make the effort. Increasingly he allowed valuable time to run like grains of sand through his fingers and, in the retrospection of his own medical opinion in later years, he was quite deeply depressed. He began to escape what had become his prison in Cambridge to spend every weekend in London with Alice and the St Thomas's set, illegally, as he never asked his tutor for the exeats which would permit him to leave Cambridge during Full Term. He hoped that he would squeeze another Upper Second in Tripos but when confronted by his experimental psychology practical exam – which he did not even attempt through lack of knowledge and experience – he left the examination hall fifteen minutes after turning over the paper. Alone, he walked back to Magdalene feeling abjectly miserable by letting himself down so cruelly.

When the results were posted outside Senate House some days later his eyes locked onto the list of Upper Seconds, his habitual Cambridge label. His name – Butland, J C M (for Magdalene) – was not there. His eyes, like leaded dolls' eyes, dropped to the Thirds. He scanned quickly, not logging his name. Perhaps he had failed completely. It was possible after his psychology performance. No. Lower Second.

His spirits were shattered although he knew he deserved no better after his sloth-like third year. James telephoned his old confidant, Father Montague Haydon, his prep school headmaster.

He had remained in touch with Mont over the years and he was a good sounding board for his problems. Mont had given him gentle but firm advice several years before to continue history. He felt that medicine was an inappropriate false idol – a fad, an infatuation, not a deeply held conviction. Mont had been wrong. He also tried to insert into James's turbulent mind that this apparent need to change direction was a subconscious awakening of a vocation for the priesthood. James did not comment but rejected such a bizarre thought. Mont knew that he was not one of the conformist boys who swallowed all Anglo-Catholic perversions of belief and practice. Perhaps Mont really did know that he refused to kneel in the Good Friday service when the prayers were chanted for heretics and schismatics.

James rationalised his failure as a poor choice of subjects in his final year. Perhaps he should have read history as suggested by his tutor. No. He had been offered an opportunity at the end of his second year to study Part II Pathology which was only available to those who had done very well in the second year exams. He had rejected this offer. He still doubted his scientific abilities and convinced himself that it would be too difficult for him, that it would drive out all other Cambridge life and that it would prevent him from spending weekends with Alice in London. These weekends were also deeply disappointing as James knew that they were stolen time. Alice could not raise his spirits. He began to think more about the past, his past, the successful past and not the future. Those were critical factors, he now realised. James was disgusted with himself for his sheer pessimism and lack of courage and for allowing his plans to be affected by an emotional attachment. He was angry with Alice for compromising him and for wrecking his third year in Cambridge and perhaps his whole future in medicine. James reflected on his last year in Cambridge. He had been given superb rooms at the top of Left Cloister in the Pepys Building. The window seat overlooked Second Court and he spent so many hours just looking through windows, watching the progress of the clock over the Hall. Picking up books and discarding them after so few minutes of study.

The headmaster's study at Dayton Hall had not altered since James and his parents had sat on the edge of the deep sofa reserved for visitors that summer in 1926, when they were seeking his transfer from the primary school. All three were anxious and afraid that they would be swallowed up by the sofa if they dared to sit comfortably. Mont, reclining in the matching sofa facing them, had no such qualms in his own study with his shoulders only a marginal height above his knees. He always smoked throughout interviews with boys and parents, his right arm resting high on the arm of the sofa with smoke rising in a thin column to the tobacco-soured ceiling above. Twenty-one years bracketed the two scenes. Now James relaxed into the same posture as his friend and poured out his disappointment in his recent performance in his final year in Cambridge. He had lost all objectivity, inflating the importance of this academic stumble over his wartime experiences of his injuries, his own near death and the loss of so many friends and soldiers for whom he had been responsible.

"James, the last few years have been wretched for us all. I have had no biological sons or daughters to suffer and die, but I have lost 11th Harrow scouts in the war who were just as dear to me. Bill Creak, a sub-lieutenant in the Navy, was the first to go. He brought his ship through the shoals and minefields in the fog and smoke of battle bringing hundreds to safety from the Dunkirk beaches. Anthony Brackenbury was only eighteen when he was shot down. Peter Bluett was killed in the thousand-bomber raid on Berlin in May 1941. Arthur Hamilton was an air gunner who perished in the Channel a month later. The rear part of his aeroplane was shot away and he fell into the sea without being able to open his parachute. Arthur was the cub who handed me a twenty-first birthday present on behalf of them all.

Peter Cordy, Anthony Thornhill, Ian Hewlett, Howard Forster, Ronald Valters, Roy Hocking. Clyde Watts was in the Merchant Navy and was last heard of as the officer in charge of one of the lifeboats from the Avila Star in the Med. Edwin Tonge, Arthur Matthissen, Robert Mountain who died on the Russian convoys. Harold Tickle, Jack Bell, Bill Cooper, Patrick Morrow, Stanley James, Ivor Pattison. James Feacey and Dennis Blessley, both of these two on D Day, Bill Upson in Burma – he went out under fire to scout for forward Japanese positions. He would have put his scout stalking skills to good use. What his men thought of him was shown by their devotion in going out under continuous fire to recover his body. Ken Taggart, Barry Gwatkin, Dennis Carlson, the Braund twins, John and Paul, Brian Lambert and Burns McKenzie Wright. Burns served all over the Med and Middle East. In a shack in a remote spot in Persia, he found an 11th Harrow Rover Crew bulletin in the officers' mess. How it got there he had no idea. Not long after sending me this news, he was killed in Italy. He was the best patrol leader the Swifts ever had, ruling them firmly with humour and friendship, which cemented the gang together until the war sent them on their separate ways…"

Mont's voice tailed away. The deep bass thinned and rose into a higher register which merged into wheezy sobs of living grief. James had never seen Mont cry before. He had recalled every name and relived the news of each new death in his Dayton family.

"Mont, I'm sorry to be grieving over my exams when there is so much more to grieve about. I lost many good friends. The first to die was the hardest knock. After that we all encased ourselves in a carapace of steel to prevent any penetration of human sympathy which might have reduced us to boneless jelly and dissolved our will to carry on."

"Come to Moggiona – I haven't invited anyone yet. It's time to go back. Giuseppe Corsani has written to say that the house is in one piece and awaiting the return of the English priest and his young men. It will heal us. Perhaps Philip and Roger would come too."

"I should love to. I am free until I start at St Thomas's in September. I haven't seen Philip and Roger since before the war. I do hope they can make it. It's a wonderful idea."

"I'll track them down tomorrow."

Philip Grainger had been destined for the life of a medical student at Guy's Hospital in September 1939 but volunteered for the RAF at the outbreak of war. Initially rejected for aircrew training for less than perfect eyesight, Philip moved from one admin post to another at airfields from Cornwall to Scotland. As the war struggled on, and as the supply of pilots dried up with losses and the declining enthusiasm of those who could see the end of the war in sight and their improving chances of survival if they avoided the furnace, opportunities arose. Philip, who had spent so much of the war at airfields near the sea, managed to convince the sceptical medical staff that he had a particular visual skill over water. With a firm place at Guy's after the war, he inserted the idea that they owed him a favour. He was posted to an Empire Flying School in Nova Scotia for pilot training and emerged as the skipper of a Sunderland flying boat in Coastal Command. He spent the rest of the war on long patrols from Islay, hunting for U-boats in the Western Approaches, and he ended with a creditable tally of three. With his medical career well mapped out, Philip had been allowed to leave the RAF and start at Guy's in the autumn of 1945. In the middle of his summer vacation in 1947 Philip did not hesitate to accept Mont's invitation to return to Moggiona in the company of his old friend and fellow medical student.

Roger Trenchard had spent the war as an engineer officer in the Royal Navy and had been sunk twice – off Crete in May 1941 when he had spent twelve hours in the water before rescue, and then he had been torpedoed in the North Atlantic on convoy duties. On that occasion, he boasted, he had kept his feet dry as a cruiser nearby had taken off the crew before the ship went down. At the end of the war Roger started a science course at University College, London, and was looking forward to a career as a school master. All three had faced their own death and witnessed the death of many others. All three found themselves in the summer vacation of 1947 free to retrace their route to Moggiona with Mont.

Mont had contrived to keep the old school Bedford van running through the war, bullying the officials who would not increase his generous petrol allocation inflated by his school and scout responsibilities. He argued that he should have had yet another allowance for being a priest. He was also ruthless in obtaining the unobtainable on the black market and boasted of his successes. It was nine years since those four war-blasted survivors had collected at Dayton Hall for their first expedition together to Moggiona. Then they had been one man who had experienced some life as a curate in the slums north of King's Cross Station, and as priest and headmaster, and three boys on the threshold of life eager for their first taste of France and Italy. They had all inhaled ashes and choked on the bitter taste at the back of the throat which they could not erase by swallowing.

Retracing their old route offered the comfort of familiarity. They expressed surprise at the lack of evidence of the war in the villages and towns of rural France. Enriched by the strength of the pound against the franc they lunched and dined in more auberges than in 1938.

After its prolonged rest during the war years the Bedford van struggled up the Gotthard Pass without boiling. With no hunger for the city they did not delay in Milan but pressed on to their retreat high up in the Apennines. After each hairpin bend climbing up from Poppi they expected to see Moggiona across the valley clinging to the hillside it had claimed for a thousand years. Signor Corsani had described no war destruction in his letters to Mont. They swung round the last curve before Moggiona, praying that it was still 1938 and not 1947. They wanted to nuzzle down in the past and be healed by the sheer unchanging familiarity of the little world that recent history had ignored, and by the simple friendly folk who had ignored Mussolini and his Fascists. People who wanted to till their fields, harvest the timber for their barrel making, raise their children and conduct their lives to the rhythm of the church calendar.

As they drove over the bridge into the village they could see no evidence of the nine years. The barricading pine forests exuded the same sticky fumes that they all inhaled with pleasure in 1938. Mont's house on the outskirts of the village bore no obvious scars. The shutters were closed but they had not sent word of their impending arrival. The stone drive off the road up to the house had been overwhelmed by tall green-brown grasses. Mont produced his heavy key which turned the only mildly resisting lock. They imagined the little puffs of rust inside which would succumb to a little oil.

They stood on the familiar chipped ochre tiles of the hallway and, as one, climbed the stone staircase which led to the room at the rear of the house which overlooked the valley. The shutters opened with a thin groan and they gazed down on Poppi on its breast-like hill. This world had survived. All would be well. They each split off into the same rooms they had occupied nine years before. The pre-war routines would heal their souls and maintain a pretence that war had not occurred and was a cruel creation of dreams. Mont, now alone, knelt with the less confident knees of middle age and gave thanks in prayer. The others rested on their sheetless mattresses and watched the flies on the ceiling readmitted after so long a banishment.

At about seven o'clock they strolled down to the centre of the village for their dinner. The villagers had heard from the Corsanis of the return of the English priest and his young friends and soon collected outside the *ristorante* with warm smiles and greetings.

"*Buona sera, Padre.* Welcome back to Moggiona. We are very pleased to see you all again."

As the four Englishmen stood with their backs to the *ristorante*, smiling and waving in return, they saw behind the enthusiastic group a gap in the terrace of buildings across the street. The walls of the adjacent structures had been smoothed off and patched by new bricks. The exposed ground had been healed with new concrete. Signor Corsani and his daughter, Margherita, came out of the *ristorante* and shook hands with all four of them, reluctant to relax their grip so that the greeting lasted minutes rather than seconds.

"You are most welcome, my English friends. You have been away too long."

"It was a long war," Mont replied. "Moggiona has not changed and you have not changed either. Except, Margherita, you have grown even more beautiful."

"No, we have not changed much." Corsani's smile melted away.

"Come inside. You must be ready for your dinner."

James, who could speak no Italian, asked Mont to enquire about the missing house. Surely there had been no bombing up here in the hills.

"It's a sad story, my friends. Perhaps another time."

They felt uncomfortable but soon their spirits rose with the peppery Chianti, the generous pasta and the thin strips of lamb impregnated with the chemistry of local herbs. Down in the valley a light in the tower of the Castello di Poppi winked in the swirling summer haze of the maturing night. They ambled back to the house inhaling the breath of life of the yellow broom and elderflowers that surrounded the village. The track was littered with pine cones which they kicked ahead of them. James picked up one larger than most and ran his fingers over its contours.

"Just like a miniature grenade," he murmured. James continued:

"The pine cone was a symbol of eternal life in the classical world – new life growing out of the dead seed. Now death only breeds death. Do you know the old German legend of the natal tree? At the birth of a child a tree was planted. The child and the tree grew up together. After death in old age the tree was felled and hollowed out and the body was buried in its tree coffin. All too few allow the natal tree the years to develop its girth these days."

"Come off it, James. You see the war in everything."

"Don't you?"

After breakfast they set off up the road to Camaldoli to see the Baron and Baronessa, who would disapprove if she heard of their arrival before their first call on her. They left the old Bedford van in the street opposite the monastery guarded by the statue of San Romualdo, reasoning that it would not be harmed or stolen if watched over by the local saint. Before their social duty, Mont led them down some steps into the monastery, a set of enclosed quadrangles of the 11th and 12th centuries. As they entered each quadrangle the monks, dressed in rough cream-white robes, scattered through doors, clearly avoiding the intruders. The Camaldolese were not an enclosed order but wished to preserve their peace from the world. The church was a seventeenth-century Counter-Reformation baroque extravagance. James and Roger acknowledged this with only the faintest flick of their eyes but Mont, closely followed by Philip, processed around the aisles. There were two paintings by Vasari. James considered the Nativity scene to be the more accomplished but poor meat when compared with the pictures in the Uffizi. The barrel roof painted with angels, saints and floating clouds offered insights into the presence of heaven on earth.

Adjacent to the church was a medieval pharmacy filled with jars and presses to extract the juices from herbs that would comfort the sick. As they left the precincts of the monastery early on that summer morning in the Apennines a breeze sprang up, bothering the leaves, and was answered by murmuring insects and cuckoos camouflaged in the woods.

"Welcome, welcome. Signor Corsani informed me that you were blessing us with another visit, your first since the war, of course. The Baron is in Rome on business as usual. Now, I know that I met you all when you came before the war. Was it 1937 or 1938?"

"1938, Baronessa." Philip spoke for them all.

"I hope your house is as you left it, Father Montague."

"Yes, just as we left it. I can see no damage. It could do with a fresh coat of paint but all in God's good time."

They settled down with their coffee and glasses of Vino Santo fermented by the monks. Mont thought that the war should be embraced early and should not be left unspoken.

"Baronessa, I hope the war did not impose too harsh a burden on you up here in the mountains?"

The Baronessa drooped and hunched her shoulders, belying her middle-aged years.

"It was dreadful but you don't want to hear about that on your holidays, do you?"

"Madame, all four of us have had a very hard time but we are all alive and recovering in our different ways. It is best to confront the past and not bury it in a place where it decays and smells and creates more disease." Mont now spoke for them all. James, for the first time in many months, was conscious of his eye and its glass reincarnation.

"Well, I can tell you some of it, if you can spare the time."

The monastery church bell tolled once, summoning the monks to their prayers.

"During the first years of the war, we were barely touched by it up here. The Fascists would hold an occasional parade in the village and the young men disappeared into the army but we had plenty to eat. Although I am English, no one spoke against me. I suppose the Baron as a Dutch citizen offered me some protection. Everything changed in September 1943. The Italians surrendered to the Allies and we all thought the war was over for us. But the Germans were not having that and swept down from the north. They occupied the whole of Italy and prepared to fight the British and the Americans.

"The Italian guards in the prisoner of war camps released their prisoners and there were soon 80,000 milling around and hoping to be rescued by the Allied troops advancing from the south. About half of these were quickly recaptured and were transferred to camps in Germany and Poland. The other half dispersed into the countryside. Some went north hoping to reach Switzerland but were mostly recaptured. Most tried to move south in the direction of their own front line. To make themselves as inconspicuous as possible, they headed for the Apennine hills and the mountains. Perhaps you would all like a picnic up at the Eremo?"

Gabriella, though not even Mont would dare address her so, began to collect bread, prosciutto and cheese from her larder without awaiting an answer. She was given the place of honour in the front seat of the Bedford van and they began to climb the three miles of steep, winding track through woods, up to the Eremo. The Baronessa pointed at an imposing villa clad in the white stone of Fascist Roman revival style, so hostile to Tuscan warmth.

"That was the HQ of the SS and local Fascists. It has many stories to tell."

The Eremo was the hermitage for the monastery down the hill in Camaldoli. Monks isolated themselves in their single cells patchworking the hillside.

"It was September 1943 soon after the surrender. One evening a group of very senior British officers – two of them were generals, General Neame and General O'Connor – arrived with their junior staff officers in Camaldoli. After their release from their camp in the north they were taken to Florence where they were surprised to be cheered by the crowds who had been their enemy until days before. They bartered cigarettes and chocolate for old clothes and caught a train to Arezzo. The Italian commandant wanted to get rid of them as soon as possible but the Germans had cut the railway line to the south. They were handed over to the prefect of Fascist police and they were sure that they would then be handed over to the Germans who were moving south at a great pace to confront the Allies. To their surprise they were hidden and then driven in trucks up here to Camaldoli. The monks fed and housed them in the monastery. The Fascists and their sympathisers were still strong and offered rewards of about £25 for information about escaped prisoners. Two officers briefly lived at our house and enjoyed listening to the BBC on our wireless. We were only too pleased to help.

"It was not long before word arrived that the Germans were on their way to round them up. The monks led the officers up this very track to the Eremo and hid them in the monks' cells. There were too many officers to house at the Eremo. One monk, Don Leone, with many years of beard, flashing eyes and inseparable from his flask of wine, led the more junior officers to surrounding farms over a wide area. Even the Eremo was not immune to traitors. One late evening they heard the rumble of heavy German vehicles making their way up this road from Camaldoli, gears grinding on the tight bends, sometimes quieter, sometimes louder, as they twisted around the hillside."

The van drew up by the little chapel next to the gate of the Eremo. They could see the baroque church behind, dominating the hillside and the monks' cells. The Baronessa led the way up a track to the side of the Eremo. She stepped lightly picking her way around the bigger rocks and they were soon in the woods looking down over the hermitage. The track continued further up the hillside behind them.

"They escaped up there," she pointed. "As the German lorries pulled up outside the Eremo, the generals were scampering away, led by good Italians to safety in the villages above here. From what we heard later, they had a very difficult time hiding with the simple people of these hills. These were not English villages like the Cotswolds. The houses are mainly a ground floor divided between the kitchen and the cow sheds with an upstairs room for sleeping. In the kitchen the copper pot hangs on a long chain in the deep fireplace. Sometimes one end of a tree branch smoulders on the fire while the other pokes out into the room. They live on soup with macaroni and spaghetti with a rabbit or chicken on Sundays and Feast Days. Sometimes polenta made from sweetcorn poured onto the table with tomato and meat scraps added to be devoured by all the family members with their own fork. No sanitary arrangements. Usually only a nearby path on a steep slope served as a latrine and rubbish dump, identified from afar from the cloud of flies above it. Those British officers will have really learnt about Italian peasant life.

"We heard later that most had managed to escape, although the winter up here is devilish. Many joined or were helped by the partisan groups which were forming. Many were communists but many were young Italian men with no political views, escaping from the Germans who wanted to send them to labour camps in Germany. The Germans became more and more angry with the bands of escaped prisoners and Italian partisans and organised *rastrellamenti*, when they cut off whole valleys with large numbers of German soldiers and Italian Fascists. They then moved in and collected all the insects they could collect in their nets. Whereas the Allied POWs who were caught were sent back to POW camps, the Italians were usually murdered. In August 1944 the partisans killed sixteen SS troops. In retaliation the Germans burned twenty villages and killed all the men, women and children who lived in two of them. In one, fifty young men were dragged behind vehicles and then lined up with steel wire round their necks so that they had to stand upright. The SS then machine-gunned their legs so that they died of strangulation. Over 400 died there. In September 1944 near Marzabotto on Montesole, south of Bologna, they murdered 700 civilians including a priest."

The four Englishmen had remained silent during the Baronessa's account, not daring to believe that in these hills among these simple brave people such things could happen under this same blue sky overhead. The insects hummed more loudly. The two-noted cuckoos competed with their song up and down the hillside. James's head and chest pumped to the threshold of pain, well practised from Calais and Tunisia. Each would never forget, nor ageing memory ablate, that early afternoon above the Eremo. He ate his picnic, chewing and swallowing without taste, as if one of his senses had been wiped out. In contrast his hearing was able to isolate each insect. Each breeze and leaf threatened to deafen him on that Tuscan hillside.

They retraced their steps down the track and climbed into the van. Roger drove very slowly, listening for the grinding of German gear boxes concealed round each bend in the road. They did not speak until back in Camaldoli, where they delivered the Baronessa to her house. Their farewells were brief and formal. At dinner that evening in the restaurant in Moggiona, James gathered his strength and asked Margherita about the missing tooth in the parade of houses across the road.

"What happened to the house opposite the restaurant, Margherita? Surely there was no bombing up here?"

"No, there was no bombing but the war did not completely ignore Moggiona."

Surely the Baronessa would have warned them if Moggiona had been tortured like the other villages in her account. Perhaps she hoped to spare them by describing the crimes in distant villages.

"Have you heard of the Gothic Line?"

"Of course, I fought in Tunisia but was then wounded and invalided out."

James was aware that Margherita was trying to avoid looking at his glass eye.

"My battalion, 10th battalion Rifle Brigade, clawed its way up Italy, Monte Cassino, the Liri valley, the lot. One of my good friends, Lieutenant Ralph Stewart-Wilson, won the MC knocking out an anti-tank gun in the Liri valley northwest of Cassino on the Gustav Line. That was to the south…"

His voice trailed away. He had exposed too much. In dark moments he could not excise the gnawing pain that he had spent the war deserting his fellows in Calais and then Tunisia, always managing to extricate himself from danger and leaving them to fight on without him. If he examined his conscience with as much honesty as he could contrive, he realised that his concern was unreasonable. But sleepless nights are enemies of reason.

"Then you will know that the Gothic Line was one of Hitler's defence walls extending from just south of La Spezia on the west coast to Pesaro on the east. The line ran just south of Moggiona along those heights overlooking the plain at Poppi. At the beginning of September 1944 the Germans arrived in Moggiona and ordered the evacuation of the village. They did not want Italians, probably some of them partisans, getting in the way of their defence preparations. Some left but many stayed on to continue their livelihood making barrels and looking after their animals. One evening the Germans arrived in trucks and without any provocation murdered twenty-two villagers. Grenades destroyed the house opposite and one boy was left alive in the ruins. In spite of his injuries he remained very still by the dead bodies of his family and did not utter a sound. Nine killed were from one family, the Menchinis. The two Acuti sisters were taken into a room by the Germans. One managed to escape through a window. The other, aged seventeen, was raped by ten Germans. She was left alive but was killed in the street in

Camaldoli one week later by a car. The driver said she looked as if she were in a trance. We think she took her own life, reasoning that no real life remained for her."

That night James could not sleep. They had come to Moggiona to be bandaged and healed but they had arrived in an inferno which had swept through the peaceful hills about them. On the following day Mont led them down to the village cemetery and they stood among the graves of the massacre of September 7th 1944. The pictures of the dead on the tombs, so alien to British eyes, stared back at them. James thought of his dead chums. The face of Sergeant Tom Woods was no less vivid than the black and white images in the cemetery.

"No escape from reality here in Italy, chaps." Mont spoke uncharacteristically softly that evening. "We've heard tales of evil to end all evils. We're on the ropes. It's time to stand up and fight back. We'll achieve that by devoting the rest of our lives to doing good and what's right. It's what God would expect from us. I know that the 11th Harrow, the Chapel of St Francis and civilising all you ignorant townies who've come through Dayton Hall, is God's work. James and Philip – you are going to serve as doctors and I know that you will both be great doctors. Roger – teaching is the profession of true service par excellence and the pay is almost a schoolboy's pocket money. But penury brings its own rewards."

During the following days they combined art with religion in the pattern that all anticipated. In Arezzo they stood in awed silence before Piero della Francesca's frescoes, *The Legend of the True Cross*, dissolving the evils of recent experiences with the solvent of art. Mont watched the faces of his young friends just as set and vivid as the faces of Piero's characters on the walls of the church of San Francesco. His eyes swivelled from one to another, probing their minds and their immunity to the experiences of the war. They had preserved their sanity and humanity, thank God. He did not want to disrupt the web of silence which they had spun for themselves in this place. When he spoke, each visibly and as one altered the balance of weight distributed between their legs.

"Do you know the Legend of the True Cross?"

"No, Mont." Only Roger replied, although James and Philip were equally ignorant.

"Solomon felled the Tree of Life in the Garden of Eden. He used the wood to make a bridge, two beams from which would one day form the Cross. The Queen of Sheba, who was visiting Solomon, had a premonition that the wood spelt doom for the Kingdom of the Jews. She warned him of her fears and Solomon ordered the bridge timbers to be buried."

Mont pointed at one wall. "There, you can see the Queen of Sheba shaking hands with Solomon. They are both overwhelmingly sad with downturned eyes and the faces of their attendants resonate with this gloom. Hardly the cheerful way to welcome a guest."

The three younger men did not travel with reluctance to the sites of St Francis in La Verna, Assisi and Gubbio which had provoked such cynicism in 1938. Mont's old stories of St Francis, repeated throughout their years at Dayton Hall and now retold with a new fervour during that ochre Italian summer, comforted and did not reproach them. G K Chesterton noted that St Francis did not "love humanity but men" as individuals: "From the Sultan of Syria in his pavilion to the ragged robbers crawling out of the wood, there was never a man who looked into those brown burning eyes without being certain that Francis Bernardone was really interested in him." His anthropomorphic interpretations of nature – he called the sun his brother and the moon his sister – exalted all natural objects and animals to pinnacles of affection. From the perspective of St Francis, the sun, moon, stars, wind and water, the flowers, birds and animals all serve as evidence of God's creation of the world. But there is a reciprocal spectrum from evil and hatred at one extremity to the misfortune of illness and accident at the other. St Francis began to lose his sight and submitted to the application of a burning iron to his eyes.

"When they took the brand from the furnace," wrote Chesterton, "St Francis spoke: 'Brother Fire, God made you beautiful and strong and useful. I pray you to be courteous with me.'"

They each began to incorporate recent war experiences into memory with acceptance and without anger. Their conversation was of history, art and politics and the Italian countryside, but when drifting into or out of sleep, each weighed those bad times and constructed a scaffolding of life for the future.

On the day before they left Moggiona for England, Mont spent all his remaining lira on crates of wine and tobacco which were stowed in the empty space below his bunk for the first post-war duel with the British Customs, which he enjoyed so much. They all laughed and remembered their confused reactions to Mont's little games in 1938.

"I have paid the full price and Italian taxes for all of this. What right do the socialists have to tax it all over again? There is no justice or moral principle to support their legalised larceny."

"Absolutely, Mont."

James recalled how flat and depressed they felt during the drive from Folkestone to Harrow in 1938. They had been deprived of their freedom and were returning to routine and hard work. It was déjà vu in 1947 but all three were on the verge of a new life and a break with the painful past. They returned from Italy with hope and anticipation.

October 1947 to 1962

James, bruised and disappointed by his final year in Cambridge, but healed by Moggiona, started his new life as a clinical medical student at St Thomas's Hospital in London. His recovery would be with his patients, the real reason for his abandonment of history. He soon developed a calm, easy manner and spent as much time as possible with them on the wards and in the operating theatres.

St Thomas's had not changed very much since 1944. The evacuated country branch had returned to London and the hospital seemed much bigger and busier than before. The scars of war were still there. One pavilion facing the Thames remained in ruins with wild flowers, mainly colonies of Oxford ragwort, insisting on their own life amongst the rubble. "*Senecio squalidus.*" James massaged the word for effect and could not resist a brief seminar for the other students who could be bothered to listen. "It lived as a native on volcanic ash in Sicily. It somehow found its way to the Botanic Garden in Oxford – hence its common name. During the Industrial Revolution it gained a new habitat on railway embankments. It liked the limestone ballast under the lines. It was reminded of its home in Sicily. It seems to have made a special beeline for bomb sites which aren't so different from volcanic lava. I expect we shall soon see bunches of its loathsome yellow flowers at our patients' bedsides. You can repeat the story to them if you like."

Later, alone, James spoke softly to himself. "Now why did I say all of that pompous nonsense?" He felt foolish. But the victory of the Oxford ragwort over the bombs against all odds was a symbol of renaissance and James banished his self-reproach. There was an atmosphere of hope and the rebuilding of the future.

Clinical medical education was essentially apprenticeship with few lectures and little formal teaching. James was keen and recorded brief details on most of the patients he had seen so that he could read about their diseases in the evenings, accumulating knowledge based on experience, which he found most effective. He lived in St Thomas's House which he knew well from his First MB year. Although he began to spend less time with Alice than before, they thought about their future together after he qualified. They assumed it rather than planned it. Alice was gentle, stable and loyal and neutralised the diluted manic depressive personality which James now realised was his sentence. He often thought that he should attempt again to contact Agnès and he wrote more letters to the doctor's house in Calais but never posted them. Just as he feared returning to history in his final year in Cambridge for its threat to his equilibrium, so he was terrified to see Agnès again and of what might follow. But he would have loved to be able to tell her that he was a doctor, or almost one, and that she had been the catalyst.

He worked very hard throughout his three years of clinical study. He was relieved that the old methods, which had brought success, had not deserted him and the three years passed quickly. He was in the top flight of students in his year and made close friends with other students more addicted to medicine than beer and rugby. In the summer of 1950, with final examinations to qualify as doctors, students were appointed to posts as housemen, assuming that they passed. James had enjoyed all specialities and found it very difficult to decide what sort of a doctor he might become. Loudly and alone he would declaim: "Deciding to do medicine is no decision. Deciding what to do in medicine is the difficult one."

The early front runner, to be a physician in hospital medicine, had dropped back during his final year and he was now more attracted to obstetrics and gynaecology or possibly surgery. During his midwifery course he had delivered eighty-two babies and had become quite adept at normal and forceps deliveries. He sensed that the qualified doctors and midwives liked him and trusted him and he enjoyed the responsibility.

In his final year he was posted from St Thomas's to the Norfolk and Norwich Hospital for extra experience in surgery. With his old family connections in East Anglia and the long months on coastal defence during the war, this created a happy and fulfilling time. For two weeks he acted as locum house surgeon during the leave of the qualified houseman and he had performed very well. His consultant offered him the post after he qualified and James gratefully accepted. Alice visited him in Norwich and the vision of her running out of the gates of the fussy, embroidered Victorian Norwich station into his arms formed one of those permanent pleasant memories that punctuate life and return during sleepless nights. Infuriatingly he was offered a post as house surgeon rather than house physician at St Thomas's which prevented him from accepting a similar post in Norwich. Their Norfolk dream evaporated. James and Alice had hoped that a house physician's post at St Thomas's would be followed by the surgical post in Norwich, which would have been an ideal way to embark on his career.

James qualified as a doctor in July 1950 and began the monastic life of a house surgeon at St Thomas's. They married later that month, very soon after his exams. Their early life together was one of poverty and brief periods of exhaustion which did not build a strong foundation for the future. Alice continued to nurse at St Thomas's until Alasdair was born, followed a year later by Sarah.

Although he was married with two small children James's life was medicine. As indecisive as ever, he did spend a year in obstetrics and gynaecology delivering yet more babies and learning the common basic surgical techniques of the trade but found the work arduous and unfulfilling. From his Harrow days he knew the Hawkers, a husband and wife team of general practitioners, and he then spent some months as an assistant in their practice. The combination of the long surgeries of patients with their unfounded anxieties and of the arrogance of the young doctor convinced him that the hospital was where his future lay and he embarked on the long training to become a hospital physician. The obsessive interest in common and even better, rare diseases, consumed him. The diseases were well described in books but the same diseases in different patients were all so different. It was the huge variation created by the patients that enthralled him and never caused him to question his apostasy from history.

At home in the brief periods off duty he was exhausted and often in poor temper. He never formed close relationships with his small children. Alice gave up nursing and provided the dominant love and stability for which children crave.

James ascended the hierarchical medical ladder at St Thomas's with the usual well-chosen steps: the Membership of the Royal College of Physicians, some research and enthusiastic teaching of medical students which he enjoyed and at which he excelled. He was a kind, conscientious and efficient doctor at the hospital, good at diagnosis and patient management, but cool and tired at home.

In 1962 he was confronted by another career crossroads. The choice was between staying in London with the prospect of a consultant post at St Thomas's or another London hospital or a career outside London. A post at Addenbrooke's Hospital, Cambridge was advertised in the British Medical Journal. James gasped. Of course he knew Addenbrooke's on Trumpington Street opposite the Fitzwilliam Museum. Preclinical students in the university had no reason to enter the hospital. Their priority was to accumulate the scientific tools to equip them to see patients as clinical medical students in one of the London teaching hospitals. The Victorian additions at Addenbrooke's had been imposed over an original Georgian façade. James hesitated to apply for posts outside London but Cambridge had never lost its almost Oxford magic and it would be a civilised and beautiful place in which to raise a family. Always conscious of his East Anglian heritage he also thought that it would reinforce the old continuities of life on familiar soil.

Three months later he was appointed consultant physician. They found a suitable house in a village near Cambridge and Alasdair and Sarah settled into their gentle but demanding new schools. All seemed set fair for the next stage of Butland life.

January 1963

It was a typical January evening of rain, wind and Siberian-steppe cold. The common Cambridge cliché is that the highest ground to the east is the Ural Mountains but this ignores the East Anglian heights on the border of Cambridgeshire and Suffolk which can compete with the Arctic. As an undergraduate, James had sometimes written essays with gloved hands as the apologetic gas flames in his rooms had hardly raised the temperature in those draughty spaces.

James drove home from the hospital at about 7pm. The house was in darkness and, as he turned the key in the front door, he stiffened with an experience of visceral chaos which with medical objectivity he immediately identified as a panic attack. The rapid, regular racing pulse, cold sweating and head hammer blows that he recalled from France and Tunisia created an overwhelming sense of utter disaster. He entered the house, turning on lights as he ran from room to room. He left no room in peace. The house was now ablaze with light. He fought to think straight. He had not felt like this even with German soldiers within fifty yards threatening his life. James stood very still looking out at the drive in front of the house. It was Tuesday. It was scout night. Alasdair must be there. Alice, Sarah and Shandy, the recently acquired mongrel from the animal strays' home, must be there. Collecting him. But it was too late for that. Why did they all go? Shandy was usually left in her basket. Perhaps the car had broken down.

James ran out of the house and threw himself into the

Jaguar. At the crossroads half a mile towards Cambridge police cars blocked the road to the right that he wished to follow. He stopped and wound down his window to speak to one of the policemen.

"I must go up there, officer."

"There's been a terrible accident up there, sir. The road is closed."

"But I think my family is involved."

"Statistically most unlikely, sir."

He now drove fiercely straight ahead along the road which led to Addenbrooke's. He parked outside Casualty and ran in without locking his car.

"I'm Dr Butland."

The receptionist knew that already.

"Has anyone with the name of Butland been admitted, please?"

"Please wait a moment, sir, and I'll find out."

A nurse appeared.

"Please come this way, Dr Butland."

Alice was sitting upright on a trolley, pale and short of breath with an oxygen mask over her face.

"Alice, where are the children?"

"In the car… in the car."

"Where are my children?" James screamed to anyone who passed by. He now began to run, run around Casualty, trying to find them in any of the cubicles. Patients with their fractured wrists and lacerations watched him with a mixture of fear and disgust. A casualty officer took his arm firmly and told him to calm down. In the middle of this fit of complete loss of control James saw an ambulance draw to a halt outside and the sight of a stretcher with, clearly, a small girl with blond hair with a high neck collar brace being lifted out. He ran to the ambulance.

"Sarah."

"Hello, Daddy."

"Thank God." He realised that she could not be too badly injured.

"Where's Alasdair?"

"I don't know, Daddy."

James ran back to his wife.

"Sarah's here but there's no sign of Alasdair."

"In the car… in the car."

James once again struggled with his turmoil and then to think calmly, logically. He spoke out very loudly: "If Alice and Sarah are here, and if the accident happened on their way back from the scout hut after dropping him off, then Alasdair must be there, waiting outside in the cold, expecting to be collected."

He would be frozen and very worried as the Butlands were never late for anything. Except in a real emergency. This was certainly one of those.

He began to walk out of Casualty to find his car and drive to the scout hut. A nurse gently took his arm and said:

"Please wait a little longer. It will be all right."

He was taken to a quiet room, to which Alice had also been taken. They waited and exchanged no words.

"He must be dead." James spoke softly. Alice did not reply. An older doctor entered the room. James knew him slightly.

"There was a boy in the car. Tall, fair-haired."

"That's Alasdair. That's my son."

"I'm afraid he's dead."

"I don't believe it… I don't believe it… I don't believe it… I don't believe it…" James repeated hopelessly. But he did believe it. He had reached the same conclusion himself already.

A police officer and the hospital chaplain entered the room and led him out of Casualty along the main corridor of the hospital to the Pathology block. There was a staircase leading down from the ground floor with a large notice stating: NO PATIENTS OR VISITORS ALLOWED BEYOND THIS POINT.

James knew this corridor very well. Addenbrooke's was his

second home, his wife thought perhaps his first. He certainly spent more time there than at home. Voices were attenuated by the whirring vortex within his head. He was not listening anyway. He passively followed the policeman and the chaplain who had not explained their purpose to him. If they had, and they probably had, he had not listened. There was Alasdair lying with a bedspread rather than a sheet pulled up just below his chin. James noted a few minor cuts. James felt his forehead. Cold. But it was January. He lifted the cover and felt for his right hand. Very cold. Forever the doctor, he even opened each eyelid in turn. Both pupils were fully dilated. He wanted to test whether they were fixed and dilated with a torch and he asked for a torch. He received no response and he did not repeat his absurd request.

"Oh, Alasdair, Alasdair."

He kissed him on the forehead and never had his lips touched such cold flesh. His son's flesh. He was taken back to his wife. Sarah needed an operation to reduce her fractures and he signed his consent for this. He then followed the trolley taking her to the operating theatre until they reached the entrance. He held her hand and kissed her as she was wheeled away. He did not want to see her go. He could not possibly lose two children in one night. James was later informed that his daughter had been found unconscious with obstructed breathing but she rapidly regained consciousness when her airway was cleared at the roadside. He could easily have lost them both that night and that added more haunting to the sleepless nights.

James telephoned his friend and colleague, Jumbo Tennant, and blurted out a skeleton of facts. Jumbo was there in what seemed like thirty seconds but was really fifteen minutes. The complete abolition of normal time perspective that night never ceased to impress him but the physics, or metaphysics, were beyond him. He stayed that night at his friend's house and he was plied with whisky and brandy until he could fall asleep. Next morning he contacted his team and reported that he could not attend that day. He had never had a single day off for sickness since he had qualified as a doctor.

He returned to the simultaneous cognition of his arrival at home and Alasdair's death about a mile away that night. He had read of wives and mothers who had known that their husbands or sons were dead on overseas battlefields at the precise moment of their deaths. He now believed them.

The next few weeks were occupied by sitting helplessly in the room provided for both Alice and Sarah. The procession of visitors trying to be supportive was stressful. All they wanted was solitude but instead they had the nauseating insight that the whole world was sorry for them.

On the day after the "accident" he drove home and forced himself to enter the house. All lights were switched on. He had never extinguished them in his panic. Once again he visited every room, calmly and quietly this time, except one. Alasdair's room. It was two weeks before he could enter that room and look at his son's clothes, possessions and unfinished prep. He had been given an old kitchen table from Harrow to use as a desk and had carved wedges and his name on it with a new penknife. James wept as he ran his fingers over these perfect imperfections.

The funeral ten days later. An ambulance ferried Alice and Sarah, neither of whom could walk at that stage. The village church was full of friends and relatives. James had a deep distaste for burials with the mind's eye images of human decay in coffins leaving a skeleton as the eventual evidence of a life. Better to incinerate and forget. After the funeral service the ambulance took the three of them to the ovens and the other mourners just melted away. Unfed. No wake. Just emptiness and the shocking sense that it could happen to any of them.

He always arrived at Addenbrooke's at 7.15 am. James was always at his best in the morning and at his nadir in the evening, arguing against his self-diagnosis of depression. His secretary was already there organising everything before the medical staff arrived to interrupt her real tasks. After periods of leave there was always the strong sense of never having been away.

Monday morning was always a busy outpatient clinic and James enjoyed clinics. Patients walked in and described their problems. He listened, wrote notes and performed a carefully selected examination appropriate to the problem. Not the blunderbuss comprehensive general examination instilled in medical students and junior doctors – an excellent discipline for the inexperienced who had yet to grow their medical antennae. He arranged blood tests and x-rays and a plan of treatment. The nurse ushered the first patient of the week out of the consulting room.

James sat still. He reflected on his walk along Regent Street in Cambridge several days before. He had strode through a group of foul-mouthed yobs, far more deserving of obliteration than Alasdair, and had heard himself muttering, "There should be better methods for selecting candidates for premature death." His mind switched to the disabling, explosive sadness of seeing Alasdair's attractive and personable friends continuing their lives when he was only history.

James wept. He wept openly in the interval between the patient leaving and the arrival of the next. The nurse sensed this through the door just ajar and slipped away. She delayed the entry of the next patient. Ann Hall, ten years older than James, had been delegated to look after Dr Butland after the accident. She combined nursing with a mothering role for her consultant. Ann was a lighthouse in a tossing blue-black sea of despair. She had sensed that he was far away with his thoughts. She had caught him sobbing uncontrollably on several occasions. He would never sob at home. The patients knew it too and understood. They would see his red eyes and never once accused him. Some would break into tears themselves in his presence and he would comfort them in a reversal of roles. If he had to break bad news to patients and relatives, his eyes could flood and tremors of his lips and hands communicated too easily that their goose was cooked. It was an uncontrollable response because empathy and sympathy had merged in his disordered mind.

During the following months a nightmare recurred. He was walking through a dark forest looking for his son whom he had lost. When he was about to give up the search, convinced that his son was lost forever, he found Alasdair with his knees drawn up to his chest sitting at the foot of a tree in a clearing.

"Daddy, I knew you'd come and find me, I'm lost. So I waited and waited until you found me."

On some days James would awake feeling happy, almost ecstatic, after another recurrent dream with Alasdair vividly alive. For a few awaking seconds he was convinced that it had all been some huge mistake and that Alasdair really was alive and all was well. But it was just another cruel hoax on a desperate mind. With full awakening he was dashed back against the rocks of despair with another ghastly day to face. Or perhaps Alasdair had been present in some paranormal sense, reassuring his father that all was truly well?

James began to reason that only by his own death could he ever see and rescue his son, abandoned in some post-death-state forest. There could be worse fates than suicide – this nightmare-infested life for one. He had never taken any steps to end his life so far, but as a halfway house he had developed an utter contempt for his own death. He would not have been upset if one of his consultant colleagues had broken the news to him that he had terminal cancer. He did, though, hope for a sudden heart attack which would conveniently dissolve the misery of staying alive. James never accumulated massive doses of paracetamol or bought hoses to connect the exhaust to the inside of his car but he did speculate on the most effective and least unpleasant method to achieve the result.

James, Alice and Sarah gambled with a holiday in Italy in an attempt to camouflage their unhappiness. Usually when an aircraft lands safely even the most travel hardened notch up a little register of relief. When James and the remnants of his family landed safely, his hopes that the plane would crash were dashed. He did not balance the thought that others would die in this reckoning.

At home the dining table with four chairs reproached them. Family behaviour, as in all families, decreed that Alice would sit nearest to the door which led through the hall to the kitchen. James at the opposite end of the table, Sarah on his left side and Alasdair on his right. They would not remove Alasdair's chair. It remained empty, unoccupied, accusing the remainder of the family who had survived. Their reduced family had become an object of mass pity which James found throttling and disabling. He had always firmly controlled his life and events, bending them to conform to his altering and unpredictable objectives, with obsessional hard work and planning. He had always determined that anything could be achieved if he willed it. That self-belief and old confidence evaporated in the winter of 1963.

Mont had done his best. He had held a special requiem mass for Alasdair in the chapel of St Francis at Dayton Hall soon after the accident. James could not bear to attend. Some months later Mont invited him to lunch on the pretext of asking him to administer cortisone injections to his arthritic knees which were making it increasingly difficult to genuflect and kneel during his religious observances.

"James, you must understand and accept that Alasdair's death was God's will. It is the only way to make sense of it. I shall include your family in my prayers every day for the rest of my life. Be assured of that."

"Thank you, Mont."

What residual faith he still possessed was extinguished on that day. When Mont died suddenly some months later he blamed the pressures of work at the hospital, real enough, for his failure to attend the funeral.

May 1964

The coach with Colonel Belchamp's Battlefield Tours proudly emblazoned on both sides and rear drove onto the ferry at Dover. The party had left the coach during the crossing. James did not fall in with any of his fellow travellers but stood on the bows with his eyes fixed on Calais. That May, twenty-four years before, the crossing had been calm but cool with intermittent rain showers but now it was bright. The French coast seemed at peace with itself without the vertical pillars of smoke that had suspended the town from the sky at his last visit.

He had barely survived 1963, which had been more destructive of his equilibrium than 1940. He felt profoundly low. It had been counterintuitive to return to Calais after Alasdair's death but he had illogically thought that reliving 1940 might blunt 1963 and help him to recover. Distraction therapy. The argument had no logical structure but he had grown used to disordered thought. Twenty-four years ago. He could see the prominent town hall clock which had survived the war and ached for his son whom he now knew he would never see again. They climbed back into the coach before the ship docked and drove off onto the quay. James sat in silence thinking not of the QVR and 1940 but only of Alasdair. James was ashamed if he did not spend at least a few minutes in every hour thinking about his son, wherever he might be or whatever he was doing.

Colonel Belchamp stood surveying the party from his command post at the front of the coach next to the driver, obediently focused on the road ahead and his conscious resolution to apply his right-sided wheels to the road gutter on the right in contradiction of all his driving instinct.

"Plan B."

Everyone swivelled heads and identified their companions. James again felt relieved that he was sitting alone with no immediate neighbours but dutifully he confirmed that the heads two rows ahead and the faces behind were conforming to the blueprint.

"No one AWOL? Very good. We're off. We shall not delay in Calais now but will return in two days and will then discuss the heroic defence of Calais in May 1940. Plenty of time for a recce then."

James felt his hands and his thighs loosen. He was not ready to confront Calais quite yet. The coach headed for Dinant and Sedan where the Germans had crossed the Meuse in the forests of the Ardennes in May 1940. The French had considered the Ardennes to be impenetrable to tanks and heavy vehicles and had defended thinly, expecting the main German assault to come further north over easier tank country. The Germans broke through the weak French defences and struck northwest against weak opposition, reaching the Channel coast at Abbeville. The British Expeditionary Force and the French First Army had advanced into Belgium to anticipate the expected main attack, leaving their well-defended positions which had been established since the autumn of 1939. The German advance through the Ardennes and then towards the coast effectively cut off the BEF and French First Army and threatened the Channel ports supporting the northern armies.

All the discussion in the hotel that evening was of 1940. Most had served in the war but there was a handful of younger men hoping for another war and the opportunity to test themselves. They would of course have denied this. The now middle-aged veterans exchanged stories of their own experiences.

"What was your war like?"

Dinner was at communal tables and James diffidently joined a table of probable ex-officers. He concentrated on his food and said little. Many doctors, like James, led a Jekyll and Hyde existence, warmth and cheerful bonhomie leading the consultation at the hospital or surgery, chiding junior doctors and nurses with gentle humour and encouragement. At home, off duty, many reverted to become reserved introverts. In their training and earlier monk-like employment they had spent so much of their lives with other doctors that they had lost the social skills to relate fully to those who were not doctors. Conversations with patients were structured and almost scripted, not acting, which would be insincere, but somehow not as intimate as with other human beings. James could not avoid the direct question when it was fired at him by one of the more voluble members of the group. RAF officer type, probably not aircrew, who had polished more office chairs on East Anglian airfields than a Whitehall civil servant.

"I spent most of the war defending the coast of Norfolk from the waves. Never saw a German in anger."

"Really? A quiet war for you then?"

James swore not to reveal himself on this expedition but then he heard himself say, almost as if someone was speaking on his behalf:

"I was also at Calais in May 1940. In the QVR. Queen Victoria's Rifles. Twenty-four years ago. It doesn't seem possible. I was only eighteen, just left school."

There was silence. Colonel Belchamp was sitting at the next table but overheard the confession.

"Dr Butland."

Colonel Belchamp maintained the pretence of military formality and had been rehearsing the names of the group.

"I assumed that you would have served as an MO and enjoyed yourself in a nice, clean field hospital somewhere."

"No. I was too young. I qualified in 1950 after the war."

"You must give us all the benefit of your experience when we return to Calais the day after tomorrow."

"I'm not sure about that. I don't have much to say."

"Nonsense. No false modesty. Firsthand experiences make these trips come alive."

"We'll see. If you'd seen me trembling when we drove off the ship at Calais you might not find me in a fit state when we return."

James forced himself to smile, and then laughed. Having opened up a little to his new acquaintances at dinner he became a new focus of attention. Some sought his company at briefings and coach stops as they retraced the advance of the German armour from the Meuse to the coast. Belchamp had a deep, professional understanding of this campaign and they all threw themselves into the past, studying the actual ground where actions had occurred. Each hour of each day was rich with intense interest. James slept fitfully for two nights without nightmares. He began to enjoy himself and when he realised this he felt guilt and disgust that he could feel, briefly, obscenely light-hearted. He was not entitled to these emotions following Alasdair's death.

It was time to return to Calais and the coach approached the town from the southeast. James froze. There it was, the bridge by the canal. They were driving along the Rue Madeleine which had been the German line of advance to the QVR position. The coach driver turned right at the end of the road. Not over the bridge. Thank God. He could not have borne it if the coach had crossed the bridge then. He would have sobbed and the group would have thought that he had cracked. James gazed at the higher ground on the opposite side of the canal where he and his chums had lain for so many hours squinting along the sights of Lee Enfields and Bren guns. They would have riddled the coach with bullets if they had still been there. James felt the painful throbbing hum in his head and his ears that he knew so well from the bad times. Then the bridge disappeared behind them and they were driving along the road by the canal.

They arrived at the hotel in Calais for their final night in France. After dinner Colonel Belchamp stood and described a long and accurate account of the defence of Calais in 1940.

"We are honoured to have in our midst a soldier of the QVR, one of those battalions ordered to hold Calais and reduce the German pressure on Dunkirk. It was a territorial battalion and more than held its own with the illustrious Rifle Brigade and Kings Royal Rifle Corps or 60th Rifles as its friends like to call it. He has modestly kept very quiet on this tour but I am sure that Dr Butland will entertain us with some colour and insights into their heroic stand. Dr Butland."

James stood up very slowly. He had prepared no speech in spite of warnings. He did not know where to start or what to say. The bare facts of his experiences made him sound rather brave but he must not shoot a line. He knew the truth. Court martial for desertion in the face of the enemy would have been more appropriate than the Military Medal. Agnès. That was Calais for him. Agnès. *Agnès. Where are you? Twenty-four years is nothing.* James realised that he was standing. The vacuum of silence. Waiting for him to speak.

"I was eighteen years old and had just left school. With several of my school fellows we had joined the QVR, Queen Victoria's Rifles, which was a territorial battalion in London. Not much happened to us at the end of '39 and early '40 but we had a great time on our motorcycles as we were supposed to be a mobile reconnaissance battalion, not really an infantry battalion, although we were riflemen. Our parent regiment was the 60th. We often joked that the War House really did think we were a proper Rifles battalion though many of us had no rifles and not all our officers had pistols. Funnily enough that misconception turned out to be true. We were in camp in Paddock Wood in Kent when one night we received orders to proceed to Dover without our motorcycles as they thought there would be no room for them in the ships. Rather oddly, they had changed the name of Dover to Port Vic in the code designed to confuse in those crazy days. Our CO had to ring around to find out where Port Vic was.

"It was like a dream when we found ourselves sailing into Calais. We could see shells falling in the town and the Luftwaffe were dropping bombs though they left us alone then. When we landed we were the only proper troops in Calais to defend it. There were a few stragglers, mainly French soldiers and sailors but very few British troops. Our Company was ordered to march southeast to hold the part of the defensive perimeter we had been allotted. Later we were told to hold that bridge over the canal we saw as we drove in this evening. What more can I say? We defended that bridge and the canal for two days against several attacks but eventually we were ordered to withdraw to an inner defence line based on the old bastions surrounding the town. The QVR reinforced the line held by the 60th. I copped a little wound in the head and don't really know very much about the final stand at Calais. I was rescued by a French doctor's family who dressed my wounds and then gave me their boat. I managed to escape back to England. I was one of the very few who were lucky enough to get back. Most were captured and were POWs for five long years. I later heard that Admiral Bertram Ramsay, who was in charge of the Dunkirk evacuation, wanted to take us off from Calais. He even sent destroyers on several nights into Calais for us but Churchill forbade him to evacuate us because he wanted to impress the French that we were fighting to the last, at least in some part of France. Last man, last bullet, that sort of order. Perhaps our stand made it easier for them at Dunkirk. Someone claimed – it might have been his secretary, Jock Colville – that Calais was the grit in the German machine. I don't know. I suppose we kept 10th Panzer Division busy but, quite frankly, Churchill sacrificed us at Calais to let the French know we were not deserting them completely."

James remained on his feet. Not speaking. He imagined that they were all staring at his unspoken glass eye and speculating on its loss. He wondered whether he had sounded overcritical of Churchill's decision. He had not openly expressed this thought before, even in private to his family. But it was true. Those three battalions were deserted at Calais even though the Navy could have evacuated them. This militarily well-educated group might have been comparing Churchill's decision with Hitler's order to the defenders of Stalingrad to fight to the last against the Russian hordes.

He sat down. There was no applause. Bulldog-like heroism implicit in the Dunkirk miracle had been questioned. He had embarrassed his new friends. It was more palatable to remember Dunkirk and forget Calais. He began to drink heavily, finishing his glass almost as soon as it had been refilled. He said very little for the rest of the evening and his new acquaintances spared him questions. James staggered off to bed. He awoke very early and breakfasted alone. He turned left out of the hotel and walked down the road by the canal back to the bridge, the QVR's bridge, no more than half a mile away. He crossed the empty bridge and climbed up to the grass bank where the QVR had lain twenty-four years ago, where he and his fellows had fought hard and killed Germans. James tried very hard to find the exact spot where he had lain. He lowered himself down onto his chest, sniffed the grass, and looked up the street on the other side of the bridge where the Germans had approached. He could identify where his first German victim had died. Two bullets and he was done for. With shame he remembered the exhilaration of that first kill and how he had enjoyed it, savoured it and rehearsed it in near dreams before waking. Not so very different from the glow of scoring a try or flattening the stumps of a batsman – only a thousand times more fulfilling. He began to understand how some men enjoy killing and why war is a deeply well-disguised addiction of the human race.

There were no signs now of that battle. The world had moved on. Lying down, gazing at the bridge and the street he knew what he had to do. James walked north and soon found the old familiar bastion. His legs without orders took him along the streets until they traced their way to the side street which led into the little square. It was about nine in the morning when he approached the house in the corner of the square. The same iron gates with the green solid panelling below topped by railings with finials. The monkey-puzzle tree was taller with more green limbs budding off from the thin trunk. James knew that they grew about one foot a year. Twenty-four years. Twenty-four feet taller.

"About right," he mumbled.

His eyes sought the brass plate on the pillar by the gate. It had gone. The rectangle of wall where the plate had been fixed was lighter than the surround, leaving its ghost. James was undecided. Perhaps he should wait at the far end of the square and watch for anyone who might enter or leave the house. Or should he pull the bell? Perhaps it too had gone, replaced by an electric buzzer. He could not bear that. Agnès would now be… forty-five years old. Would they recognise each other? He was relieved to see the well-polished brass bell pull knob there. Standing still he circled the bell pull with his fingers. He fondled it. Then he heard the bell ringing, ringing in that tone of exaggerated acuity that he recalled so well. No answer. He turned away almost relieved. He had tried and failed. As he turned away to retrace his steps down the path back to his fellows and to 1964, he heard the door open behind him.

"*Bonjour, Monsieur.*"

He did not recognise the voice.

"*Bonjour, Madame. Je m'appelle Dr James Butland. Je suis anglais. Parlez vous anglais?*"

His French was very rusty and it would be easier to speak English.

"*Un peu, Monsieur*, how can I help you?"

"I was here in the war. In 1940. This was a doctor's house. I was wounded and the doctor, no, his daughter Agnès, treated me."

James was saying too much and too quickly.

"*Lentement, Monsieur.*"

"Is Dr Hugo or his daughter Agnès still here?"

"*Non, Monsieur.* Dr Hugo and his son were killed in the war and Agnès returned to the university in Lille to complete her studies. The house was empty for many months. Calais was a very sad and battered town. And then we bought it."

"Do you know what happened to Agnès?"

"*Oui*, I do know something. Come in and we can talk with coffee."

"Thank you very much."

"My family have always lived in Calais and we were patients of Dr Hugo."

"I knew Agnès so briefly, only a few days."

"Agnès qualified as a doctor in 1945 and decided to set up a practice in Saint-Omer rather than return to Calais. She had lost her whole family and wanted a fresh start. She might still be there. We exchanged a few letters and in the early days she occasionally visited the house to make sure we had not altered too much of it. You know that those who have loved houses hate to see much change after they leave. It is an unspoken insult to them."

"What is the best way to go to Saint-Omer, Madame? By bus or train?"

"The bus runs every hour. It is very easy. You must have liked Agnès very much."

She began to suspect something.

"Yes, Madame. To say that she saved my life would be

exaggeration. I was not too severely wounded but she did arrange for me to take Dr Hugo's boat which I sailed to England."

"*D'accord.*"

"Do you know her address in Saint-Omer?"

"I can try. It is almost twenty years ago. She may not still be there."

She left the room and returned with her address book.

"Number 30, Rue Jacqueline, Saint-Omer."

"Thank you, Madame. I am so grateful to you."

James returned to the hotel and left a message for Colonel Belchamp informing him that he would not be returning to England with the party and would make his own way back. Belchamp would understand. Last night's catharsis needed more exploration. He would think the poor fellow was mildly unhinged by his wartime experiences.

James found the bus station and bought a ticket for Saint-Omer. It was about an hour's journey through rather flat countryside, less attractive than Kent. As he left the bus station in Saint-Omer he asked the driver:

"Can you direct me to Rue Jacqueline, please? I have never been here before and I am trying to find an old friend."

"Certainly, Monsieur. Straight down the road. Take the second – no third – street on the left. That is Rue Jacqueline."

He walked slowly, trying to discover why he was there. She may not be pleased to see him.

"Why am I here?" he shouted. No one else was in the street to reproach him.

He must keep going now he was there. He wanted to tell Agnès he was a doctor and a reasonably successful one. He wanted to tell her about Alasdair. She would listen and he would feel a little better. Perhaps he still loved her. He would know when he saw her. He did not dare to spend more than a few seconds with that threat. It would create new problems and he had more than enough to cripple him.

Rue Jacqueline. He walked slowly trying to identify numbers and then fifty yards away he saw a house with more than a resemblance to the doctor's house in Calais. A large stone house. No monkey-puzzle tree. He was disappointed. He was now within a few yards of the house. Ivy covered the pillars on both sides of the gate. Then he saw a rectangle carved out of the ivy which still pushed fingers into the space. A brass plaque.

Dr Agnès Hugo MD
University of Lille

He stood completely still. He realised, as if there had been any doubt, that he still loved her. She must be happily married, with children. Comfortable in her medical practice. A respected member of Saint-Omer society. Her husband was probably not a doctor, probably a lawyer or businessman who would not need a brass plaque. Only a doctor would need one. Although forty-two years old, James felt like an infatuated schoolboy.

He turned away from the house. He gazed up and down the street pleading for someone to order him what to do. He did not want to decide, now, on his own. The consequences were too immense. The familiar pounding in his head, the cold sweaty palms, the gymnastics of his intestines. He had suffered enough. He could not take on any more burdens. Yet meeting Agnès could be the beginning of his recovery, something positive and powerful that could reverse the inertia of hopelessness. He turned to his left, his gaze fixed on other houses, any home other than this one, anything to delay a decision. James was terrified of decisions. He faced the house again. He read the brass plaque again, slowly, so that he could not be mistaken. James stepped briskly to the door. No brass bell pull. An electric bell. The note was rough and dismayed him. At times of such stress sounds were either magnified to intolerable levels or attenuated to unreality.

Footsteps. Not Agnès's, he was sure.

"*Bonjour, Monsieur.*"

"*Bonjour, Madame. Est-ce-que la maison de la docteuse Agnès Hugo?*"

"*Oui, Monsieur.*"

"Is she here, is she in?"

James switched to English as the strain of translation was too much.

"The surgery hours are from five until seven this evening."

Thank goodness, she speaks English.

"It's not a medical, a professional matter. I'm not a patient. It's a personal matter."

"The doctor is on her afternoon rounds visiting patients. She will not be back for about an hour."

"May I wait for her?"

"If it is so important, Monsieur. *Entrez. Attendez ici, s'il vous plait.*" She reverted to French to put him in his place. She indicated a waiting room just off the hall.

James sat very still in an upright high-backed chair with his legs trembling. He forced his heels hard to the floor to stop this incontinence. He could not keep still. He massaged his thigh and calf muscles to rid them of their random electrical impulses. He picked up a magazine. There was an old bookcase with leather-bound volumes, some paperbacks and even old medical textbooks. In England patients would steal them. Even quite upright people "borrow" books with the intention of returning them but rarely do. *Do I recognise this bookcase from the old house?* James could not be certain. This table and these chairs were not there. Agnès must have bought them in Saint-Omer. He looked hard at the net curtains, at the street, the gate, the box hedges.

"Why am I here?" He spoke quietly, in case the maid might hear. "Perhaps I should prepare what I'm going to say."

Agnès would have every right to be angry. He had ignored her for twenty-four years. Why arrive now without warning or invitation? Without a letter in advance or at least allowing her the opportunity to say, "*Merci, mais non merci.*"

The hour passed more quickly than he had feared. At least three times during that hour he had risen to his feet, walked towards the door with the intention of leaving and avoiding the encounter. The sense of time passing, like the acuity of hearing, can be accelerated or retarded by the intensity of the occasion. What determines which of these two perceptive options?

He stared at the street, yearning for and dreading Agnès's arrival. His mind flew back to those few days in May 1940. He then wanted to stay and not leave. Agnès stood still by the boathouse, holding her bicycle, waving vigorously at the start, then subsiding to a few random jerks of her right arm. He had focused his eyes to look north to England but he could also see the still figure waving no longer. He deceived himself that he could see her riding off but in truth he could not. The boat was already veering off ten degrees to starboard in the direction of Calais. He over-corrected the tiller and the boat swung abruptly to port and dipped alarmingly. He must concentrate or all Agnès's efforts to help him would be wasted.

James was facing the street but it was footsteps on gravel that awoke him from his trance and not his eyes. The footsteps had passed and there was no one in sight. The bell. He heard the maid walking quickly, almost running through the hall – certainly more eagerly than when he called an hour before. The door was opened.

"*Madame. C'est un Anglais qui vous attend.*"

"*Un Anglais?*"

"*Oui, Madame.*"

James stood very still, facing the door. The door opened very slowly.

"*Bonsoir, Agnès.*"

She faced him, gasping, grappling with her reactions, struggling to make sense of this scene.

"What happened to my father's boat?"

"I'm sorry. It disappeared at Dover. I tried to locate it but it must have been stolen or requisitioned by the Navy."

"I hope it was put to good use."

Agnès offered her right hand. He grasped it and shook it with a single downward stroke. She kissed him coolly on both cheeks, in the French manner, without emotion; a ritual which always takes Englishmen unawares.

"It's twenty-four years."

"Yes, it must be."

Patients were now walking through the gates and crunching up the gravel path.

"It's time for evening clinic."

"Yes, it must be," he replied lamely.

"Can you come back at seven o'clock? You must stay for dinner. Where are you staying?"

"Nowhere, or at least I have been with a party visiting the 1940 battlefields. They returned to England today. I decided to stay and look for you. To explain…"

"Then wait in the drawing room. My patients wait in here."

"Thank you, Agnès."

The maid, with an unconcealed frown of disapproval, showed him the way. He sat down in a deep armchair and almost immediately, as an escape from this reality, fell asleep. He may have dreamed but could not recall any when he awoke, quite abruptly. He had slept fitfully for the past two nights with alternating sensations of nightmare and peace. He may have dreamed of the past but could recall nothing through this anaesthetic.

The door opened and he lurched to his feet as Agnès entered. He had not dared to look at her closely earlier. He was afraid to meet her eyes. She must be forty-five now, given the three-year gap in 1940. He rediscovered the red hair, a lighter shade now, the thin figure, the taut elegance of middle-class French women. She shook hands again, more confident now, more firmly than before. No kiss. James deflated.

"An aperitif?"

"Thank you, Agnès."

She handed him a glass of dry vermouth.

"Well, now that the shock has passed, you must describe twenty-four years of history. If my patients complain that I was not listening to them attentively this evening I shall blame you, James. I almost forgot the correct dose of penicillin."

"It's a very long story."

He felt ashamed at such a weak introduction. Agnès, and twenty-four years, deserved more.

"We have a whole evening to tell it. Please follow me to the dining room."

James followed, puppy-like. He recognised the dining room furniture easily. The heavy Third Empire table and chairs with the same upholstery, deep blue brocade with a pattern of hand-embroidered gold outlined squares. The deep red curtains came from Calais, he was sure. The oak dresser. He relaxed at this familiarity with old friends, old props from 1940, which had been only brief acquaintances. Some memory pictures are stencilled into the brain ineradicably, the very best and the very worst, and can be conjured up like ghosts rising from tombs on All Saints' Day. By paintings, sounds, smells or just by escapes from the locked safe of memories, the codes are cracked too easily and too painfully. They sat on opposite sides of the table. The maid served.

James had not planned how to tell his story or how to prepare his excuses. For deep guilt was there too. The story came out rapidly with too much detail in places and wafts of mere suggestion in others.

"After Calais, the rest of the war seemed tame. I spent the next two or three years guarding beaches, waiting for the invasion which never came. In early 1943 I was posted to North Africa, Tunisia, and did see some action then. In fact, I was wounded – you can see I lost an eye – and spent months in hospital. I was never in action again after that. I decided to become a doctor and the Army gave me leave of absence to go to medical school at the end of 1943."

"A doctor, James, surely not. You were a student of history. I remember it well."

"If I had not met you, Agnès, it would never have entered my head. You had that inner calm, that confidence in your role in life that I found infectious. It was a powerful disease. No, it was an addictive drug. Once you had caught it or tried it there was no escape. The infection or addiction just grabs you. There was then no decision to make.

"I knew no science. At school I had a visceral hatred for it. I had grown up with languages, history and maths and this interloper into my life at thirteen was most unwelcome. Science seemed so soulless and spartan, so cold, after history and literature. If you remember, I was going up to Oxford in October 1939 to read history. I wrote to Wadham College in 1941 requesting to switch to medicine after the war. The dons thought that I had lost my marbles with the strain of war and that I had somehow discovered that I should "help people" rather than indulge in intellectual gymnastics. Apparently all sorts of selfish young men and women suddenly decided that they should become doctors, priests, nurses and social workers after the war to wash off the odour of killing. I suppose similar impulses made people communists and certainly the rejection of Churchill in 1945 and the overwhelming choice of socialism was all part of a pattern. The truth was that I had fallen out of love with history and into love with medicine because of you. You seemed so sure of yourself and your place in the jigsaw. I envied your focus and your certainty."

"Surely you did not change the course of your life because of a love affair?"

"Agnès, that is what love is. A change of life. No one is the same person after a love affair as before. Many experiences are buried deeply and essentially forgotten. Perhaps Freud or drugs can release them. But love affairs are never forgotten. The problem was that Oxford would welcome me to read history but would not waste a place on a non-scientist to read medicine. I wrote to the Dean of St Thomas's Hospital in London and made my case. I left your part in this out of my application, Agnès, as he would have been as unconvinced as you seem to be. And so I went to St Thomas's Hospital Medical School in late 1943. They could have called me back to fight but I think they had forgotten all about me quite quickly. The doctors looking after me in Algiers were very helpful in recruiting me to their ranks. I was a student on the First MB course for those with inadequate sciences to bring them up to speed. They indulged ex-servicemen in those days. It was a real struggle but it was a means to an end and I stuck it out. Oxford had been my escape plan from 1930s suburban drab but was now closed to me. I began to settle down and see my medical student days in London stretching ahead.

"'Why not Cambridge?' I quite often spoke out loud to myself at critical moments. It seemed worth a try. I wrote to the admissions tutors of every college in Cambridge and explained my predicament. All but one replied with the same reflex response as the Senior Tutor of Wadham. About two weeks later a letter arrived from the Master of Magdalene College inviting me to visit him and discuss my application. He had already contacted the headmaster of my school and Wadham to check that I was genuine, gaining evidence that I had a brain of some sort, though it might be historical porridge rather than scientific steel.

"It was in May 1944 that I caught the train from Liverpool Street to Cambridge, ambling through the flat lands of the East of England. I walked from the station to Magdalene and was soon sitting in the Master's Lodge. It was not the aggressive prosecutor's interview I had experienced at Wadham in 1938. It was a gentle conversation about the war and the essential flexibility of the mind that can meet any challenge if motivated to do so. The Master must have decided that I would do, as a week later I received an offer of a place at Cambridge in October 1944 if I passed the London First MB."

Neither of them spoke for several minutes. James sensed the intrusion of the unasked question. Agnès had said so little. She had responded to his story with full engagement of her eyes and her face and with brief inspirations at moments of extra tension. But she never asked the question that James had expected since they first faced each other earlier in the evening.

"Agnès, I did write to you at the end of the war but clearly you never received my letter. I sent you another letter and Christmas card in 1945 and these were returned to me, stamped 'Gone away. Address unknown. Return to sender.' I even thought that you might be dead, murdered by the Nazis, or killed by Allied bombing around D Day. I wrote further letters but did not post them as I reasoned that, if you were still alive, you wanted to forget all about me. I have no excuses. The war was over. We had medicine in common though you would have been qualified by 1945 and I was only a junior student. There was another reason which has tortured me ever since. After you patched me up, I should have somehow rejoined the QVR, the Queen Victoria's Rifles, my regiment. They were almost all killed or captured at Calais. While I was with you, in love with you, they were dying. I still feel ashamed. I have avoided QVR reunions because I could not face the questions. Of course, they know that I had been one of the very few who escaped by boat but in those few days there would be many gaps in my story that I could not fill without exposing myself. I could have rejoined them somehow and shared their fate. Why should I have been so fortunate? They even gave me a medal which you deserved more than I.

"And there is something else that I must tell you, Agnès. I teamed up with a St Thomas's nurse during my years in Cambridge. I used to escape to London to see her. It sounds ridiculous as I had done everything to leave London, but it is true. We had to return to London for our clinical medical training and I thought long and hard whether I should return to St Thomas's. It's very difficult to analyse. I suppose I wanted to retain some independence from Alice – that's her name – and St Thomas's was the most traditional and conservative medical school with an unhealthy obsession not only with the medical roots of one's family but especially with the St Thomas's roots of one's forebears. Something of a perceived disadvantage to those of us who could not claim this lineage. I considered very carefully whether I should go to UCH, University College Hospital, meritocratic, cosmopolitan, multicultural, almost the antithesis of St Thomas's. I was tempted, but decided eventually to return to St Thomas's. I never had any doubts about my chosen life as a doctor or regret that I had relegated history to a hobby like cricket or stamp collecting. When I qualified in 1950, Alice and I married. You see, Agnès, I could not contact you then though I sorely wanted to. It would have torn everyone apart. I thought that if you were alive, you must have married by then too and would not wish to be reminded of the English soldier who invaded your life for a few days in 1940. I worked hard and even found myself back in Harrow where I was born and raised. Yes, it's crazy, isn't it? I spent years working so hard to escape from Harrow and its stifling existence but worked for some months at the hospital on the Hill, dominated by the great school. I had decided to become a hospital physician with a life of theatrical ward rounds, the intensity of treating the very sick and dying and the relative calm of thoughtful outpatient clinics. We had two children, Alasdair and Sarah. I've rambled on far too long, Agnès. What have you to tell of twenty-four years?"

"Our son, Alexandre, was born in February 1941."

James's bowels writhed. The pulsing loud head. The cold sweaty hands. He had already noted with relief that she wore no wedding ring.

"Oh, I'm so sorry, Agnès. You should have told me before, letting me ramble on about my life…"

"Don't be sorry, James. Alexandre has brought me so much happiness. I have never revealed the name of his father which made some suspect that he might even have been German. My aunt looked after him so that I could continue my studies in Lille. He knows that his father was a soldier, a wartime love affair. Not so unusual. He always understood. He never blamed me for giving him no father. For all he or I knew, his father might be dead. Alexandre is now a medical student too, at Lille. He qualifies next year if he passes his exams. Yes, I had many friends in that closed, non-celibate monastery of medicine but none came to mean anything special. I thought you might come back some day and we could pick up our lives again which had been left behind, like the clothes of a bather on the beach at Blériot-Plage.

"I left Calais at the end of the war. My father and brother were dead. It was a sad town. What was left of it after 1940 was demolished by Allied bombs in 1944. I moved to Saint-Omer and set up my practice here. It's a full and happy life. I am well respected. I have that clear role in the community of which you spoke. I am a good doctor. I never speak of Alexandre's father. Most assume that he was a Frenchman who did not survive the war. Or perhaps he had left me. I never imply anything different. James, you are shell-shocked, I can see."

"No, it's not as you think, at least, not entirely. It's just that my son, I mean Alice's and my son, was killed in a road accident a year ago. He was nine. Alice and Sarah had many fractures but survived. I now realise that I do have a son, another son. I don't know whether to laugh or weep. I'm so sorry, Agnès, for convulsing your life."

"It was not you. It was the war. I am so sorry you have lost your son. That is a far worse experience than mine, James. I remember every detail of those days, as I am sure you do. I came to your room, remember? I undressed. I climbed into the bed of a frightened young soldier, younger than me. He was my patient though I was not yet a doctor. I needed warm, human, male company that night. Most unethical."

They both smiled and James gripped her left hand with his right, across the table.

"I was only a medical student then and exempt from the rules. You just flicked a switch which I have never tried to explain. It happened. It was not your fault. You must feel no guilt. To lose your son, only nine years old, is beyond insanity. How do you survive?"

"I have not survived. I am almost dead in spirit. I have been existing and working like an inanimate machine, with the cogs going round but with no soul. Two years ago I was appointed a consultant physician at Addenbrooke's Hospital in Cambridge. It was a new start for the four of us."

It was about ten o'clock but in this exchange of lives it seemed like dawn after a very prolonged night. James had drunk almost a bottle of Bordeaux and a cognac while Agnès had drunk very little.

"You must stay here tonight."

"Oh, I can't. Your maid."

"Constance lives here. She is my chaperone. I don't think you are in a position to threaten my virtue – what's left of it – tonight. We have so much more to discuss but only in morsels that we can swallow. Otherwise we will choke to death. Follow me."

James had a suitcase which he had left in the hall.

"No night rambles tonight, James, I promise."

James smiled, looking at the floor, embarrassed.

"Goodnight, Agnès."

They shook hands. She turned and closed the door behind her.

He slept throughout the night for the first time in a year. Alasdair's death had destroyed his sleep pattern. At every sudden awakening, and there were so many, he snapped on the bedside lamp and read hungrily until he thought he could sleep again. Often having tried to sleep again, within seconds he was fighting for the lamp to escape back into a book. It was his technique to fight off the demons of recall and memory.

He awoke as Agnès pushed open the door with a tray of coffee in large bowls. 1940 again. She smiled and patted his forearm. *She does not accuse me. She may even be pleased that I have come.*

"No time to chat this morning, James. Go downstairs when you are ready and Constance will prepare your breakfast."

He was confused. He knew where he was. Saint-Omer. Agnès. The surrealism of it all was drowning him. He crept guiltily along the corridor with small steps, feeling the way with his toes, avoiding all sound, as one does in a strange house. He found the bathroom. He shaved and bathed and crept back to his room. He found one last clean shirt as he should have been back in Cambridge by now. He descended the stairs almost one by one like a patient with arthritis but then forced himself to walk down with the regular, well-timed footfall of familiarity. The stairs would not stay silent. Constance, who had clearly been hovering in the kitchen awaiting him with her door ajar, showed him into the dining room.

"*Bonjour, Monsieur.*"

"*Bonjour, Constance. Merci.*"

"Doctor Hugo works at the hospital on Fridays but she requested that you lunch together at Les Trois Cocques at one o'clock."

"Very good. Thank you, Constance."

James managed to stretch out his breakfast for an hour as he had no plans for the morning. He did not want to go for a walk around Saint-Omer as thoughts would pursue him and punish him. He did not want to face these thoughts quite yet. *Alexandre, my son. My only living son. A son I never knew I had. Alasdair's brother.* Would they look alike? No. His only son was Alasdair and he was long dead. In the hospital mortuary he was yellow-white and cold like the corpses in Calais and Tunisia. The old dead, in hospitals after their heart attacks and strokes, looked so normally dead. The young dead after traumatic death looked so surprised to be dead. Doctors are accustomed to dead bodies but not to dead bodies they claim as their own.

He found Les Trois Cocques easily in the centre of Saint-Omer. He was fifteen minutes early. He had never been late for anything in his life with an almost obsessive compulsive respect for time. If he feared that he might be late a diluted version of panic would taunt him.

"*J'attends Dr Hugo, Monsieur,*" he stuttered to the patron.

"*Asseyez-vous ici, Monsieur.*"

He was shown to a quiet table at the back of the restaurant.

"*Vichy, s'il vous plait, Monsieur.*"

James needed a clear head for the lunch which would define the rest of his life. Agnès walked in swiftly just after one o'clock, bowing to the patron. She did not hesitate before marching to the table. He leapt to his feet too eagerly like a new prep school boy when the headmaster entered the classroom. They shook hands but Agnès pulled him by both forearms towards her and kissed him on both cheeks. Two glasses of cool Sancerre were placed in front of them.

"James, why have you turned up after twenty-four years? You clearly did not want to complicate your life with me after Calais. I was pleased to help you. My father and brother were away at the front and I wanted to help too. In the dark days after Alexandre was born I convinced myself that it was my sacrifice for France – I had helped a gallant ally and produced a son for my country to replace those who were dying."

"I thought about you so often, many times a day during the war and always when I was in physical danger. I thought of you, Agnès, not my family, not my friends, but of you. Your courage. The risks you took to help me. I could not write to you during the war as my letter would never reach you. I did think about writing to the British Embassy in Berne asking them to forward my letter to you but that seemed crazy. I was afraid that the Germans would intercept the letter and arrest you as a British spy. I had also caught the medicine bug from you which completely changed the direction of my life. How could not I absorb you into myself for good? I suppose at the end of the war I was utterly obsessed by medicine. It is no exaggeration. It is common in young doctors full of ideas and optimism. Alice had become a good friend and sticking with her seemed the only way then. I convinced myself that you would be married and have children. If I found you I feared it would be destructive to us all. After the war we all craved certainty and stability. I was terrified that you would resent my very existence for those few days we spent together. That would have been intolerable. It was safer to do nothing and pretend that it had all been a dream. As one grows older you can stumble on memories and genuinely not know whether you have dreamt them or whether they are true. At times I wondered whether you had really existed. The fact of your existence and those May days was too disturbing to accept. I settled into a hospital and family routine that brought a sort of peace. I convinced myself that you were far better off without me in your life."

"You should have allowed me to judge that, James."

"I know and I'm deeply sorry."

"Would you like to meet Alexandre, or would it be easier for us all if I do not tell him of your visit to Saint-Omer?"

"I just don't know."

His face fell into his hands and for the first time since Agnès arrived he had looked away from her. He was aware that the patron and the other customers – probably all Agnès's patients – were looking at them, at him. What was this Englishman doing visiting their doctor and upsetting her?

James thought of rushing out and running for the bus back to Calais, never to return, never to face this tribunal on his life.

"I had a son. I lost him and now I have another son of whom I know nothing. I would be afraid to see him. He might be too like Alasdair but much older of course. Agnès, if you think that some good to you and Alexandre could come from it then of course I would like to see him."

"I don't know what is right. Like all doctors I am very good at dispensing advice on diseases and treatments, and even on the problems of living life to everyone else, but I am hopeless at judging my own life. If I thought I would never see you again after today I would say that it would be best to say nothing. The status quo is not unpleasant. Alexandre and I are content and happy. He is studying hard, very keen on medicine – like both his parents. He is ambitious to succeed in hospital practice and not be just a country GP like his mother. That is a good thought, a warm thought, is it not? He has a girlfriend, another medical student. You would like her, James. You could grow to love him too. He would never replace Alasdair but he would help to fill the vacuum in your heart."

"Do you want to see me again, Agnès?"

James trembled to ask this. He knew now that he could no more run out, mumbling apologies, and run for the Calais bus than he could deny that he existed here, now, in this little restaurant in Saint-Omer.

"I do not know yet, James. You must give me time. You have Alice, your wife, Sarah, your daughter. You must love them so deeply after what you have been through together."

"There's no such thing as an accident. I used to say this as a mild repeated joke that my children would recount to their own children in the years ahead. Truth is, I really believed it. Medicine does not give up on you. It is always testing you and beguiling you; yes, seducing you to do your best. After Alasdair was killed we attempted some perfunctory love-making with the cool, almost cynical objective of replacing him. But it was hopeless and even more destructive of our own marriage breathing its last gasps."

"You have been so unhappy, James. I am so sorry for all of you. For you, for Alice and for Sarah. It's good you are a doctor; working hard for your patients is respite, a worthwhile distraction for your own life. It's almost a justification, a defence of unhappiness…"

Her voice trailed off. James realised that Agnès was also speaking of her own life. Behind her confident professional exterior she was incomplete. Was it because of him? Could someone else have filled his place? The lack of a large close family to support Alexandre through his growing up. He would not press her on these questions.

James could not recall later what they had eaten. He certainly could feel the thick white linen tablecloth, lightly starched, with textures exposed to his fingers. He was back lying on his chest, fingering the salt grain-like imperfections of the trigger of his Lee Enfield rifle, feeling its tiny pits and hillocks, waiting, waiting for the exquisite pleasure of the shot. There must have been cheese, and yes, there was a lemon tart. The bill was tiny.

"I must return to the hospital. I am already late for the gynaecology clinic. When are you leaving Saint-Omer?"

"Now, Agnès. I must. I'm due back at the hospital after the weekend. If I leave now I shall be back in Cambridge tomorrow afternoon. Let us decide nothing now. We are both too sensible and middle-aged for that. Write down your address and telephone number on this menu."

He tore it in half and gave her one half. He wrote his own address and number on the other half. The patron ignored this contempt for his menu and offence against good manners.

"Is that agreed?"

"Yes, of course. We have exposed ourselves to each other far too much already. Doctors are not supposed to be so vulnerable."

They left together. James kissed Agnès on both cheeks with dry, in-turned lips. They both grasped both hands, his right to her right and his left to her left. Agnès walked off towards the hospital, turning several times to wave and then for the last time as she turned a distant corner. James was back in the boat, watching her on the shore, despairing as she disappeared from view. James too turned away, trying to recall the way back to Agnès's house. He hesitated, trying to extract every drop of choking juice from the scene. If he left too soon he would weep. He did not walk away. He stood outside the restaurant. He could not leave her again. After several minutes he started walking slowly and deliberately back to the house to collect his suitcase.

"*Merci, Constance. Au revoir.*"

"*Au revoir, Monsieur. J'espère que nous vous rencontrerons.*"

"*J'espère aussi. Au revoir.*"

He felt desolate. He would not return to Saint-Omer. The consequences were just too immense. He found the place where he had left the bus from Calais and hoped the bus to Calais would soon appear. He could not integrate all his thoughts. He cursed himself for deserting Colonel Belchamp and overexposing himself to the past and this present.

In just over an hour he was back in Calais walking to the Gare Maritime and the Channel ferry. He could not recognise much. Post-war building had abolished most of the Calais that he remembered except for the Hotel de Ville clock tower. The air was fresh. No stench of burning buildings and clouds of roasting oil. No cordite perfume and death. No QVR.

Dover. The QVR had sailed on May 22nd 1940 and he had returned in the Hugo family boat in early June. Dover had been as chaotic as Calais in the midst of the Dunkirk evacuation which had camouflaged his escape from France. He could now smell oil which often tainted the salty pheromone of the sea. James did not delay in Dover. He found his car and drove silently alone back to Cambridge, fighting off the demons of negative thoughts. In spite of his best efforts his defences crumbled and he heard himself letting out deep sobs. He felt tears falling down his face and dripping off his chin onto his shirt. He was unshaven and exhausted and hoped that no one who knew him would witness this condition of despair.

Alice and Sarah were at home. James described the skeleton of the expedition which was of negligible interest to them.

"We expected you yesterday, on Friday."

"I decided to stay an extra night in Calais just to tramp around and see if I could recognise any of the scenes of my heroics."

His persona, his act at home, was of a confident, almost arrogant man in full control which was remote from the truth, as Alice understood.

"I'm thinking of writing a book about Calais in 1940 – the forgotten brigade. We had a whole forgotten army in Burma but everyone seems to know plenty about it. Who's ever heard of Calais? Dunkirk, Dunkirk, Dunkirk – that's all we hear. Without Calais there might have been no Dunkirk."

Alice and Sarah looked at each other and responded with thin smiles. James knew that they were uninterested. It was all so long ago. Alasdair had been interested. He would listen to his father's stories without sham interest. He knew that Alexandre would listen too.

"I need more trips to Calais for research. I need an interest outside medicine. It's too stifling, allowing no other interest in life to breathe."

Not even one's family. He left this unspoken. He would not even admit it to himself.

"Is your French up to it?"

"No, it's not. It's still rusty schoolboy. But I shall improve. It's not buried too deeply below the surface."

He reflected on how limited his conversation had been in France, planning and rehearsing such simple sentences before uttering them. Agnès spoke fluent English which made him feel defensive and embarrassed. He could never play this arrogant role with her. She knew him only too well even after such a brief time together. He must see her again. He had refused to debate this question between Saint-Omer and Cambridge but there was no decision for him to make. It was fixed, predestined, irrevocable, just as his first meeting with Agnès was inevitable, inescapable with no room for human error or intervention. James knew that he still loved her. There was no other possible translation of these emotions.

June to September 1964

Cambridge is a beguiling town but James was immune to its beauty. On Saturday walks in the spring he would see the snowdrops, crocuses and daffodils of new life emerging from winter hibernation. They were an adrenaline infusion to him as an undergraduate but no longer moved him. They were just painted on the landscape in pre-Renaissance two dimensions with no perspective. Alasdair would never be an undergraduate ambling through the Cambridge courts with his friends, laughing, planning the future. He would not have wanted to study in Cambridge anyway, too close to home. He would have been happy at Exeter or St Andrew's.

In his consulting room at the private hospital, a mile from Addenbrooke's, he would hear the chirruping of the boys at the adjacent school. *My son, I want my son*, he thought to himself and sometimes he spoke this out loud, repeating it like a mantra. If repeated enough the wish might even have been rewarded. On one occasion a nurse had intervened by slamming down the window to blot out the intrusion and went away crying herself. James had been quite hard on Alasdair. He was not a natural book man like his father and struggled at a school that was too bright for him. An unfortunate choice. It had placed unwelcome pressure on him. He was a desk dreamer and not a swot or a grafter and this caused conflict. James admitted all of this to himself but much too late. There was now no chance to make amends, no opportunity to say, "Don't worry old chap. Many have never passed an exam in their life but have had happy and worthwhile lives. Don't worry, be happy." When James now rehearsed what he should have said to his son he folded in half like a pen-knife blade snapping into its trough. He despised himself for trying to mould his son into his own image. "Agnès," he murmured to himself. "Agnès, save me." For the first time since Alasdair's death he sensed a warm gentle breeze of optimism brush over his face.

He telephoned the number scribbled on the half-menu he had folded in his wallet.

"*La résidence de la Docteuse Agnès Hugo.*"

"*Bonjour, Constance. C'est* Dr James Butland calling from England." He merged and mangled his French as usual. "May I speak to Dr Hugo?"

"*Oui, Monsieur.*"

"James, it is good to speak to you. It is almost two months since you were here. I thought that you had decided that sleeping dogs should lie."

"I've had a tough time, Agnès. Lots of dark thoughts about my son – about Alasdair," he quickly corrected himself. "I've been drinking too much and not concentrating properly at the hospital. I've been feeling very low and confused about what is right. About what I should think. What I should do. I have almost telephoned you on many occasions and then fled from the phone. I do my best but have little time for the worried well and the trivia that some patients present to us. How so utterly insignificant their worries and concerns are when set against… what you and I have experienced. May I come and see you again soon?"

"I look forward to it, James. Yes, do come. I too have been thinking hard and I hoped you would telephone. I phoned you once at Addenbrooke's and spoke to your secretary. You were not able to speak to me, she said, and I left no message. Did she ever tell you that a French doctor rang?"

"No."

"I dared not call you at your home."

"Oh, why not, Agnès?"

He regretted his reflex response.

"Have you spoken to Alexandre about me?"

"No, James."

"That's probably right until we have mapped out our future."

"That sounds presumptuous, James."

"It was not meant to sound presumptuous. But we must meet again very soon."

"The weekend after next."

It was a statement of fact and not a question.

"I'm planning French lessons so that you do not have to keep patronising me with your perfect English."

"Patronise… I do not understand that word, James."

"I'll explain one of these days."

Those two weeks dragged by but several friends at the hospital thought he seemed brighter. "Time heals" is the clichéd mantra. It is not true. He knew that decades after trauma acute attacks of despair can be provoked by unexpected incidents – meeting a patient with the same birthday as Alasdair's or seeing a young adult male of the same age as Alasdair – if he had lived – and who could be a son, even if physical appearance denied that possibility. A chance sighting in the street of a young man so closely resembling Alasdair that James's eyes flashed to him, away again, and back to him several times. Could there have been a mistake? Could Alasdair have escaped from the accident, lost his memory, become lost and built a new life with someone else? In his panic could James have misidentified his son? The passage of time brings new experience, new insulating layers of asbestos, to obstruct access to the dark times. But they are still there. Burned under layers of self-deception.

October 1964

It was late October when James almost reproduced the journey that he had undertaken to join Colonel Belchamp's 1940 tour in May. But instead of taking the battle bus at Calais he found the local bus to Saint-Omer, the birthplace of le Maréchal Pétain he had learnt since, when dipping into a French guide book. Saint-Omer was not such a backwater after all.

The red-brown autumn was still warm and the windows of the bus were open, sucking in the savoury smoke of leaves in the first stages of decomposition. The air was windless and the smoke from bonfires climbed vertically before vanishing into infinity. He felt that he was just waking from a very long deep sleep. A field of lavender well past its zenith with fading purple and scent. Two bees in the last throws of summer had navigated unwisely into the bus and were now angry with their unwanted journey to another galaxy. They groaned heavily, almost unable to make height, resorting to parabolic sorties from one passenger to another. James jerked his head out of the flight path of the more aggressive bee and almost missed the town sign announcing Saint-Omer. He stiffened in his seat. This time it would be even more difficult, although he walked to the house more confident of his way. He pushed the white knob for the electric buzzer. He still mourned the loss of the Calais bell pull. Constance did not come. He heard Agnès's steps in the hall. Lighter, more rapid, more impatient. Perhaps he imagined that. He kissed her lips. Not the ritual handshake and double-cheeked franking of their previous meeting. Agnès did not reject him. He moved his hands to her shoulder blades and pulled her towards him.

"Where's Constance?"

"She's spending the week with her sister in Amiens. She wanted us to have the house to ourselves."

"Does she know about me, about Alexandre?"

"I don't think so. She knows that we met before, many years ago, perhaps in the war. Constance has been trying to find me a suitable husband for years. James, you haven't changed much, you know. A little older of course. You were such a boy, with several days of fur on your chin rather than stubble. I loved you then and I love you now in spite of your unforgivable neglect of me for half a lifetime."

He wilted.

"I exaggerate of course."

"I do not think we should tell Alexandre very much now, do you agree? It could force us both into corners from which we might want to escape."

"I know, James. It is too early to disrupt your life in England. You are a doctor with a growing practice in Cambridge. Work must come first for us both. I could not work in England. The patients would be too suspicious of their French lady doctor and the women would not trust their husbands with her. We must share some time together and not face the future. All will become clear sooner or later."

James relaxed a little. On that January night of Alasdair's death he had been an innocent party, completing the last few tasks in the hospital before driving home for a relaxing evening. Instead he drove home and into an Armageddon with no end in his lifetime.

"Are you hungry, James? Have you eaten since leaving Cambridge?"

"No, but I'm not hungry. Let's walk. Show me Saint-Omer. I've only seen the bus station, the restaurant and your house.

Did you know that the RAF pilot, Douglas Bader, who had lost both his legs, was in hospital here in Saint-Omer after he had been shot down in the war? He escaped from the top floor by climbing down knotted sheets using only his arms. He was taken to a house where he could hide from the Germans but he was betrayed. He was recaptured and the couple sheltering him were sent to a concentration camp."

"I know. I'll show you the hospital and the window he climbed down from. But let's walk first. Saint-Omer is beautiful, perhaps not as beautiful as Cambridge, but it is my home. The tourists all rush south to the Dordogne or Provence and have little time for poor little understated Picardy."

Agnès steered James around a corner into the Rue Gambetta where the tall chapel of the old college of the Walloon Jesuits loomed above the drab street. The ochre brick front absorbed the autumn light just as the impenetrable white classical stone columns reflected it back. They followed the old cobbled streets into the Place Victor Hugo and James, who had never visited Venice, exclaimed:

"What a fine old fountain – it would be more at home in Rome or Venice."

"That is Saint Aldegarde's fountain built in 1752. Just as good as anything you might see in the Renaissance south."

Concealed by the dark, dense houses of provincial northern France, Notre Dame transfixed James as they rounded the next corner. An expanse of ghost-white stone, by its very size and complexity, was evidence of the importance of Saint-Omer as a centre of religion and education on the borders of France and old Flanders. They leaned on the heavy door and stood very still inside. Autumn leaves followed them in and after their eddying resistance to gravity, settled on the mosaic floor. From above, oblique organ pipes of light touched the floor and seemed to disturb the restless leaves refusing to lie still.

"Yes. I saw it too," said Agnès, as James stood staring at the simple, unpredictable leaf dance.

"We'll spend more time in Notre Dame another day," she added.

They walked through the streets and were soon outside the little hospital. James had always relished historical sights, piecing together the past with books and maps. Recreating Blenheim, Bussaco, Waterloo and the Alma had reversed his insomnia on many a night tortured by the past. Because he had been there in Calais in May 1940 he found it difficult to see the bigger picture. James focused on his own walk-on part in that scene. Twenty-sixth spear-carrier at best. Thin red line defensive stuff for a few hours only and then a minor wound that should have kept him off the field for a few hours at most. He never faced the Germans with his friends at Calais again. He was AWOL – absent without leave – with his French lover when he should have been back in the thick of it. This guilt tumble-dried his guts. He was ashamed of his desertion and was, in his own estimation of himself, only half a man. And now, back in France, he was deceiving his family when they most needed his love and support. He was no doctor of the highest integrity. He was second rate, no, third rate and should be dead. If he had been killed in Calais in 1940 beside his friends, there would have been no Agnès, no Alexandre, no Alice or Sarah… no Alasdair to lose his young life so senselessly. He despised himself. The world would have been a better place with his blood on a Calais street than it was now with all the consequences of his actions since.

"Here's the hospital, James. You have been very silent. Do you wish you were back in Cambridge after all?"

"No. I was just back in Calais only a few kilometres away but decades away in memories. Bader was here later in 1941."

"Saint-Omer is one of the best kept secrets in France. The people are quite reserved, quite English really, until you have gained their confidence and then they expose themselves a little. It's been a battlefield for many centuries for the French, the Hapsburgs, the Germans, the English. There has been so much human blood spilt here that the soil has turned into one great black pudding. It is quieter than Calais where everyone is rushing from boats to trains, trains to boats, along the streets – no one really stays in Calais. No one belongs there which is why I moved here. Most of the old buildings of Calais were destroyed in the war and the dull grey concrete of the new ones depresses rather than inspires. We've buried the past but the future has not yet been born. This time is a ghastly limbo between world wars and the remote possibility of a happy and peaceful future. It is easy for doctors. We do our best to improve the human condition, tend the wounds, stroke the brow and say smugly to ourselves that at least we know what we are doing and why we are doing it. But, on a bad day, I think we are only providing temporary solace and amusement for our own patients on their journey to their deaths."

"Lives could be spent in worse ways. I've never regretted my mutation from history to medicine. I know that if I were a historian now rather than a doctor I would find an escape route to something else."

"Perhaps I have done you at least one good deed then."

"You probably saved my life in 1940. I suppose I could have been captured and could then have spent five years in one of Adolf Hitler's Butlins holiday camps. But I think I would have been killed in the line on the embankment. I also think you are now saving my life again. Despair was breathing its fatal breath over me before deciding whether to eat me raw or incinerate me with its flames."

"Melodrama does you no credit, James."

They walked the streets and parks of Saint-Omer until darkness fell and they returned to the house. James carried his suitcase to the same bedroom in which he had slept in May.

"Run a bath if you like, James. Treat this as your home. I'll prepare dinner."

He obeyed orders like the good soldier or junior doctor.

He lay still in the deep warm water. His back and legs ached a little which always happened when he ambled along in the manner of those with plenty of time and nothing to do. When he walked quickly, or marched, there was no stiffness. *Probably the consequence of the rapid clearance of the products of anaerobic muscle metabolism. I don't know. Who cares?* His eyelids drooped and his body jerked in that myoclonic spasm that precedes sleep. He did not hear the bathroom door open but he stirred and Agnès was there kneeling by the bath, her head tilted to the left with a thin smile.

"People drown in baths."

"Not grown ones in six inches of water."

Her fingers were skimming the surface of the water like flat pebbles. She kissed his forehead turned slowly towards her.

"You have me at something of a disadvantage here."

He did not say 'darling'. He hated this insipid word on his own lips and on the lips of others. It was a cheap, glutinous word, more appropriate for a mother to her tiny infant than between sensate adults. His penis did not stir. It floated in the water with the random movement of flotsam. Agnès's fingers continued to disturb the surface tension of the water and brushed his left hand and thigh nearest to her. James lay perfectly still. He knew that if he moved he would lose self-control. *Perhaps that is what she wants. It is too soon.*

"Don't worry, James. I shall not disturb you anymore. Dinner will be ready in twenty minutes."

She stood up and left, smiling at him with just faint concern as she closed the door. He dried himself and dressed quickly and was in the dining room well before the appointed time. He heard Agnès leave the kitchen and she arrived with a tureen of strong-smelling lobster bisque which she placed before him. James sprang up and embraced her with all his strength so that she could not breathe.

"I know I love you, Agnès. Always have. Always will."

"Methinks he doth protest too much," she replied with that English erudition which belittled him. "It might just be an acute attack of nostalgia. They say it's endemic in the middle-aged with their increasing awareness of their mortality."

"Nonsense, Agnès. At least consider the hypothesis that it might be fate offering a lifeline rather than disaster."

"I have considered that, James."

They sat facing each other across the table. James could sense the texture of the food but it seemed tasteless.

"Delicious. Thank you so much."

They drank the same Bordeaux as in May.

"I'm exhausted. It's been such a long day."

"Yes. A very thoughtful day. Bedtime. You go up first, James. I have some work to do in the kitchen."

James had hoped that they would climb the stairs together and that she would lead him to her room, depriving him of making the decision and therefore of guilt. He was in bed, well trussed in corded pyjamas, when he heard Agnès climbing the stairs. He heard her trying very hard not to make noise on the landing, in the bathroom and on the few steps to her bedroom, clearly not wishing to wake him. She assumed that he was asleep. Silence and darkness. Clearly Agnès was delegating to James the next move. She had moved her opening pawn two squares in the bathroom earlier. In May 1940 Agnès had come to him. A deep humming silence surrounded him in his room. The street was not lit and he could have as easily lain in a field under a cloud-covered moonless sky in remote moorland. This torture of sensory deprivation, yet all his senses were competing for his attention.

What James decided to do in the next minute would determine the pattern of the rest of their lives and the lives of those closest to them. Their happiness or despair. Their unspoken loneliness. He was achingly lonely in spite of family, friends and patients jostling around him. With Agnès he would never feel lonely again. James forced himself to lift the sheet and climb out of bed, feeling his way with his toes to the door. He grasped the doorknob firmly before turning it very slowly in silence. He was pleased with his achievement. He saw light at the foot of the door to Agnès's room. He knocked.

"Agnès, it's me," he whispered pointlessly.

"Well, I don't know who else it would be. Constance is away. My spare lover from Amiens could have climbed a ladder and entered through a window but he usually gives me some notice. Come in."

He felt deflated and timid as he stood in the doorway. His erection had melted under the glare of humour. Agnès was holding a book.

"Agnès, I could not sleep. Would you like to talk?"

"I would much prefer it if you came here and hugged me. Surely you did not expect me to come hunting for you again? You could then let me take all the responsibility for the past twenty-four years. That wouldn't be fair, would it?"

James kissed her gently on her forehead and rolled the duvet down to the foot of the bed. She was wearing a plain white silk gown and he slid the silk over her dry form without skin resistance. With the advantage of ageing he could sustain this gentle exploration for hours. They fell apart exhausted and slept till dawn.

James was still dozing as the dawn light crept around the curtains.

"Alexandre is coming to lunch today. It is weeks since he has been here. He has been so busy at the hospital."

James awoke abruptly. It was too soon for this. His son. His first son. Alasdair was his second son.

"Do you wish me to stay, Agnès? Is it too soon?"

James realised that he was dreading this meeting.

"Of course you must meet him, James, but I suggest we do not explain anything today. I have told him that a very old friend from England is visiting. He is probably curious. As he has never heard of you before he assumes that you are not a crucial element in my early life."

"No," he answered meekly.

Alexandre pressed the bell at the front door. To James, this was now a reassuring and benign note. Agnès left the room and walked to the front door. James heard the mildly resisting door open and he constructed the scene of mother and son in warm embrace. He noted his right leg trembling so that once again he had to force his heel to the floor. Agnès had refused to describe their son, leaving James to make his own judgement. He heard the desynchronised footsteps in the hall and made one last effort to grind his heel into the carpet. Standing in front of him was his son.

"Alexandre, may I introduce to you Dr James Butland, a very old friend from England."

"How do you do, sir. I am very pleased to meet you."

His English was as good as his mother's. James had exploited the last grind of heel on floor to propel himself to his feet and he stood as still as he could with outstretched hand and uncomplicated smile. His deepest fears were confirmed. This young man, twenty-three years old, much older than Alasdair when he was killed, was Alasdair's surrogate. He was taller, of course, but shared the same round face and fair brown hair without the red tones of his mother. His eyebrows were so transparent as to be almost invisible. His skin was fair. Neither thin nor fat and James knew that Alasdair, allowed fourteen more years of life, would have been a convincing half-brother for Alexandre. Even if the voices of nine- and twenty-three-year-old males cannot be compared it was not too speculative to trace the evolution of the soft, firm timbre and the precision of the language. James was aware that Alexandre was appraising him too with the cool objective eye of the physician taught to make provisional diagnoses on the entry of patients to the consulting room – to be revised later, of course, with more data. This discipline of careful observation was shared by all good doctors.

Alexandre had already reached the conclusion that he had suspected when his mother informed him that he would meet a very old English friend. If this friend had been so unimportant his identity would have inserted itself into conversation with his mother over the long years of growing up. His crucial importance had been consciously suppressed by his mother. Alexandre could also see the physical resemblance to himself.

"Forgive me, sir, if I am mistaken. But surely you are my father?"

James turned to Agnès with anguish and she rapidly intervened.

"Yes, my son. James is your father."

James advanced and shook his son's right hand once again, now with both his hands and with the intention of warmth. He could not, yet, offer the embrace that his son might have expected.

"Alexandre, I had a son, another son, just like you. He was only nine when he was killed in a car accident but he would have grown up to look like you. This is quite a shock for me as you will understand."

"Yes, I suppose so. Why have you come back after such a long time, over twenty years?"

"Twenty-four years. I was visiting Calais with a history group and just could not leave without retracing my steps to your grandfather's old house. I have explained to your mother why I have stayed away so long. I was given her address in Saint-Omer and I knew that I wanted to, had to, see her again. I was sure that she would be married with a large family. Trying to be unselfish, I hoped that she would be surrounded by such a family. I never expected to find her here with a son, our son. I knew that I would never have another son to replace Alasdair, but to now find that I have you, Alexandre. That is remarkable. It must have been hard for you to grow up without a father."

"As I never knew my father, I never knew any different. So many children conceived during the war years had no fathers. I was not so different from many others. But what do I think now? Mother, are you happy with… all of this?"

Agnès smiled.

"Of course, Alexandre. After the war I had given up all hope of meeting James again. I assumed that he was most likely dead. He was a soldier. I was sure that if he was alive and had survived that he would have returned to me."

James reddened and concentrated his gaze on the patterned circle near the corner of the carpet.

"Or perhaps he had made a new life in England and did not want to spoil that with old memories and mistakes."

"You are married, Dr Butland?"

"Please call me James. Yes, I am married but unhappily, especially since the death of our son. Our marriage really ended a year ago. Meeting your mother again has been wonderful."

"I must prepare lunch. I must leave you two men to get to know each other. And if that is too awkward you can easily swap medical stories."

James did not want Agnès to leave. Now that he had found Agnès again each separation unnerved him. He was alone with his son.

"I am pleased you are studying medicine, Alexandre." He was grasping for something to say to avoid the vacuum of silence. "I only chose medicine after meeting your mother in the war. She was one of those dedicated, focused medical students and I found this infectious. I am now a physician at Addenbrooke's Hospital in Cambridge. What do you plan to do after you qualify?"

"I don't know yet. I may join my mother in the practice but Saint-Omer is a little quiet. I shall probably continue in hospital practice, possibly psychiatry."

"That's interesting. I thought about psychiatry too."

"Do you plan to stay in touch with my mother… and me… now? Or do you wish to return to Cambridge and forget all about us now that you have done your duty and revisited old battlefields and the scene of your conquests?"

There was more than a hint of bitterness in his voice. James reeled and sought the solace of the carpet but only for a few seconds. He forced himself to meet Alexandre's eyes which were fixed on his own.

"I only want good to come out of this, Alexandre. I think your mother is genuinely pleased to see me again. You must ask her yourself. I am still in love with her. I have loved her since 1940 but life submerged this, buried this love. Only the blessings, or curses, of memory allowed me to meet her again."

It sounded strange when spoken. Clearly Alexandre realised that his mother's life would be disrupted after so many years of stability. He was concerned for himself. How could he tell his friends that his father had turned up twenty-four years after deserting his mother? He would be an object of pity or even derision. Although he had avoided open discussion with his school friends he had always offered enough clues to suggest that his father had been killed in action. Sometimes he constructed elaborate stories in his head that his father had been with the Maquis and had been ambushed by the SS somewhere down in the south at the time of the Normandy invasion. Or that after the fall of France he had managed to escape to North Africa and join the Free French army and had died at Bir Hacheim in 1942. Alexandre never openly lied to his friends about his father's heroism but he had given enough for them to construct the stories for themselves. At least they would know that he was not a German bastard, the fruit of a liaison between his mother and one of the occupying forces. Surely his mother did not now need this man. They were better off without him.

He could also see the alternative hypothesis. His father was now a senior doctor in Cambridge with an interesting life. Even his embryonic psychiatrist's mind could see the benefits of this new relationship. His mother, who had always seemed content, could be even happier. He also realised that he had a half-sister, Sarah, in England now, which made him feel less solitary, less independent. Children without siblings presented a barrier of insulation between themselves and the world outside. They developed less reliance on others and were content with their own company. It could create antisocial instincts. Alexandre could see that in himself and he was not proud of it. His mother's happiness must be the first consideration. He could cope without a father.

Lunch passed almost in silence. It was clear that Alexandre resented his presence and that this could easily expand into hostility. James considered leaving after lunch and allowing events to take their own course. When he made fully conscious and reasoned decisions they were often faulty with adverse consequences. When he allowed thoughts and ideas to incubate, rather than forcing himself to make decisions, the path ahead usually became clearer. Decisions were determined by external influences and not by internal debate. James could not take the blame and responsibility for the future. If he took his leave now, one day earlier than planned, all would become clear in the following months.

Agnès sensed this and spoke very little for the rest of the day. They dined early and all went to bed well before ten. Early the following morning Alexandre left, returning to the hospital in Lille, without taking leave of his father. He did slip into his mother's room, very early, like a small boy with an agenda.

"This has been quite a shock for you, Alexandre."

"Yes, Mother. I want you to be really happy if possible but can James offer you this? You have coped so well on your own, with me, over the years. Life must have been very difficult for you at times."

"Of course, my dear boy. I do not think James can or even should move to France. He is a very English doctor with little French and a great career ahead of him in Cambridge. I am a rural GP in a small town in France who could never be transplanted to England. We have grown in two soils, acid and alkaline, and plants do not flourish in the wrong soil. At the very best we can visit each other and tell stories about the war and medicine, the glue of our lives. James's marriage is terminal if not dead already and so that should not be a big problem. But it will not be easy. Would you not value having a father?"

"Perhaps, but I fear that where there has been order, there is now a real risk of chaos for you, Mother, for us both. But I also know that once the cork is out of the bottle the wine has changed. One cannot replace the cork and drink the same wine two weeks later. You and I have already changed. It might be for the good of us all but I can't predict that now."

James returned to England later that morning. When he parted from Agnès they both left all unsaid, neither wishing to commit the other to any course of action. They hugged each other for hour-seconds and kissed with the fervour of the liberated-repressed but dared say little.

"*Au revoir,* Agnès, and thank you for a weekend of earthquakes."

"*Au revoir,* James. Let's wait and see."

As he sat on the Calais bus, unconscious of other passengers and the world outside, he wondered what he had done. He had opened up cracks in the lives of at least five people and Alice and Sarah were still unaware. The voyage across the Channel and the journey back to Cambridge were almost invisible. He supposed he was what lay people called "in shock", traditionally treated by large volumes of hot sweet tea. James felt empty, a flat battery, an airless balloon.

He arrived very late at his home and slept in a spare bedroom, leaving very early for the hospital before Alice and Sarah awoke.

The unfailing routine of the hospital left little space for his mind to wander. That evening he said very little to his family. That was not unusual. He had become deeply introverted at home since Alasdair's death and long empty silences were the norm. Thoughts of Alexandre could not so easily be suppressed. He tried to think positively about him but had to admit to himself that it was the idea of another son, and not the son himself, that attracted him. He was detached from his son but felt no guilt about this. No one could replace Alasdair. Alexandre was an imposter trying to insert himself through a gap in the fence, invading his garden, his private space, his memories.

"Grossly unfair analysis, Butland," he spoke loudly.

That night he dreamed a new dream. He looked down on a circle of fifty dead rats, each with its head lying across the whip-like tail of the adjacent one.

January 1965

Addenbrooke's Hospital did not teach clinical medical students. The university offered a three-year science Tripos for prospective doctors but these students joined one of the London teaching hospitals for their practical clinical training just as James had left for London in 1950. Occasionally students from other universities spent one or two months at Addenbrooke's for experience. Shortly after his return from his second visit to Saint-Omer James approached the ward, expecting to meet his house physician and registrar for his ward round. An obvious student was waiting for him.

"Excuse me, sir. I am Edward Barnes from Bart's. May I join you on your rounds?"

"Of course, my boy."

James enjoyed teaching medical students and had missed the experience since leaving St Thomas's. He would tease them about their entirely reasonable ignorance of the details of diseases and tried to convey the real secrets of medicine: diseases do not vary much but their manifestations in different human beings are of infinite variety. He had always been aware of a platonic love for many of his patients and liked to explore details of their lives and not just their symptoms. Many men appreciated questions about their military experiences in the world wars and on one occasion James even prised out of one old man that he had charged on horseback at Omdurman in 1898 in the last cavalry charge of the British Army in the Sudan war with the young Winston Churchill not far away along the line. James became well known for the expectation of his juniors to include a "military history" as well as a standard "past medical history" or "social history" recorded by all students. This ward round lasted twice as long as usual as James assessed each patient in ever more detail than usual to impress the visiting medical student and he needed extra time to teach. The ward sister, who regarded doctors' rounds as obstructive to the proper work of the ward, could barely conceal her impatience. Most consultants viewed the occasional visits of students as a chore to be avoided if possible. Rounds ended in Sister's office for coffee and biscuits. It was also an opportunity for James to make the student feel welcome and part of the team. He might direct him to read up about one of the rarer diseases that he had just seen for the first time.

"Tell me about yourself, Edward. Where's home?"

"My mother lives in Hampstead, sir, but I live in Charterhouse Square, near to Bart's."

Of course James was asking where his home was and not his digs but Edward Barnes nervously offered no more.

"Is your father a doctor?"

"No, sir. He was killed in 1940 in France. I was born in 1941 so I never saw him, obviously..."

He blushed as he had stated the obvious fact.

"What regiment was he in? Or perhaps he was in the Royal Navy or RAF?"

"No, sir. He was in the Queen Victoria's Rifles, a lieutenant."

"At Calais. D Company," James replied.

"Yes, I think so, sir. Calais certainly but I am not sure about his company. How did you know that, sir?"

"Your surname, Barnes, and the QVR connection. I was there too. I was a lance corporal in the platoon. I was just eighteen years old and just out of school. Your father seemed so much older though he was probably only in his early twenties. What an extraordinary coincidence. It was a very difficult show with just three battalions holding off a whole panzer division with taxi ranks of Stukas trying to dislodge us. I was wounded and managed to escape in a small boat."

"My mother told me all about the QVR. She always said that no one escaped. All were killed or captured. I must tell her that I've met someone who did."

Sister impatiently had left the office, leaving the doctors to their conversations with no relevance to her patients. James was uneasy. He had tried to bury the charge he had made against himself that he had deserted his fellows in the QVR, in that compartment just beyond memory, but he could still stumble into it without provocation. He prayed that one day, Alasdair's death would settle in that same compartment; accessible, but not too accessible. Old soldiers, who chose to recall their stories rather than bury them, repeated them until they began to believe they were true.

On the following day Edward Barnes was chatting to the secretary when James entered.

"I phoned my mother last night, sir. She is very keen to meet you and talk about Calais... and my father. Do you mind if she contacts you?"

"No, of course not. If I can help in any way. I don't suppose it would be comfortable for either of us, but I should be pleased to meet your mother."

Mrs Barnes telephoned later that afternoon.

"Dr Butland, this is Philippa Barnes. I am so sorry to trouble you. You must be a very busy man. Edward has been telling me all about you. Well, not all, obviously, but something."

James could sense that she felt a little awkward and there were pauses when he knew she was swallowing her tears but she pressed on.

"I should very much like to meet you and hear your account of Calais and anything you can tell me about my husband. I understand you were in his platoon."

"Yes, Mrs Barnes. I knew your husband quite well though I

was only eighteen and a lowly lance corporal. He was an officer and presumably in his early or mid-twenties. I knew that he had served in the QVR for a year or two before the war."

"He loved it. He was an insurance broker in Lloyd's but his real love was the QVR. He wanted to leave Lloyd's and become a regular officer but the salary was too generous to give up and so he pressed on as a broker by day and a territorial officer at weekends and camps."

They arranged to meet a week later. James waited for the London train at Cambridge station. He examined the college shields above the entrance for the first time in his life to direct himself from the fear of meeting the widow of one of those soldiers he had betrayed. In the throng of twenty or so leaving the London train James easily picked out Philippa Barnes and she too showed no evidence of indecision.

"Mrs Barnes," James almost sang her name with the message of warm welcome, "I'm James Butland. How do you do?" He noted her resemblance to her son; confident, her black hair a little longer than he would have expected, almost invisible make-up and dressed in a long blue suit and coat that defied the 1960s. He estimated that she was in her mid-forties but that was not too difficult to calculate. They drove to the University Arms Hotel on Parker's Piece where James had booked a table for lunch.

"What would you like to drink, Mrs Barnes?"

"Oh, do call me Philippa, please."

"James, please," he immediately countered.

"Something dry and white, I think."

She continued: "What can you tell me about the QVR and my husband, Geoffrey? I heard quite a lot from those who became POWs at the end of the war but any new information would be wonderful."

James went over the events of the chaotic embarkation from Dover, embellishing his account with warm, friendly anecdotes about Geoffrey Barnes. It was not difficult. He did not need to protect his widow. He was an excellent officer who took infinite trouble to look after his platoon. On their side the platoon responded warmly and put in maximum effort. They were mostly educated, middle-class soldiers with very little military instinct but keen to prove that anything their fathers had done in the Great War they could do in the present one. It was Lieutenant Barnes, after a successful exercise, who had suggested to James that he should apply for a commission. He recommended him to the colonel and it was agreed that James's name would go forward at the next opportunity. The QVR spawned many officers from the ranks and the colonel, with split loyalties to the battalion and the army as a whole, realised that they were losing so many first-rate men for officer training. They were diluting their own strength. After officer training before the war they were always posted to other regiments to avoid any possible embarrassment.

James described the days in Calais in May 1940 in the greatest detail he could muster, ending with his head wound which, of course, was little more than a graze. He had suffered worse injuries on the rugby field. James resorted to the story which he had told many times, omitting the elements which tortured him. After his treatment by a French GP he was unable to trace his company. By that time the Germans were swarming all over Calais Saint-Pierre. The doctor's family hid him and then gave him their boat. He somehow managed to sail it back to England and that was the end of his Calais story. He saw Philippa Barnes shudder.

"Have I said something to distress you? Or at least something new, of which you were unaware, that has caused you new pain?"

"My husband apparently – according to the POWs whom I met after the war – had been very worried about one member of his platoon who had been wounded in the head. He never reached the regimental aid post and he was afraid that he might be unconscious in some ditch behind the line. He left his sergeant in charge of the platoon and went off to try and find him. They were under intense fire from the Germans and he could not delegate this to one of his men. Apparently it was as he turned away on this quest that he was shot in the back of the head by a sniper."

James raised his hands slowly and watched them trembling in front of him before clamping them to the sides of his head.

"I could have been the soldier he was trying to find. Your husband was killed looking for me."

Geoffrey Barnes could have been trying to find another soldier. But James knew it was him. He had enticed another man to his death, this woman's husband and Edward's father.

"You weren't responsible for his death, you silly man. Oh, I'm sorry but you look as if you are imagining that you murdered him. He was doing his job as a good officer."

Philippa Barnes had sensed that this realisation had turned James into a fly squashed by a hostile newspaper on a window. He had seemed to buckle and slump into despair. She had gained strength and pride in meeting the man who had attracted her husband's concern. He had survived and was now leading a useful life. Her husband had not saved him but, who knows, his good intention may have added weight to the random events in war that make men live or die.

The short car journey back to the station was silent. They shook hands and declared their intention to meet again, neither believing that this would happen. That night James reviewed the events of the day. Sleep was broken by not only visions of Alasdair's death, in which he had played no part and over which he had no control, but also by Calais visions of desertion and betrayal. He was once again in Tunisia with his sergeant, Tom Woods, pressing his fist into Tom's thigh to try and stop the blood pumping from the severed artery, watching him as death blanched his face.

James.

He called me James as he slipped away. I should have saved him. I shouldn't have left him. I deserted them all. They suffered in Italy while I was tucked up in bed in the hospital in Algiers.

Dreams, with their remote logic, torture with flames of perverse memories. So many of his actions in life were flawed. Those around him were harassed or harmed by his presence in their lives. He pretended that as a doctor he could do only good works but, in truth, his interaction with those closest to him brought only disaster and death. His selfish imposition of himself on Agnès and Alexandre could only produce unhappiness.

April to May 1965

My Dear Agnès,

Months have slipped by since my last visit to Saint-Omer and those few days I spent with you and Alexandre. My mind has been in turmoil since then, deciding what to do. I discovered that the officer of my platoon in Calais was killed trying to look for me. Although it is a crazy thought I cannot escape the conclusion that I, in a safe place with you, was somehow responsible for his death. I don't cause death but seem to attract its attention to those around me. I am sure that I can do some good to my patients but I can only cause unhappiness to others. When I started writing this letter to you, dear Agnès, it was my intention to say that we should not meet again. The distress that I would cause to my family here and, let's face it, to Alexandre who clearly resents my arrival on the scene, is too much.

May I visit you just once more to talk over everything and to say a proper goodbye? If I just cast you off by letter I could never forgive myself and this guilt would be heaped on all the others.

I look forward to your reply.

With much love,
Yours sincerely,
James

My Dearest James,

I am so pleased to hear from you after so many months. Clearly you were despairing and depressed and I hope you are seeking help for this. I am sure you are not. Doctors never do. Equally clearly Alexandre and I are the cause of this, following on from other terrible events in your life. It required real courage to seek me out after so long and so you must never feel too badly about yourself. You must believe that I am so glad that you did find me in Saint-Omer. You have awoken me from a long deep sleep and I have been praying that you would keep some part of your life for me and Alexandre even if you cannot offer us your whole life. Alexandre was certainly full of resentment for your breaking into our lives but he too now realises how much good you have done us. Please try and believe this.

Yes, please come and visit us again. If you feel, after this next visit, that Alexandre and I have no part to play in the rest of your life, then so be it. Your presence on this earth has been a blessing for so many. No, not only for your patients, but also for those closely around you who have suffered too in different ways.

Alexandre would not exist without you. He is a fine young man with a great future and I am not going to take all the credit for this. You are in him too.

Do come soon.

All my love,
Agnès

James read and reread this letter. He folded it and placed it in the secure zipped compartment of his wallet so that he could return to it at random times at the hospital. He could soon recite every word in his head. It overlapped with nightmares and calmed him when he awoke in cold sweats. He could not predict his emotion from hour to hour. At the hospital he could act his part without difficulty. If necessary this could be his whole life, cutting free from his ties outside the hospital. He reflected that he had led an extraordinary life, the stuff of novels if it were not so damnably true. James had decided to write about Calais one day. He had invented this as a pretext for his visits to France but now he knew he must write something. The men who fought and died at Calais deserved the telling of their story. The "miracle" of Dunkirk had drowned the disaster of Calais. People only want to hear good news and historians prefer to write about success, especially success which supersedes failure. James wanted to indict Churchill for one bad decision in refusing to evacuate the QVR and the other Rifle battalions from Calais. Hitler could have withdrawn von Paulus's army from Stalingrad and saved them. Churchill could have saved the QVR.

James had always enjoyed writing. Unless events are recorded, set down on paper, they may as well have never occurred. Events are real for those who are present and are preserved by the power of memory until memory inevitably fades. They do not exist for those who are not. They have no existence or reality or historical worth after the participants are dead. Without a record it is as if the players had never existed. Recording events makes them live for others too. James determined to write an account of his experiences for Alice, Sarah, Agnès, Alexandre and for everyone who was not present at Calais in 1940 and Tunisia in 1943 and Saint-Omer in the 1960s. Writing it down would also be cathartic, helping to bury the demons which tortured his sleepless nights. Only he could write it.

My Dear Agnès,
May I visit you during the first week in May? I have so much to say to you but I shall save it up until we meet again.
With all my love,
James

James explained to Alice that he must undertake another of his research expeditions to France. She knew that he had been deeply depressed in recent weeks but, of course, he did not discuss it with her. She was pleased that he had found a new project and diversion from their obsession with their own misfortunes. She did not imagine any other explanation.

As the long weekend in France approached James decided that he would rather take the Jaguar on the ferry instead of leaving it in the car park at Dover. He sat at the desk in his study, gazing at the path down to the fields. Over the fence for a fleeting second he again convinced himself that he could see Alasdair and Sarah playing in the field beyond and this inserted the bayonet into his chest, forcing his ribs apart. The field was empty. He pecked Alice on the forehead, checked his wallet and passport for the last time and strode off to the Jaguar with the noisy boot and the sticky lock.

On the deck of the ferry James alternated between ecstasy and despair in minutes and began, for the first time, to fear that he was losing control of his mind. Perhaps he was on the verge of a true psychosis that would deserve treatment. Self-diagnosis was always difficult, lacking balance and objectivity.

Calais was busy. He missed the signs to Saint-Omer but, navigating by the position of the sun, he struck southeast and knew that he would not be far wrong.

He drove in the intuitive, automatic way that sees no details of the road but which is cancelled immediately on any instinct of danger. Although he had travelled this road by bus before, he had ignored the road. He now saw hedgerows and signs to interesting sounding villages off his route. He was tempted to choose a random left turn off the Saint-Omer road, anything to delay his switch back into his French life. He sat in the car outside Agnès's house for several minutes, afraid to leave its leathery familiarity and its Englishness. Concerned, seeing his car outside, Agnès walked down the path to receive him at the gate rather than await his gravelly footsteps.

"Agnès," he whispered, almost with questioning surprise, rather not expecting her to be there.

"James, welcome back."

He hung back and did not reach out for her. She grasped him with both hands, avoiding the now almost awkward formal handshake. She led him inside. James, standing in the hall, was aware of others though there was no sound. In the sitting room both Alexandre and Constance were standing with smiles and warm handshakes.

"*Bonjour, Monsieur*, welcome back."

"James, I am so pleased to see you again."

This was not going to be easy. He had returned with the clear agenda to make formal farewells to his Saint-Omer life. It was clear and the final, easier option.

"Let me show you to your room, Doctor." Constance moved towards the door.

"I'll fetch your suitcase from the car, James."

Alexandre left the room and James could hear the rapid steps down the path and the heavy thump of the boot of the Jaguar.

"Constance and Alexandre are staying here this weekend, James. You don't mind, do you?"

"Of course not. It's their home, not mine."

He was aware that this remark placed a barrier between them and he immediately regretted what he had implied in that dismissive phrase.

It was now late in the afternoon. After some coffee with all four of them chatting about the journey and the weather, Agnès suggested a walk. James and Agnès followed their old route to the hospital and they stood looking up at Bader's window.

"It deserves a blue plaque saying 'Douglas Bader slept here in 1941'," suggested James.

"What is a blue plaque?"

"Where famous people in England have lived. The local culture beavers erect a plaque on the home to record it. It is becoming so commonplace that most of the names have no significance. It is probably a conspiracy to increase the value of the house."

"I thought the English only recorded where Queen Elizabeth I slept. If all the records of her bed-sleeping were added up her life would have lasted for 200 years."

"What a curious fact to teach French children about the English. We were taught – or perhaps we weren't – that Napoleon Bonaparte was, well, so poorly equipped that he could not satisfy Josephine. To compensate for his inadequacies he decided to conquer countries rather than conquer women."

"The English," Agnès laughed. "They have always felt at a disadvantage to Frenchmen in the bedroom and so they make up silly schoolboy stories to mask their lack of confidence."

"You're right, Agnès. Every Englishman remains a schoolboy at heart and never wishes to grow up or grow old."

The breeze stiffened and the evening cooled. Agnès shivered inside her coat. James slid his arm around her waist, pulling her towards him in a gentle repeated motion. Agnès turned to him, face to face.

"Is this really your last visit, James? I do not think I could bear that. Surely you can see that Alexandre's decision to spend the weekend here is a sign of his approval? Constance also wanted to stay and not escape to her sister. She wants to cook and clean and wait at table so that the "two doctors" can spend as much time together as possible. She is almost part of the family and the nearest to a mother I have had since I was a child. Do not leave us, James. You have brought such texture back to my life. Medicine is wonderful but, as the years pass by and when one has seen everything and tried all the treatments and seen their successes and failures, it becomes a rather thin soup."

"You know that I could not move to France and practise medicine here just as I know that you will not give up all of this. Do you think that I can live two lives, one here and one in England full of deception?"

"It is for you to decide that, James. I – Alexandre and I – would like to have a part of your life, probably not a very big piece but one that would enrich our lives."

"It's possible." James weakened. "It is not what I came to say to you, Agnès. I thought it would be kindest to us all if I did not come again. It is honest and the correct thing to do. We must all live with our consciences. I do not regret 1940 and I do not regret the present. We all have to face up to the past and its consequences. We must all stay strong and live."

"Perhaps, James. Let's go home."

James bathed and changed. The dinner was one of Constance's best. Alexandre opened a bottle of chilled Sancerre which served as an aperitif and lasted through a cool vichyssoise. Then lamb served with a concoction of herbs accompanied by the excellent Bordeaux which James now knew so well. The stocks had survived a war and had dwindled and this was the final bottle in the cellar. He ate and drank with a continuous smile which left her in no doubt of her success.

After dinner, they sat in front of the fire, superfluous in May, and said little. Constance was breaking this silence with a cacophony of pots and pans in the kitchen and James was grateful for it. Complete silence, and things unsaid, were too painful.

"James," Alexandre broke the silence. "James, I know that I did not receive you very well when you first came here. It was a shock and I was not prepared. Yes, I was afraid that you would bring unhappiness to us all. We were a family, a tiny one I grant you, but a family that functioned well without any great trauma. I want you to know that I have seen with my own eyes how my mother has been revived by your arrival in our lives. She was working very hard and performing all of her duties but inside she was dry. I have always wondered why she did not marry. There have been other men these years who have appeared at the door, and even at the dinner table, but never for more than one or two visits. I now know why. Mother was comparing them with you and none compared. That is the truth, is it not, Mother?"

"If you say so, my dear."

"Then you do not deny it, Mother. My case is proven."

"Agnès, Alexandre… You know I love you, Agnès, and I know I would learn to love you too, Alexandre, with more time to know you, but I cannot resign my job in Cambridge and start a new career in France. I cannot even speak good French. When I decided to become a doctor, I gave up much and I would not throw all of that up to lead a different life here. I could live a divided life, one part in Cambridge and one in France, but it could not possibly work. I really cannot see how we could all survive, no, not survive, be happy with this."

"We could try, James. If it does not work then we all are free to opt out. We would feel better having done the experiment."

"Perhaps. It is true that if I thought I should never see you again I would despair. But from despair sometimes comes strength. I never thought I would have any life again after Alasdair but I have had a useful and constructive life and knowing you both has been an enormous help to me."

"Let's say no more about it tonight."

They all stood at once. Constance was still hard at work.

James lay in bed trying to read the same line of his book many times. Whole pages passed but he had no recall of a single fact and had to start the chapter again.

"We could do the experiment," he spoke out loud, quietly, so that no one else would hear.

"It probably wouldn't work but you never know until you have tried."

He switched off the light and fell asleep. He awoke some hours later and realised that the room had changed. Agnès was in his bed, breathing regularly and deeply. He wanted to touch her, run his hand up and down her arm, her back, touch her toes with his toes, but he dare not. She was deeply asleep. With difficulty he tried to sleep again and moved away from her towards the windows, rattling in the night breeze.

The early morning light was now framing the curtains. He was alone. Agnès had gone. Had he dreamt her presence in the night? He was certain that he had not. He felt warm and reassured. It was a calming sensation to share a bed with someone you loved without any physical contact. He slept again until the door opened slowly. Agnès entered with bowls of coffee.

"Agnès, good morning, thank you."

"Did you sleep well, James?"

"Yes, very well. The dinner last night was truly excellent. I must thank Constance again."

"Yes, she will appreciate that."

Agnès left him to bathe and dress.

At breakfast all four sat together at the table.

"Only one roll for me today, Constance, after that truly excellent dinner. It was magnificent. Thank you very much."

Constance smiled.

"I have some work to do for my exams today," Alexandre sighed, "and so you will not see very much of me. You must enjoy yourselves today without me."

"I thought James and I might drive to Lille. I do not think you have visited there before, James. It is a fine city with an excellent art gallery and the university and the hospital which have played such a part in our own lives, have they not, Alexandre?"

"Yes, Mother. Lille is more attractive than Paris. Not so many cars. A more subtle place. You'll enjoy it, James."

"A great idea. When do we leave?"

"Just give me twenty minutes to get ready."

James and Agnès sat in the car outside the house. He made no attempt to start the engine.

"A very English car, your Jaguar. Just like you."

"Did I dream it or did you come to my room last night and sleep?"

"Of course I came, James. That might have been our very last night together and I did not want to spend all of it on my own. You were deeply asleep and I did not want to disturb you. It was good just to be there together but, on the other hand, apart. I thought that it might even be an allegory for the rest of our lives. Together but apart. It appealed to my turn of mind and I am so glad that I did."

James leaned across and kissed her. She wriggled.

"Stop, James. We are like two teenagers sneaking a kiss away from the grown-ups. Constance might see. Madame Corot across the street might see and she is one of my patients."

James laughed and started the engine. He drove slowly out of the town, following instructions from Agnès.

"Agnès, let's not go to Lille. I prefer the countryside to the city. It's such a fine day and we should not be hiding from the sun. You would probably want to show me your old dissecting room and laboratories and other favourite haunts from your medical student days. Let's go to Cassel. It's not so far and the views from the top must be worth seeing. It was a crucial place in the First War and in 1940."

"You just cannot avoid 1940, can you, James? We should live in the present and in the future and not in the past."

"I shall always live in the past, as the future always disappoints and does not live up to its promises."

"What a depressing thought. Perhaps, though, you have a right to feel like that."

He smiled at her.

"Sometimes, when I am with you, I do allow myself to peek

through the keyhole in a dark room and see light in the room behind the door."

They altered course to Cassel. The town covered the wide plateau on the top of the high ridge which dominated the flat plain stretching away from it in all directions. With only a meagre understanding of military strategy one could envisage its obvious importance. The Jaguar wound up the gentle hairpin bends leading to the centre of the hilltop town. They parked in the main square and then climbed the little path up to the site of the old castle which gave the town its name. No evidence of the castle had survived. The space was dominated by a windmill and by a statue of Maréchal Foch who sited his headquarters in Cassel during the First World War. On all sides the flat countryside, map-like, stretched away divided by long straight roads seeking infinity.

"Agnès."

"Yes, James?"

"You know I fear the future. If it is half as terrible as the past, it will not be worth waiting for. But, if you and I spent more time together, it might not seem so bad."

"What a compliment to me."

"It was not supposed to sound like that. I meant that, if we enjoyed each other's company sometimes, life might change direction and create some undeserved happiness that might blot out some of the past."

"You may be right."

"It means that I would have to lead a double life with all that entails. But it might be the way to avoid new layers of unhappiness in those around us. Who knows how it might all turn out?"

"Who knows? Let's not rush our fence, if that is the correct English idiom. You come and visit me when you are able to. Alexandre will grow to love you as I have loved you. Perhaps you will even learn to speak better French."

They made no pact that day but, as they walked down the

path back to the square, they held hands and kissed in the shadow of Maréchal Foch.

The Jaguar reluctantly edged away from the old town and eased down the now familiar hairpin bends in the direction of Saint-Omer.

"Take the next turn left, James."

He drove slowly, gaining confidence on unfamiliar roads, and began to relax. Resisting the temptation to turn onto the British left side of the road James accelerated. They drove in a haze of unexpressed warmth and contentment. They were on an expedition together as an old familiar couple on their way to visit friends.

The single lane road was lined by columns of poplars. James could see the ridge of Cassel now low in his mirror and did not want to transfer his sight of the friendly town back to the road ahead. He saw a tall hedge on the right running up to the crossroads. As he approached it, a huge lorry, which had been concealed by the hedge, pushed out its bonnet into the road. James was sure it would not press on without clear vision and would halt. But the lorry accelerated hard, with clouds of black smoke billowing above the hedge, and turned right. It began to fill both sides of the road ahead of them. James braked as hard as he could. He could see that they would still hit the side of the lorry. Deep ditches bordered both sides of the road behind the poplars. There might just be room to steer around the front of the lorry before it completely obliterated the road. Agnès screamed and grasped for James's left arm. She had seen another car travelling towards them but invisible to James, whose vision was blocked by the lorry.

"James, James!"

★

Alexandre was uneasy as he tried to study. Something was not quite right. He rose from his desk and paced around the room. He walked into the garden to look at the shrubs and hedges

240

although he had never shown much interest in them before. He walked back into the house and through the front door towards the green gates on the street. As he was turning back towards the house a police car drove slowly along the road trying to identify a house. It stopped outside the doctor's house.

"Can I help you, officer?"

"Is this the house of Dr Hugo?"

"Yes."

Alexandre felt sick and a little faint.

"Can we go inside?"

He led the two police officers up to the house.

"Are you related to Dr Hugo?"

"I am her son but tell me what has happened."

"Then I am afraid I have some bad news. Dr Hugo and a man, an Englishman, were involved in a road accident an hour ago. Neither survived the crash with a large lorry. I am very sorry. We identified your mother's address from her belongings. We shall have to ask you to identify her. Do you have any information about the man she was with? An Englishman. We have his name. Dr James Butland."

"Yes. He was my father."

Alice, dressed in an old coat and wearing thick gardening gloves, was dead-heading roses. Sarah was in her bedroom doing homework. Alice could just hear the doorbell ring and she hurried inside. She opened the door and two police officers, one male and one female, were standing there.

"Mrs Alice Butland?"

"Yes."

"May we come in, Mrs Butland? I am afraid that we have had some bad news from France. Your husband, Dr James Butland, has been involved in an accident."

"Is he badly injured?"

"I am afraid that he is dead, madam. We're very sorry."

"It can't be true. Our son Alasdair was killed in a car accident a year ago. It can't happen to one family twice. There must be some mistake."

Statistically most unlikely, Alice recalled the account that James had given her of the... the accident of which she had no memory.

"Thank you for letting me know."

Sarah was there sitting at the foot of the stairs saying nothing. Crying no tears.

Alice walked into James's study and looked around for evidence that he was still there somehow. It must be a big misunderstanding. His packed shelves of history and medical books stared back at her.

"There's no such thing as an accident. Only incompetence," she shouted at the top of her voice. She sat at his wide, deep oak desk which faced the garden and the grass path down to the field. The musk of the olive-green leather top seemed more intense than before. A ream of fresh A4 paper, just unwrapped, bleached bone-white, with corners neatly squared off, defined the middle of the desk. At the head of the top sheet, neatly hand written in capital letters, and carefully underlined by a pen clearly controlled by a ruler, she read:

COLONEL BELCHAMP'S BATTLEFIELD TOUR